Snow

behind the door

V KNOX

Library and Archives Canada Cataloging in Publication
Knox, Veronica, 1949-
'SNOW BEHIND THE DOOR' / V Knox
ISBN 978-1-7750471-6-2

Silent K Publishing
Victoria, British Columbia, Canada

www.veronicaknox.com

ALSO BY V KNOX

ART HISTORY MYSTERIES

Lisabetta — a stolen glance

*Lisabetta series — books 2-4**

Adoration – Loving Botticelli

Disapp'earring Twice

Woo Woo

The Indigo Pearl

Pearl by Pearl

MAGICAL REALISM TIME-SLIP SERIES

THE BEDE TRILOGY +

Twinter - the first portal

Time Falls Like Snow

Tomorrow Again

+ the 'stand alone prequel summary':

Snow Behind the Door

HISTORICAL TIME-SLIP FANTASY

The Unthinkable Shoes

POETRY

I Was There

** works-in-progress*

"There is the dream,
and there is the dreamer of the dream.
The dream is a short-lived play of forms.
It is the world – relatively real but not absolutely real.
Then there is the dreamer,
the absolute reality in which the forms come and go.
The dreamer is not the person. The person is part of the dream.
The dreamer is the substratum in which the dream appears,
that which makes the dream possible.
It is the absolute behind the relative,
the timeless behind time,
the consciousness in and behind form.
The dreamer is consciousness itself – who you are.
To awaken within the dream is our purpose now.
When we are awake within the dream,
the ego-created earth drama comes to an end
and a more benign and wondrous dream arises."

- from **'A NEW EARTH'** by **ECKHART TOLLE**

permission to print this excerpt was granted by Namaste Publishing
Vancouver, British Columbia, Canada

for sarah and david

TABLE OF CONTENTS

PROLOGUE

Before time existed,
the constellations displayed
a gallery of divine portraits in space
formed from points of light.
And when time began,
the stars fell to earth, the skies opened,
and rain and snow nourished the land.

History comes and goes. Empires rise and fall, civilizations flourish and cultures collide. The laws of probability converge and stir up trouble. Geological time advances. Volcanoes explode and cool, seas flood and subside and turn to ice. Ice melts. Species evolve and mutate. Land rumbles into hills and valleys, and grass grows over everything. And in spite of the flowering of art and the inevitable clashes of war, science advances and retreats, and Bede's heart continues to animate each new age, according to its true nature.

But before all of it… before Bede Hall inhaled its first thought as a stone pyramid, it was a primordial hill emerging from a timeless sea. A mound of muddy memories, sheltering the seed of a dying civilization where the human race could sprout anew.

Long ago, Bede's natural water features, its sources of ancient power, had been stolen by the Romans for their formal spas and new temples. Springs and streams were rededicated, displacing the old guardians, renamed to merge with a pantheon of Roman gods – immortals 'borrowed' from the Greeks without permission. They built forts over the shrines of the green gods and clogged the sacred wells with sacrificial animal bones and amulets, vanquishing the local water spirits to trickle away underground in disgrace.

In time, their abandoned pagan settlements were absorbed by the dark ages and subsided into shallow impressions left in the clay underbelly of the rich topsoil. Stone circles tilted out of kilter in tired fields, straining valiantly to mark the solstices. Hadrian's great wall stood as a gallant reminder of the long-gone glory days, keeping out marauders while Bede remained steadfast under an ancient spell of protection.

Left to themselves, the old nature gods silently returned to Bede from the netherworld. The face of the Green Man, overseer of the growing seasons and lord of the harvest festivals and woodland creatures, began appearing again in the barks of trees. Flora, the Green Woman, consort to Jack-of-the-Green, gathered the scattered fairies into colonies and fanned their waning magic into sacred fire.

The elementals rallied their weakened whorls of energies into vortexes of great power. Comets, falling stars, and solar flares revisited the skies above the rumble-grumbles of the earth as it stretched and cracked its skin. Fresh waters bubbled anew from sacred springs. But comeuppances long overdue still blew hot and cold out of season.

Vengeances lying dormant for eons, slithered from the withered skins of mummified enemies in a fresh colony of eager snakes in the grass. The Green Man retreated, and Bede Hall, savvy to the magnitude of old scores and subtle reprisals, trained its youngest champions and prepared itself for war.

If time stands still anywhere, it's at Bede. If ghosts haunt anywhere, it's in Bede Hall.

PART 1

good mourning

> *"To sleep:*
> *Perchance to dream*
> *Ay, there's the rub,*
> *For in that sleep of death*
> *What dreams may come?"*

– William Shakespeare

'Hamlet' – act 3, scene 1

Chapter 1

UPON WAKING

I know WHERE I am
But not WHY I'm here
And WHEN I'm here, changes.
I am nine years old. My name is Snow.

The year is unfolding completely out of order.

THE HOUSE OF REINCARNATIONS

Hadrian's Wall, Northumberland, England

I died a very long time ago or was it yesterday?… I think maybe it was both. My new name is Snow – a name that suits me even though there are days I wish it didn't.

Apart from a few self-possessed phantoms, I live alone in a house of shadows. My father said they were memories of the past and foreshadows of things that might have been. But that was in the 'high-winter' when he'd been out of sorts, and as soon as he saw my eyes brim with tears, he enfolded me in a bear hug and told me not to worry because he had plans to capture the happy shadows of wonderful things yet to be… and then he left to find them.

Bede Hall is my family, now. I 'live' inside its walls and peer through them into grand rooms full of brightly-colored people. I especially like to stand behind the great mirror in the dining room, the twin of the one in my Winter Room, and study the girl named Beryl who looks as lost and moody as me. If anyone could see me in the gilded frame, I would look like a painting of a nine-year-old girl, sometimes smiling, but intently searching their faces for my father who once lived there.

I slip unnoticed into times that overlap and fade into each other, so, I'm never quite sure *when* it is until I see Beryl, who can be my age or a teenager or an old lady dozing by the fire.

But there are days when all that greets me from the other sides of mirrors are white mounds of furniture covered in sheets, when the dust lies thick as time and it's my turn to comfort the house. It's not easy being a child or a great house after you've been abandoned.

I've learned two things since I arrived here in the House of Reincarnations. My friend, Parks, the old head gardener, who used to be King of the Trees, is a ghost like me, and that fairies are dreadful gossips.

Chapter 2

UPON MUSING

*Since lucid grown-up thoughts rarely
last more than a moment,
and before I return to an everlasting childhood,
may I state, while I still can,
that I am NOT completely nine years old!
I am a ghost. My names appear endless.
Time has no beginning or end,
And the realization of haunting for eternity
is endlessly upsetting.*

Because every year is the same

SURELY

One thing is sure and certain, in spite of my present child-like form, I am NOT, intellectually speaking, nine years-old! The grown-up thoughts and words that come through me are not borrowed from the blue. They are mine even though most of them escape me as soon as they're aired.

The thought occurs to me, that I must have lived several lifetimes, and during one of them I died as a child, and it's this *child-me* who 'lives', if I can use that word, amongst the dust and broken dreams of Bede Hall. Because the Hall *does* dream. Of this, I'm also sure. Unfortunately, this realization led to the unnerving thought that Bede Hall was a ghost haunting *me*.

Possessing me.

So, I have to ask: Why did the father in my untamed dreams bring me here? Why did he abandon me? Is he angry with me? I wish I knew. I miss him terribly. My memories come and go like quicksilver. A fleeting glimpse, and my mind goes blank. Most days, it's all I can do to remember my current name.

I'm allowed to play in the gardens of the 'House of Reincarnations' during the erratic seasons that come and go with surprising hit-or-miss irregularity. But although Bede Hall may be my surrogate family, it doesn't feel like home. I desperately want to leave. Forever is such a dreadfully long time.

But I *can't* leave.

I've tried walking out the door, heading towards the gates of freedom but after a few steps, drowsiness overtakes me and I wake up in bed, transported back to the Winter Room, like a naughty child. Perhaps I was. Perhaps I am.

But the truth is, I mustn't leave in case my father comes back while I'm off somewhere roaming the afterlife, which I'm sure must be an enormous place. He'd never find me there.

During the evenings when I sit by the fire, an endless stream of 'wonderings' pop into my head, that surely, I'm being punished. Was I banished here? Was Bede Hall the scene of my transgressions? What terrible crime did I commit to deserve an eternity teased by glimpses of a life I no longer have? Did I die here? And will my beloved father ever forgive me?

In the endless meantime, I'm resolved to accept, as best I can, being consigned to a lost childhood, trapped for eternity in an empty shell of a dying building.

Which begs the question. Who will forgive me if I can't forgive myself? And how can I forgive myself if I don't remember doing anything wrong?

Chapter 3

UPON WAKING

I am arriving in Bede with my father.
Bede Hall lies derelict in the deep freeze
of earth's accursed winter nightmare.
I am nine years old. My name started out as Anna
or Annie spelled two different ways,
but by the end of the day it was Snow.
It's no great matter
as most days I forget all four.

The year is always 2023 - more or less

DESTINATION WINTER

Before Kit and Anna broke into the decaying ruins of Bede Hall, they marvelled at the icebound blue door encased in a thick blanket of frost. Once situated on the third floor, years of accumulated snow had elevated it to ground level as the Hall's only entrance.

Its doorknob of clear glass looked like a cut diamond the size of a snowball and shone like a lantern with a pinpoint of electric blue light inside it. Its glow revealed the scowling face of a man with leaves for hair under the encrusted snow. Kit knew it only too well.

Father and daughter set down their bundles and baskets and brushed fresh snow from the door's escutcheon plate. "This is Jack," Kit said.

"Ani and I have met several times," the face announced. "In our dreams. Well, hers actually."

Kit scowled. "You can say hello, Anna. Jack won't bite. In fact, he's almost a friend. He looks gloomy because he has the weight of the world on his shoulders."

The door coughed and started to breath. "Then I'd be interested to know what you call frost*bite*," it said, sounding put out.

"There's no need to frighten my daughter, Jack. Anna this is 'Jack of the Green' – also known as Jack Frost, and one other that must remain a secret. How cool is that."

Jack winked. "Particularly apt for the guardian of an ice-age portal, don't you think. Why, it's positively glacial!"

The frozen door held fast when Kit gave it a shove, but a lump of snow crumbled away and fell down the back of his neck. "Thanks, Jack," Kit exclaimed. "Always a pleasure working with you."

For a moment, the keyhole smiled but it was a trick of the light. The face and Anna remained almost strangers.

"Anna needs to understand the truth about winter to survive," Jack said. "Given time, she may well save us all. Am I right?"

"But he's blue," Anna said. "Why isn't he called 'Jack of the *blue*?"

Kit stamped the snow from his feet. "The Winter Room is special," he said. "It changes the color of things to suit its sad mood swings."

"How can a room be sad?" Anna asked.

"Good luck explaining that," the keyhole wheezed.

Kit took a deep breath and heaved his weight against the door with his shoulder.

Jack closed his eyes, released a cascade of shattered icicles, and winked at Anna.

"It doesn't sulk if that's what you mean," Kit said. "The Winter Room is the heart of Bede Hall even though it was, is, and always will be on the top floor. It was situated under the roof for a reason."

"I expect it was so we could get in," Anna said simply.

A hollow laugh issued from the keyhole.

"Precisely," Kit replied. "This is the door that matters most. And for a while, the room behind it will be our home." He waved his hand to the expanse of snow behind him. "I have to find the maze portal that lies beneath the snow. Your Uncle Kha said we were destined to visit Bede Hall together so we could bring the summer of summers, home.”

“You mean when Bede was as hot as Egypt,” Anna declared, scraping frost from one of the windows. “Or the summer you will fight for the Hall’s life. I know where you’re going, Father. Uncle Kha told me everything.”

“Anna,” Kit replied sternly. “I make it a point to always follow your uncle’s orders. Even though they’re often dangerous, they’re never ill-timed. We’ll set up camp in the Winter Room. Perhaps Bede Hall will deign to speak to me.” Kit joined Anna at the window and tapped her nose. “No worries, young lady, we will be safe in there. That room has a good soul, as does the Hall when it wants to show it, so don’t be afraid if it speaks to you. If it sounds out of sorts, don’t worry. That goes for Jack Frost, too. He has a lot on his mind and he’s rarely jovial.”

Anna returned to the door and tickled Jack’s nose. “The Temple of Bast spoke to me all the time, back home.” Her voice faltered. “Back… *er*…home, I was never afraid. My name is…” she paused searching the sky for an answer. “Funny, I don’t always remember.”

“Quite,” Jack said. “I’ll let you in on a secret. It’s Ani, by the way, but one day soon you’ll prefer to be called Snow. So, to please you, I will call you Snow from this moment on. I reckon you’ll remember how you came by the name soon enough. There’s no point in hurrying. You can’t rush time.”

Kit kicked his numb feet hard against the door to wake them up.

“Oy, temper temper!” Jack shouted. “There’s no need to be so angry, young Sir. May I remind you this is no ordinary door. Enchanted doors can be unpredictable, they can. There could be dire consequences.” His words created a puff of white breath. “If you’re lucky,” he whispered aside to Snow.

Kit drew himself up, ready for an argument but thought better of it. He took a step back, shuffled his feet meekly, and patted the door as if it were a dog. “Sorry, your ‘Bede-ness’. May we come in, please?”

Silence.

“Bede Hall is like a grandiose temple,” Kit explained to Anna. “It’s rather full of itself. Your great-grandmother, Lady Nan, always said it was temperamental. She loved comparing words that shared what she called 'magic keys' like temple and temper and temperature and more appropriately in Bede Hall's case, temper-*mental*."

Snow raised her eyebrows which sent the message: *'And, what else?'*

"A temple is lofty," Kit continued. "Being temperamental is haughty. Lady Nan and my sister used to drive me mad with their word games. So, when the Hall *does* speak, it could be through one of the walls or the ceiling or the floor or this blue door. Just remember it's your friend. Be polite and listen carefully. Spaces are moody. You and I are about to enter a disgruntled old Hall with a heavy mission to fulfill that makes it grumpier than usual. But it has a good heart, so, think of the Hall as your benevolent great-grandfather who loves you and celebrates your many names. The Hall is our family's legacy. You'll be safe here."

Snow listened at the keyhole. "I can hear a bird in there," she said.

"In an odd way, Pigeon, my father's parrot, may *be* in there under a spell," Kit said. "No worries. It's all good."

"If Bede Hall is my great-grandfather, is it married to Lady Nan?"

Kit played for time examining the hinges of the door before answering. "Bede Hall is Lady Nan's best friend. The name of Lady Nan's husband is best left unsaid. Sometimes what dies in the past, stays buried in the past for the good of everyone. My mentor, Peregrine Brooks, is your true ancestor. I've told you this many times."

The freed keyhole issued a wheezy chuckle. "You always were an imaginative storyteller, Christopher," it said. "Welcome home, lad." Jack winked at Snow. "Pleased to make your acquaintance, baby girl," he said.

"I'm not a baby," Snow replied. "I'm nine-years-old." She paused, knitting her brows trying to catch a memory that raced by, and traced the letter 'A' in the window frost. "I think my name used to begin with an A."

Kit pushed the door in several pressure points as he rattled on. "You will come to accept, that during these uncertain times, Bede Hall and Jack are anxious. When they appear vexed it's never personal. This High Winter is a blight on the land. We're here to help Jack find summer. Now, stamp your feet to keep warm. We'll be inside in the shake of a lamb's tail. And by the way, Jack, my name is Kit."

"What's a lamb?" Snow asked.

Chapter 4

UPON WAKING

I am back at square one… again.
I am nine years old. My name is Baby Girl
And Darling Girl.

The year is pointless

BABY GIRL

"Welcome home, baby girl, it's my honor to bequeath the Winter Room to you," the Hall said. "I am delighted you're here. You have the run of the place but please honor your father's instructions to keep the door to its crawl space, closed."

"My father made me promise not to open it especially if I heard voices from the other side, calling me."

The Hall's deep sigh trembled the wallpaper roses. "Fathers can be a bore," it said. "Children need to run free. Beryl and her brother, Ben, are who they are because they defied their father's strict rules and ran wild. Your brave… *ahem*… father, your Uncle Tut, Aunt Bash, Lady Nan, Peregrine Brooks, and Taraq, who roamed my rooms in the end time, had the wherewithal to surrender, even when, in the case of your *intrepid* father, it came at the eleventh hour."

"I see them, but they can't see me," Snow said. "Are they angry with me?"

"They *can* see you, darling girl, but you're on a quest. Keeping a silent vigil over you is all that is allowed. They love you, which is why, apart from Taraq, they refuse to see you."

"Is it because Taraq is a ghost like me?"

"Quite."

"Were the rooms broken in the end times?"

"The rooms weren't broken, but for a while, the children, Beryl and Ben, were. I mended them in time. That crowd of people in the summer gardens who frighten you, helped save me. I expect your father told you all about them."

Snow shook her head. "If he had, I wouldn't be frightened. They're awfully noisy and wear strange clothes that remind me of another place."

The Hall's deep sigh animated the curtains. "Twas an odd time," it reflected. "Their clothes are called costumes. They're actors, performing their roles in an endless play, remaining in character enough to upset the Green Lady's fairies whose ancestors came from Egypt with… never mind, child. You will find these things out when your father comes home."

Snow sounded out the word Egypt slowly with a quizzical expression on her face. "Do you promise?"

The Hall replied tenderly. "More than that, child, I insist."

Chapter 5

UPON WAKING

I trip on the stairs and skin my knee.
I am nine years old. My name is Snow.

The year is partly 1951.

RABBIT ON THE STAIRS

It was dark when Snow skinned her knee tripping over something squishy on the servants' stairs. "Ow, please mind where you're going," the 'squishy something' said.

"I don't know where that is," Snow replied huffily, taken aback. "And I actually have no *'where'* to go. But sometimes, before I forget, I remember where I've *been*." She lifted the soft squishy-ness into the light of her candle. A rabbity nose twitched at her from a rabbity face under a pair of long rabbity ears.

"Then it's lucky I found you," the creature said in a rabbity voice. "I will be a gift you receive in the future from a girl you've never met. But since we *did* meet just now, it must be acceptable to meet twice. My name is Pookie."

Snow squinted hard at Pookie. "I've seen you before, haven't I? It was in the 'living' room, under a tree twinkling with fairy lights."

"And I saw you. You were in the mirror."

"Yes, I was." Snow chewed her lower lip. "I was looking for my father."

"It was Christmas Day, 2010," Pookie said. "I remember it well. The twins were nine."

"I will remain nine, forever, having died," Snow mused. "Being a ghost means I'm frozen in time. I believe this winter actually *belongs* to me. But from time-to-time, the Hall shares some of its summers with me, too. My father is a twin. I wonder if…”

Pookie twitched her ears, radar-like, to focus. “Christopher was *there* and *not there*. As I recall, he was in the red library with his head in a book– the new book his grandmother had given him for Christmas. The title had the words *'annual'* and *'believe'* in it. He was forever hiding from magic… always there and not there. Somewhere between the loneliness of Neverland and Wonderland, but always lonely.”

“Father preferred to be called Kit,” Snow said. “I just remembered.”

“Believe’ it or not, the long and short of a name is highly significant,” Pookie declared. “Oh, wait… that was the title of Kit’s new book! ‘Believe it or Not’.” She giggled. “Lady Nan always did have a sly sense of humor.”

“I believe my ‘S’ name is significant,” Snow mused to herself. “It used to begin with an ‘A’.” She peered closely into Pookie’s button eyes. “What does Pookie mean, then?” she asked in her innocent child-voice.

“Well,” Pookie began. “It’s a long story.”

“Goody. I have all the time in the world,” Snow said, sadly, tickling Pookie’s ears. “I’m all ears.”

“Dear me. I see that you have a sly sense of humor, too,” Pookie said shaking her head. She closed her eyes and took a deep breath. “In the old days, before your time, there was a talking, well, *shrieking* parrot named Pigeon in Bede Hall that had a definite fondness for words beginning with ‘P’. He called me ‘Pooh Key’, with a long space between the syllables, so I assume it’s something to do with his favorite book about a toy bear who knew things beyond his brain stuffed with fluff and a key of some sort.”

Snow perked up. “Pigeon is upstairs in the Winter Room, which is uncanny because he’s been stuffed by a taxidermist and yet he talks all the time. My father said he was under a spell.”

Pookie’s ears drooped dejectedly. “I could be wrong, then.”

“Jack says Pigeon is brilliant in his madness. But then, Jack believes everyone is.”

"Who's Jack?"

"Jack, more formally, Jack Frost, is a doorknob acquaintance of mine. Well, he's not an *actual* doorknob so much as a decorative frame that holds a doorknob in place. His name is highly significant because his door is freezing cold."

The blue Winter Door was as cold as Snow had said. "Hello Pookie, nice to meet you again," Jack boomed. "Incoming," he shouted through the keyhole. "You have a visitor, Mr. Pigeon – An old friend if I'm not mistaken, and I never am."

'I spy a little key,' Pigeon shrieked, when Pookie entered. *'As I live and don't breathe, spring must have sprung,'* he cackled merrily. *'Welcome home, dear friend. You're just in time, as it were. There's a great deal of unlocking to be done. It's about time life got interesting around here. Are you aware that keys are tools for unlocking mind puzzles as well as doors?'*

Snow stifled a yawn and checked the clock with no hands hanging crooked on the wall. "It's rather late. I'm getting sleepy," she whispered in Pookie's ear. "This is the special time when Jack allows me to ask one bedtime question, even if I don't always remember the answer. He calls it the 'snowy *hour*' but it's really only a few minutes."

Jack winked at Pookie. "And what would you like to know tonight, little sphinx?"

"I would like to know more about that sparkly tree morning when Pookie and I met without meeting."

"It was a special Christmas when the twins were nine," Jack said. "Lady Nan had given her twin grandchildren insightful gifts to celebrate their first 'nine year'. There's no need to look so lost, all will become clear, later."

"But I *am* lost," Snow interrupted.

"Yes, quite," Jack harumphed. "Now then, if I may proceed. Kit received a book about believing impossible truths, and Bash, was given your new friend, Pookie." He stared pointedly at Pookie. "A stuffed rabbit doll, and I mean that as a compliment, on account of rabbits symbolizing the rites of spring as they relate to a landscape after a particularly long winter – a special interest of mine."

Pookie nodded sagely. "Thank you, Jack. *Um…* I've never heard it explained quite so well."

"You see, life is not as orderly as one might expect," Jack said. "Time doesn't move from left to right like reading words on a page. Dreams are prime examples of highly significant unanswerable questions. Like, *'what came first, the future or the past?* And these dreams are scattered like seeds throughout time, for a reason. Dreams are meant to be puzzles. The way a bigger picture emerges from the outside-in by connecting shapes when you build the jigsaw puzzles in Beryl's old toy cupboard. The dreamtime was never meant to be recorded like a calendar, sorted by numbers in rows of squares. Calendars, like the one hanging in the kitchen, didn't exist in your birth time, Snow. The nearest thing to a calendar was the Great Pyramid of Giza."

"Never heard of it," Snow said.

"Your father showed you pictures of it, many times, and you climbed it whenever you visited Madame Sphinx. You were there a long time ago or was it yesterday."

"I wish I could remember. The only picture of my father is in my head when he was twelve years old. I think it was the day my family moved into Bede Hall."

Silence. Snow settled deeper under the covers.

"I think she's out," Jack whispered. "Please verify, little rabbit."

"I have a question, please," Pookie said after confirming Snow was asleep. "I'm puzzled why Snow has to endure this endless dreamtime when she has, you know, already won the war."

"Lady Nan always said that friends and toys can meet more than once. Case in point, her snow globe and telescope…"

Pookie sniffed indignantly. "Fine. Don't answer, then. And by the way, Jack. I'm *not* a toy; I'm a companion. And I'm not *stuffed*; I'm *filled* with wisdom."

"We're all toys sooner or later," Jack replied. "You mark my words and see if we're not."

Pookie pointed an accusing ear at Jack. "YOU lie to her!"

Jack blew a blast of icy breath into Pookie's left ear to wake it up. "I created 'Snowy hour' as a wind-down, deliberately before Snow's bedtime when she's tired. It's easier to evade the whole truth by easing her into a white lie for her own protection until she's ready to wake-up."

"So, it's only a matter of time, before Snow's ordeal is over, then?"

Jack sighed deeply. "Isn't it always."

Chapter 6

UPON WAKING

I am meeting Jack Frost again for the first time.
I am nine years old. Sometimes my name is little sphinx.

The year is fuzzy.

JACK... MASTER OF ALL TRADES

Snow stood shivering before the Winter Door for a long time, clinging to Pookie for dear life. She examined Jack Frost's sorrowful face in the escutcheon plate with his crown of acanthus leaves and vacant eyes, struck speechless by the icy silence drifting from his keyhole mouth. When Jack's chilly sigh brushed past her, she heard the words 'kiss of life' in her head.

Although Snow didn't know it at the time, she was writing her story again – an ancient child of a million years, forgetting the world precisely so she could remember it.

Jack knew all about time's perverse way of shifting at the precise moment a human reached for their invisible tail. He knew its diverse beginnings and eventual multiple endings only too well. "*Listen* to my words, little sphinx," he said winking. "Listen carefully but don't *mind* what I say. Everything you're about to dream has already happened."

Snow pouted and shook Pookie in Jack's face. "Then being here is a colossal waste of time," she said.

Jack's keyhole mouth widened slightly, smiling as best he could. "I'm glad you said that. Colossal is such a great word; however, I prefer immense or extraordinary. And what better way to dream than extraordinarily."

"Where am I? I want to go home," Snow whimpered.

"You *are* home, little sphinx. Bede Hall is a brilliant house of cards built on the liminal boundaries of time and space. A living depository of human memories and secrets and wild dreams. A house of reincarnations. Your family has always lived here. You're quite safe."

"Then why did my father abandon me, here?"

"He abandoned you so he could find you, again."

"And you are? Sometimes, I forget."

"Jack's keyhole mouth exhaled a sigh of ice crystals. "I taught your father everything he knows," he said. The blue door creaked as Jack swelled with pride. Silence followed. "No need to thank me."

Snow turned to go.

The door rattled as if from an earthquake followed by the resounding echo of it slamming shut from a long distance away. "Wait!" Jack shouted, more forcibly than he intended.

Snow waited.

Jack's voice mellowed. "Hello, little sphinx," he said. "Let's begin again, shall we. Allow me to formally introduce myself. I am Jack of the green, Jack of the clearest blue skies… Jack of the age of frost. I am a jackal of all trades – named for a wild Egyptian dog that transmutes lifeless matter into life-giving energy. I am your teacher and student… your worst nightmare and best friend." The doorknob jiggled back and forth several times. "I'm pleased to make your acquaintance. I like your rabbit. Does she have a name?"

Snow reached out to shake Jack's hand but hesitated. "I don't know her name."

Jack rolled his eyes. "Are you going to stand out there in the cold or come in?"

"We're coming in," Pookie said. "Ready or not."

Jack sighed… contentedly, this time. The door swung open revealing a cozy room with a roaring fire in the hearth and a table laid for afternoon tea. "I've been ready for you all my life," he said.

Chapter 7

UPON WAKING

I am excited. My father may have returned during the night.
I am nine years old. My name is Little Sphinx
But Pigeon called me his little banked fire.

The year has disappeared into time itself.

A ROOM WITH A VIEWPOINT

Inside the Winter Room, Pigeon ruffled his stuffed feathers and flapped his wings. His glass eyes winked mischievously as he delivered his first words of wisdom for the day… always the same: *'Wakey wakey, little sphinx. Today's a wasting'*. Canterbury, Beryl's old rocking horse, creaked slowly, whinnying with silent laughter.

Jack observed Snow listening to Pigeon with her eyes closed. She sniffed the air for the smell of frying bacon, giddy with the expectation that her father would be there making her favorite breakfast of boiled eggs and bread and butter cut into soldiers. But her expression of disappointment gave her away.

Jack entered Snow's dream to share her feeling dashed by the familiar scene of her lonely room, the white hills, the biting cold, the empty horizon, and a world where a bruised blue sun still delighted in playing tricks on the eyes.

As always, until she could sit and read one of her favorite books, Snow focused on her dreary list of daily chores – the ones her father had said were her responsibility while he was away. He had made her promise. He wouldn't be gone but a few days, he'd said, but the marks Snow scratched on the wall each night to mark the passage of time were finally too numerous to count. It was obvious to the Hall and Jack that Snow didn't want to measure her loneliness anymore.

Snow's first task of the day, before heading outdoors, was to poke the sleeping fire awake before grabbing a large, dented saucepan and the reins of a makeshift sled. She then, loaded the sled with wood and filled the saucepan with snow to melt for tea.

Kit had made a woodpile of broken furniture a few feet from the blue door and showed Snow how to stoke the fire and bank it at night so that it would never go out.

"This is *my* job now," she'd bragged to Jack.

Jack praised her and called Snow 'keeper of the flames' which sounded rather grand and put a smile on her face the rest of the day.

Whenever it was time to fetch firewood, Snow's red winter coat appeared. First the sleeves and the fur-trimmed hood, red woolen mittens, and finally oversized black boots. That's when the sad truth returned and she remembered that even though she visited other seasons when the Hall decreed, it was always winter in *her* time, as far as she could see from her small window under the eaves.

Snow heaved her shoulder against the weight of the snowdrift blown against the door during the night. Jack greeted her as warmly as a representative of wintry frost could. His door swung outwards like the arm of a giant's compass etching an arc on the threshold. The old snowman that Snow and her father had built a lifetime ago still stood sentinel at the edge of a picket fence that looked like a comb with missing teeth. How the wind loved to whistle through it, but today it was silent. Jack followed the wind's example.

Every morning, Snow tramped over a fresh carpet of dry powder that had settled on yesterday's beaten path, dragging her sled behind her. A corridor of frozen steps led to the woodpile where she collected new-fallen snow for melting and a few sticks of broken furniture to feed the fire.

Every morning, Snow scanned the horizon until she felt an icy pain in her forehead from staring too long for a first glimpse of a navy-blue coat approaching across the frozen lake.

"What do you see, out there," Jack asked.

Snow took her time before answering. "I see a white desert," she whispered, her eyes unfocused. "With flowing hills that look like sand dunes. I see shapes shifting into swirls and strange mounds that remind me of whipped-cream animals."

She held her breath as a dark dot moved slowly behind a curtain of fresh snowflakes and refused to look away until her eyes watered from the strain... but it was only a crow that landed to mock her from atop a stone circle that barely showed above a deep snowbank. Pigeon cawed back angrily, but the crow, being of a perverse nature, clicked his beak rudely and flew off.

Every morning, after the sled was unloaded, Snow's red mittens faded from her hands revealing fingers almost as blue as the phantom coat she hoped to see. She shaded her eyes and squinted through the bitter sting of icy fog.

Then, huffing on her numb fingers to thaw them, Snow shaded her eyes, and pulled her wool scarf closer over her mouth, breathing through it like a mask. Jack tuned in to her thoughts to see what she saw – the cheerless panorama of a forever Christmas without the fun.

Sad pearls of ice formed at the corner of each eye before Snow followed Jack's voice inside. "Cocoa is in order," he called out. "Right this way, Miss Keeper of the Flames."

A dreamy look came over Snow's face. "Father always made me cocoa at bedtime. I had him all to myself when he set his maps aside. He listened, then, and answered my questions. I was allowed one question each night."

"A fine idea," Jack replied. "That's why we're keeping up his tradition. Remember? You'll have time all day to think of a question, but please make it a good one. My answers are too worthy to be wasted on frivolous notions."

Snow threw her coat onto a hook to dry and pulled on two sweaters. The last of these was one of her father's pullovers that reached to her knees. She loved that she could draw her legs up inside it, release her arms from its sleeves, and sit, cocooned inside one of her father's bear hugs.

She shuffled her fur-trimmed boots to the window where the warm smoke from the fire's breath had puffed its way over to its coating of ice, causing it to glisten, slick as a puddle.

"Hello little world," she said to the shapes of crystalized continents joining hands on the windowpane. It was a make-believe world of her own imagining, and she gave it a swipe with the woolly elbow of her sleeve, fracturing the thin land mass that grew there.

Jack's eyes misted up every afternoon when Snow laid tea for two on the low nursery table. A pair of bowls painted with yellow bees sat beside a set of salt and pepper shakers shaped like Egyptian mummies and a chipped doll's teapot in the form of a beehive used for pretend cream. Snow's imaginary breath formed tiny clouds as she fussed, pulling and pushing her father's great stuffed armchair into place. She settled Pookie in her own chair. Everything was ready. She glanced at the clock with no hands and nodded to Pookie. "He'll be home soon," she said.

When the kettle whistled, a hot blast of steam hit the freezing window forming a white glaze. To make a window within a window, Snow used an old birthday card to scrape the baby ice. It was soft. She called it crystallized paper.

"I don't think he's coming today," Pookie called gently from the chair.

'I expect he'll arrive soon, my little banked fire,' Pigeon squawked. *'Tomorrow always comes.'*

Snow brightened. "He only left yesterday."

Snow's companion, an albino cat named Unicorn, stretched lazily on a worn red velvet cushion on the bed, and curled back into himself like a fluffy hedgehog. Jack remembered well, the day the two of them discovered each other. It was a thin August morning, in the red library. Snow was idly spinning the great globe looking for her father and Unicorn was chasing a bee on the windowsill that turned out to be one of the lavender fairies when he batted it. Snow had tamed the commotion that followed. Since then, cat and girl became inseparable.

Unicorn was made as she was: solid most of the time but transparent as gauze when startled.

When the food supply looked as if it was running out, Snow wanted to sleep all the time. Only Jack's folk songs and the scent of summer broke her slumbers, even though she often heard the flutter of voices from the walls telling her to be brave, promising that help was on its way.

Each night, as the sun dropped below the treeline, Jack felt Snow's pain. Whenever the north wind moaned around the moon and wrapped it in gray bandages, the high hopes of a navy-blue coat trudging over the wasteland grew as dim as the feeble candlelight from her window.

Snow's last task of the day was banking the fire into a red glow before snuggling her way under the covers with Unicorn and tying Pookie's long arms under her chin like a scarf. She slept with her nose in Unicorn's fur. Girl and cat dreams mingled together so that Snow stretched whenever Unicorn did and she felt her imagined tail twitch when the storm scraped its icy fingers on the windowsill.

Snow's final thought before she drifted into sleep, was the heavenly comfort snuggling into a blue coat that smelled of stars, and the possibility of *'daddy what did you bring me?* And a happy, *'but where have you been?'* and the best tears of all, from the waiting being over.

Tonight's 'Snowy Hour question' tugged at Jack's ice-blue heart when Snow kissed Pookie's nose. "What's whipped cream?" she asked.

Chapter 8

UPON WAKING

I am bursting with excitement.
My family arrives today.
I am nine years old. My name is Snow.
Beryl is 70 something. My father is 13 or so.

The first two numbers of the year are 20
The date might be April 14

THE RIGHT MOVE

Stanley Parks, the Hall's groundskeeper, predicted torrential rain without bothering to check the sky.

"But it mustn't. It can't," Snow argued, knowing Parks was always right. "My family arrives today. I'll see Beryl again even if she *is* an old woman."

"T'aint called April Fool's Day for nothin'," Parks remarked, cleaning his fingernails with a twig. "Weather has a mind to play tricks. And don't be forgetting these people are in mourning after a nasty shock, so, don't go larking about. Let them settle in before you play your tricks. You should know better than anyone what it's like to lose a father."

Snow sat on the front steps of Bede Hall under a cloudless sky of bright cheery blue, straining for the first glimpse of the moving van until Parks waved to her from the end of the Hall's long drive and opened the double gates. Even at his great distance, Snow heard the rattle of Parks' keys and the squeak of iron hinges.

As the van and a small car advanced towards her, Snow evaporated several times from excitement.

"Stay calm, baby girl," the Hall said in her head. "Take your time for Kit's sake. No sudden moves. He might be able to see you. Wolfhound Jack surely will. Pigeon will no doubt annoy you as much as his stuffed counterpart in the Winter Room. Animals don't play silly hide and seek games. Goodness me," the Hall groaned. "Two Pigeons under my roof at the same time. Whatever next!"

Kit fairly fell out of the car head-first, as Bash pushed past him. Rupert, the twin's older brother, lowered his designer sunglasses, took one look out the window at the Hall's crumbling brick façade, and crossed his arms in protest. "I'm being punished for something," he grumbled, scrunching behind his beloved shades. "I know I am."

Snow stretched to her full height, barely up to Kit's shoulders, and walked around him in a circle. This was the youngest she'd ever seen her father. Wolfhound Jack sniffed Snow's foot and whined through his nose, only to be hushed by Kit, who walked through his daughter three times without so much as a tremor.

Lady Nan remained arm-in-arm with Bash, gazing at her old home, grinning like a child on Christmas morning, until the van careened off to its next stop.

A small familiar voice drew Snow's attention to Bash's backpack, hidden between two giant suitcases. "I'm over here," it called.

Pookie waved from an open side pocket. "We meet again," she said giggling.

Mrs. Stratford-Smyth, in her usual anxious state, stood amongst piled boxes and suitcases, her favorite lamp, a large birdcage and a cat carrier, looking bewildered. Her lips trembled as she pulled her shawl tighter around her, chilled as always, even under blazing sunshine. "I don't know how you do it, Mother," Mrs. S whimpered to old Lady Nan. "You're fairly glowing with good spirits."

Lady Nan put an arm around her daughter, Rayne. "And speaking of good spirits…," she replied.

Mrs. S stopped her with a stern look. "No stories, Mother. Not now. Especially not a ghost story. Let's at least get settled in, shall we." She fixed her eyes on the twins. "And don't you two go setting Rupert off. You know what he's like." She looked up at the clear blue sky. "I think it's going to rain."

The twins exchanged an incredulous look and shook their heads. "Right then," Bash said. "We'd better get on. Mum, you go inside and put the kettle on before you get... er *wet*. Rupert and Kit will move the boxes."

Rupert sent Bash a pained look, pushed up his sunglasses that had slipped down his distinguished nose, and picked up the smallest suitcase. "Come along, Kitty, shake a leg. The memsahib has given her orders. We minions must obey."

Bash returned Rupert's pained expression. "I'm taking Pigeon and Feathers to the library. They'll have to stay in their cages until this lot's inside. Jack's safe enough with the boys, as long as he doesn't hare off to chase the black cat I just saw."

"Haring off is not one of my favorite expressions," Pookie said to Snow. "It's the main reason dogs make me nervous. When they go rabbit mad, they 'hare-off', and nothing can stop them."

Lady Nan lifted her head. "A black cat, you say?"

Mrs. S sighed crossly. "Please don't say it's bad luck," she chided her mother.

"There's no such thing as omens," Kit piped up.

"At least not today," Lady Nan whispered aside to Bash.

A sleek black tomcat, skulking around the base of the sundial, watched the proceedings with his ears twitching. Undetected, he crept close enough to the cat carrier to wink at Feathers. When she swore back *'where the hell have you been!'* in a fit of pique, he disappeared like a popped balloon, simultaneously reappearing by the sundial, and trotted off casually into the forest, his tail up, straight as a flagpole.

· · ·

Snow continued to watch Kit closely for any sign that he saw her, but Kit looked through her several more times without making eye contact. Sadly, she followed him into the kitchen and stood in the corner while the family ate sandwiches and cake from a picnic hamper.

Rupert, still wearing his time-honored designer shades, sulked as he dipped chocolate biscuits into his instant coffee. Mrs. S poured tea for Lady Nan and Bash, set out sugar cubes and milk, and opened a bottle of lemonade for Kit. Lady Nan stared into Snow's corner, sorrowfully. "Dearest friend," she whispered to herself, "I wonder if you're still here."

Mrs. S's deeper instincts had been spot-on. Without warning, the afternoon sky darkened as if dimmed by a switch. Navy-blue clouds, backlit by horizontal lightning bolts, turned inside out flashing fiery red and gold streaks, barely inches from the treetops.

Several overhead lightbulbs in the kitchen, exploded one-by-one, but Parks arrived in a timely manner with a box of oil lamps, matches, and a supply of candles.

The family marveled at Parks' timing, none the wiser, with the exception of Lady Nan, that Parks was a ghost. "You're still a wonder," Lady Nan said with a twinkle in her eyes. "The Hall would never have survived without you."

"I reckon it has something to do with the fairies," Parks said cheekily, stoking the stove. He lit half a dozen lamps. "Sorry, missus, there's nowt permanent can be done about the electrics until tomorrow. The Hall acts up from time-to-time." He tipped his cap, winked at Snow, and went home with a Victoria Sponge for his family – five of his former incarnations in varying ages, all named Stanley. All but one, were ghosts.

A crash of thunder shook the lamps sending shadows of the family scurrying up the walls. "It was a dark and stormy night," Kit recited in a wavery 'woo woo' voice. "Two cats began to fight."

He winked at Bash who picked up the poem their father had taught them.

"There were two little ghosts, eating bread and toast," she continued.

"You're the one who'll be toast if you don't stop with Lady Nan's haunted house routine," Rupert chimed in. "It's getting rather old. I just can't see why we have to move into this ghastly place. There's no actual heat."

"Wait till you experience the cold spot upstairs," Bash said winking at Kit. "And by the way, the correct word is *ghostly*, so I hope you're not afraid of the dark."

Rupert shifted uneasily. "Dad would never have approved of me leaving college."

Kit threw a cinnamon bun at Rupert's head and missed. "Well, if you took those blessed sunglasses of yours off once-in-a-while you might see the writing on the wall. Or hadn't you noticed that Mum has no money."

Rupert took in the kitchen's cracked stained sinks, an overhead light bulb dangling from a swinging cord, and dilapidated coal stove with scorn. "And as for Parks' *fairies*, this place has obviously gone to the dogs."

Kit retrieved the bun from the floor to give Jack. "Speaking of dogs," he said. "Has anyone seen Jack? I hope that black cat has taken shelter in the stables. I saw it hanging around the tower."

Lady Nan spoke out in a trance. "No worries," she said. "It's safe as houses. But you better retrieve Jack and give the swans some peace." She closed her eyes. "I see him by the lake."

Later, after Lady Nan had told her traditional time-honored ghost story over late night cocoa, and the power outages shattered the last surviving lightbulb, Snow tormented the thoroughly spooked Rupert with a few haunting tricks that kept him downstairs for a week. She drained the energy from his flashlight batteries, blew out his replacement candle as he climbed the servant's stairs, tapped him on the shoulder, and moaned in his ear.

· · ·

At 9 o'clock when the despondent Snow finally ascended the stairs to the third floor, peace descended on Bede's landscape. "Never you mind," the Hall comforted her. "Kit will see you when he wakes up. It's early days, child. Time has a way of being, well, timely, in surprising ways."

"You would think I'd be used to waiting by now," Snow replied.

"Time matters to you most of all," the Hall mused. "Which is why waiting is so hard."

"But Winter days move too slowly, and Summer days rush by too quickly," Snow protested. "Even Beryl couldn't see me for the longest time."

Pigeon's shriek of protest rose through the floor, which was the red library's ceiling, directly below. Hurried footsteps took the stairs two at a time. The library door opened. Kit's muffled voice soothed the bird. "Sorry old thing, I didn't mean to forget you."

'*POOH!*' Pigeon shrieked, sounding like Eeyore. '*Free as a bird used to mean something,*' he grumbled.

The Winter Room's stuffed parrot, Pigeon 2, stirred restlessly as his live counterpart, screeching rude words, flapped towards the kitchen clinging to Kit's shoulder.

'*Blustery day,*' Pigeon 2 said. '*It could snow, No matter. Birds gotta fly. Tempus fugit. Time flies like snowflakes*'. The boy behind the wall spoke gently to him. "For now, we want time to stop so Kit can catch up. It won't be easy. We'll have to help him."

'*He never listened to me before,*' Pigeon lamented.

"Better late than never," Jack boomed from the door. "Hmph. Once upon a time – *that* used to mean something, too. Didn't it, little flake… *er* little *snowflake*… baby girl, I mean."

By midnight, Bede Hall had conducted the storm into a second wild crescendo. The Hall's colony of tree nymphs clung ecstatically to the thrashing treetops recharging their elemental power. Bede's topiary zoo stampeded freely under cover of the ink dark night. Each flash of lightning revealed them in new time-sensitive formations like snapshots captured by a stop-action camera.

With the family bedded down, Snow made her evening rounds. Pigeon pecked furiously at his new cuttlebone in the kitchen, but in spite of the racket, Kit had fallen asleep in one of the wicker armchairs by the banked stove. Wolfhound Jack stretched near Kit's feet, his damp fur, steaming.

Snow poked a fresh log into the stove and sat opposite her young father. For a moment, his wicker chair shimmered into a golden throne with lion-head armrests, but Pigeon's cackling broke the spell.

Lady Nan, her daughter Rayne, Aunt Bash and *her* Pookie, and Feathers snuggled together, upstairs in Lady Nan's old four poster bed. Again, time melted, and with every clap of thunder, Beryl's nine-year old form displaced Lady Nan for an instant.

Snow stepped through an inner wall into the hidden passageway behind it where Anubis made his behind the walls rounds.

Abandoned boxes and furniture littered the cramped space once used to transport food and servants out of sight. Snow followed Anubis, slipping down the parallel corridor to one of her regular spy holes behind the living room mirror.

An old memory of fire in the grate licked the room with cold acid-green flames. An exhausted Rupert, lay huddled on the couch in a state of fitful sleep that Snow recognized only too well. He lay with his toes exposed, clutching his hot water bottle like a shield and flinched every time a fork of lightning seared the sky.

Across the room, the face of a drenched black cat appeared in the window. It met Snow's gaze and howled. Rupert twitched without waking, but Feathers came running.

The two cats pawed the glass between them. But when Feathers turned to go, she saw Snow's reflection in the mirror flickering like a candle. Her back arched involuntarily. "I know who you are," she hissed. "Lady Nan told me to expect you."

"At least *you* can see me," Snow said.

"Cats see everything perfectly," the Hall replied in her head. "Never doubt a cat's power, but it would be well to remember that a hiss does not always dismiss. Sometimes, it's a spell of protection to banish residual negativity. And negative enchantments do cling rather tenaciously. They're a bit like will-o'-the-wisps in that regard. Now, come back upstairs for a cup of cocoa, baby girl. Jack is waiting to read you a bedtime story. Not surprisingly, Pigeon has decided it's to be his favorite blustery day chapter of Winnie the Pooh."

"Blustery is not the calmest of words," Snow said.

"Blustery is not the calmest of worlds, but that's life, baby girl," the Hall said.

Chapter 9

UPON WAKING

I see the Great Wall being built.
I am nine years old. My name is Snow.

The year is 130 A.D and 1960.

THE LAY OF TWO LANDS

Whenever Snow wakes, she's usually walking the passageways of Bede Hall wearing one of Beryl's party dresses or running joyously through a field of lavender in a white nightgown to meet her. Other days, but not often, the muffled sounds of construction and skittish horses and men shouting, drew her to the third-floor window. This morning, the Summer was back. The scene far below Snow's window showed a bustling settlement of tents and lean-to thatched buildings, clear to where the maze ought to have been. In the distance, a cohort of Roman soldiers clambered over Hadrian's great wall that slunk over the hills into the horizon like the tail of a stone dragon.

The Wall was much higher than the lower crumble of stones in Beryl's childhood. When Ani and Kit arrived in the 'high-winter' it was gone completely, buried under several feet of snow that rose level with the Winter Room's blue door.

Snow sensed a lonely heart calling her from the tents, but it faded as the wind howled goodbye.

In a cold snap, the Summer dissolved, and Winter returned, full force. The blue door opened once more onto a crisp world of white as far as the glare of snow would allow.

Snow's red snowsuit materialized over a thin homespun tunic as she brushed the night's frost from Jack's eyes. "Good morning, Jack," she said freeing his clogged mouth. "I want you to know that your scowl has never frightened me."

Jack took a deep breath and coughed out a few remaining ice crystals. "Friends don't frighten each other, he sputtered. "Besides, fear is a waste of time."

"Father explained several times in his Bede lessons that you were merely a friendly winter spirit who protected the Hall by frightening strangers away."

"Merely! Why that little…"

Pookie shouted "Thin ice!", her code phrase for 'stop talking this instant'.

Jack smiled smugly. "Security guard is only one of my smaller jobs," he said. "It's dead easy, if you pardon the term."

Snow giggled and pulled the hood of her jacket over her head. "Does anything scare you?"

"Not scared, child, but I'm infuriated by chaos and prone to losing my temper, which, by the way, despite my considerable powers, gets me nowhere," Jack replied. "Chaos is unnatural, it is." The door thumped with rapid heartbeats from Jack's anger, and its fresh paint shed a quantity of blue flakes the size of beech leaves. "There's order in my forests or I'll want to know the reason why."

"*Your* forests! I believe it's true that forests belong to no-one."

Jack pursed his lips. "Now, that's where folks are dead wrong. I'm the nearest thing to a father the trees have."

"Father of the Trees suits you."

"Listen, Snow, it angers me that I've been torn away from my trees. I am quite beside myself with grief. And speaking of furies, but not to overly frighten you, the very demons that held Bede hostage, enraged me. Their unleashed jealousies fueled by hate, harmed the earth worse than all the droughts, erratic forest fires, and the general disruption of wrong-time bears, put together. It's diabolical. And if anyone, you should …"

Pookie sent Jack her 'thin ice' warning squint. "Wrong-time bears?" she interrupted, "Why don't you tell Snow about those."

Jack's demeanor softened into his rehearsed story-tale mode. "Bears have their natural seasons but when seen out of order by humans, time shifts. And when time shifts, the fairies become agitated. Wrong-time bears unwittingly churn my fairies into mischievous tricksters which isn't exactly a stretch if you get my drift, *pun intended*."

"Your fairies, your forests, your world," Snow teased.

"The correct notion of ownership is misunderstood by humans. Responsible elementals, such as *we*, that is *me, myself,* and *I*, are naturally aligned to the weather, the mating of woodland creatures, and the moon's rituals for seeding and harvesting. *We* take *our* work seriously."

Snow visualized Jack, standing proudly, free of the door – a blue 'Peter Pan' figure trying to be green. "So, you don't rule time, then?"

"Of course not, silly girl… *cats* do that! But let's be clear. Cats don't *rule* time so much as respect the rhythms of the ages created when the earth was born. Cats never *overrule* events; they bring them into the light. Ages and stages are big with the universe," he said, "and good luck to it. Order is everything. Every hour in its rightful place, I say. You will remember more about this in good time." He shrugged apologetically, "Just accept it now from one who knows what-was from what-is." Jack paused to watch an idle crow peck at the piece of toast Snow had left it for breakfast. "But then, all manner of rising and falling out of season is bothersome." Jack grimaced sheepishly and raised his eyebrows. "Especially untimely disasters that I *shan't* mention out of respect for *certain* present children, who disrupted my best laid plans. Bothers me no end, she does."

"You must hate earthquakes and volcanos."

"Dearest girl, how else is the earth to stretch and breathe."

"You seem uncharacteristically prickly today."

"The thing is, prickly is my natural self. In fact, I have perfected the art of prickly. A nuclear winter is quite beyond the pale. I am positively irked by anything that disrupts my purpose. Irks me to distraction, that does."

Snow pinched Jack's cheeks. "But never wrath."

"Wrath, little one, is for demons and human bullies."

Even though Jack told amusing stories, Snow had never seen him truly smile. But sometimes, the wind whistled a lullaby through his mouth, and she catnapped contentedly, wrapped in her father's blue sweater curled up with Unicorn and Pookie in the big armchair beside the fireplace.

Snow yawned. As she banked the fire, her nightgown materialized to replace her father's blue sweater. She tottered barefoot to the bed and snuggled under the blankets.

Pookie's nose quivered with excitement. When Snow was perfectly comfortable, she always whispered her best secrets in one of Pookie's long rabbity ears. Even old secrets were new again in the retelling.

I often daydream of a land," Snow murmured drowsily, "where golden sand dunes meet a dazzling blue sky, and a great stone lion rules over gods and goddesses and a boy king."

Pookie whispered back soothingly. "It's also good to forget for a wee while. But no longer than that."

"Yes. Forgetting *is* good," Snow mumbled. "That much I *do* remember."

Bede Hall listened to their conversation and reflected. "Remembering is vital to our little sphinx," it said to Jack. "Amnesia is a way of protecting herself. Sometimes it goes as soon as it comes. But Snow's memories are frozen stuck, and we must do everything to thaw them into the open. She's been sleeping way too long."

Jack agreed. "What is, is," he mused. "Can't be anything else, right enough."

"Not to wax too maudlin," the Hall said, "but I especially like to recall…" Its words stopped, as a fresh wintry blast howled a protective spell over Bede. Left to its nature, and because it had nothing better to do, the wind blew a clear path from the blue door, where Jack slumbered, to the entrance of the lost maze glowing green, deep beneath the snow.

The wind died down at last, to pay tribute to the time before the Hall's water pipes were frozen, and the winding staircases had collapsed into a rabbit warren of crushed rooms dripping with icicles. Close by, a shaft of sunlight twitched new life into the old sundial.

Pookie listened intently to the wind's memory. She smiled within her own dream. "Ah… rabbit warrens… lovely," she murmured to herself, and snuggled closer inside Snow's hug.

Chapter 10

UPON WAKING

I am counting stars with Jack Frost
I am nine years old. My name is Baby Girl and Ani
But I prefer, Snow.

according to the laws of hindsight
the year is 2020

ANCIENT BEGINNINGS

Snow was counting stars with Jack Frost when the Hall boomed a command so loud it shook the windowpanes. "Tell me the story again, of how you came here, baby girl," the Hall insisted. "I can't sleep."

Snow moved from the open doorway, sat cross-legged on her cot, and made herself comfortable with Unicorn curled on her lap. "Once upon several times…"

"No no no. *This* lifetime. Please begin."

Snow felt the Hall's smile inside her. "Well, I *began* several times," she said huffily. "Once with Beryl, once with Unicorn, once with my young father and Aunt Bash, and once when my father was old… twenty-seven, he said. I was nine. But then, I'm always nine, no matter how many years go by. And maybe a fourth when my great-grandmother, Lady Nan, and I were reunited. I think I'm leaving a few out. Sorry. Memories of events play out of order in my dreams which is why so many middles feel like beginnings."

"Start anywhere that shows up, child," the Hall said. "The order isn't important. It's the sum of one's beginnings that matter."

"Truer words were never spoken," Jack agreed. He sounded

cheerful, but Snow had learned from Pookie that Jack's cheerfulness masked his underlying concern of keeping her calm.

"All in good time, baby girl," the Hall said. "I want to hear about the day you met old Jack, here."

"Can of worms… you old troublemaker," Jack muttered.

Snow ignored the brewing argument. "The first last beginning I remember was arriving at Bede Hall with my father on a bitterly cold, snowy English day in the year 2023," she said. "It was August. My father called me… *um?*"

"Anna," Jack said.

"No. My father called me Ani, back then. The Hall looked like a low building with a blue door set into a row of small windows because snow had covered the Hall up to the threshold of the Winter Room's door. Father said it was a true threshold since it separated the worlds of opposite realities. He often said strange things like that. Mother said it was the magic in him speaking, because my father was a famous alchemist, and people respected his knowledge even when it made no sense. Oh… I remember my mother!"

Jack was too serious to make light of Snow's destiny. "Never make light of a plan to save the world, no good comes of it," he muttered softly to himself. He pursed his keyhole lips. "Master Kit was more or less in charge." Jack gave a weary sigh. "So close. So close. And now it begins again. But it's a good sign that you remember your Egyptian mother."

"Sorry, who?"

The Hall interceded quickly. "Now now, lass. It's your job to remember a little at a time," it said. "There's no need to get oversentimental, Jack. You'll frighten our baby girl, here." In reply, the fire in the grate flared up in a cloud of fairy sparks that flew around the room. "You and I go back a long way. We have all of time to reminisce."

"We go forward a long way too," Jack replied. His keyhole mouth returned to its familiar startled shape. "Parlour tricks. Fairies and fire. Shame on your house, Master of Bede Hall. You and your selfish thirst for memories. Great Scot, we're meant to protect this

Winter Child, not press her for entertainment. Look, she's thinning out."

Snow's voice was thin, too. She faded into the wallpaper and spoke from behind a wall. "All I remember is waking up in a strange ice-covered wasteland, wearing sandals. I'd heard of Bede Hall, but I didn't know your name, Jack, other than you were the guardian of the Winter Room, and my feet were freezing. All I wanted was to be inside and warm."

The fairy fire responded by bursting into cheery flames. A full kettle whistled on the hearth, iced buns appeared on the nursery table with toast and jam, and the teacups rattled to lure Snow back.

Snow materialized slowly from her toes up, leaned close to the door, and whispered in Jack's ear. "I remember when you weren't *on* this door. It was a rainy day or perhaps it was just overcast. Anyway, my father and Aunt Bash were close to or well past, thirteen, creeping up the servant's stairs to find me." Snow closed her eyes and her form wavered off into grey fog, again. "Beryl was 11 by then. She and I were dreaming in the garden, together. Beryl spoke out in a trance with her eyes closed. 'My grandchildren are about to meet you,' she said. That was my cue to join the twins. And so, I left her crying in her sleep."

Snow scrunched her eyes tight. "I can see them now. Jack, the family dog, is growling. My father is holding onto his collar wishing he was *anywhere* but there. Bash is excited. She's brought me flowers. Your door is chilly, freshly painted ice-blue. For some reason, I can't see you. Bash is moving in slow motion. She inserts the key and turns the doorknob."

"Go on," Jack urged. "This is good."

Snow's forehead wrinkled. "My mind goes blank after that."

Jack winked. "*Nothing* is before my time, child. I took a different form then. If you care to look, you'll find my likeness carved in several places throughout the Hall's fine woodwork."

"And now," the Hall mumbled. "Come on, Jack. Stir your stumps, guardian of the trees, or I'll pull out your hinge pins."

"Very droll. Now isn't *that* the pot calling the kettle blue."

"Hush, Jack-of-the-Green, you old geezer," the Hall admonished. "I know only too well how difficult it is to smile when your mouth has to fit the shape of a key, but Snow here needs to daydream happier things. Indeed, I'm sorry to have pressed her into missing her father. All things considered, loneliness and responsibilities are far too heavy for her young shoulders."

Jack's door creaked open wider. "You do know she's ancient, right?"

"Yes yes, of course. How could I not."

Snow, fully materialized, placed both her hands on the door, caressing Jack's face. The heat from her dreaming body sent a wave of hope into the painted wood. "That's the spirit," he said.

The Hall chuckled. "Now who's being droll," it mumbled.

"Listen to me carefully, little one," Jack said to Snow. "It's our nature to come and go, you and me. It's our birthright as well as our joy. So, don't let my glum expression fool you. Whenever I disappear, think of me deep in the Green Lady's New Forest, sitting on a tree stump warmed by a ray of sunlight breaking through the tree canopy. It's my happiest place. Think of me on a warm summer day, surrounded by fairies polishing the leaves with beeswax. Be happy for me when I disappear from your door. It's what was. It was where I had to be at the time. There's nothing sinister in the natural world, I assure you. Well, except active volcanoes."

Three things happened all at once: Beryl's voice called from the garden, Jack's face disappeared, and Snow's nightgown shone brightly for a split second before turning into a flowery dress.

Snow ran to the window and waved. "Come on up," she called. "The tea's ready and there's raspberry jam."

Chapter 11

UPON WAKING

I am eavesdropping on a tense conversation
between my father and Jack Frost.
I'm over the moon that Father is still here.
I am nine years old.
I keep reminding everyone
my name is Snow.

The year is probably 2023

JACK'S WORD OF HONOR

Snow waited out of sight in the garden yet oddly within earshot when her father and Jack asked for privacy. Unicorn mewed around her legs for attention. She closed her eyes to concentrate and saw her father shaking a fist at the Winter Room door. What she heard next was clearly a heated discussion.

Kit, feet splayed apart, crossed his arms, defiantly. "What on earth is going on, here?" he demanded in a strangled voice. "The Hall that I knew, used to be in charge. We didn't always see eye-to-eye, but now, I feel…." His face reddened as he searched for the right word. "Dismissed!"

"What on earth, indeed," Jack said. "You were far too uncooperative to be in the Hall's good books for long, if ever."

"Fine, I'll grant the Hall its temper tantrums, but I need to know my daughter is protected before I go away."

"I protect your daughter, Kit. I am the gateway to the Hall proper, now. But perhaps my keyhole mouth speaks the truth too hard for you to hear. I inhale the energy to sustain the Hall. I exhale its future and past, clearing the way for the immediate moment, listening for signs of victory or defeat from a battle you're about to fight that you've already won. Bede's story is painfully linked to the fate of Pangea."

Kit shook his head in disbelief. "A truth of which I'm all too aware, as you well know."

Snow, hearing more than enough, daydreamed herself to the summer of 1960 and sought out Parks for a more congenial conversation.

Jack sensed her go and spoke more openly. "My authority holds no jurisdiction over the portals. I didn't write the rules of time travel, Kit."

"Well, I'm the Hall's bally champion," Kit replied, miffed. "Surely, my needs deserve *some* consideration. I've done my duty by following the rules dictated by Master Kha. And since I came here within one of Ani's dreams, I'm unable to return that way. Kha made it clear that while Ani's on a mission, she must wake naturally. Therefore, I require an active time portal. I have to return to Egypt's eighteenth dynasty and conquer Megeara, yet *again*, before time runs out and this wretched winter becomes permanently fixed in time."

"Not to mention conquering your fears," Jack interrupted. "As I recall, they were too numerous to count. My criticism is not meant to be personal."

"Thanks. Mentioning them is really helpful."

"I'm under orders."

"The Hall refuses to speak with me, and its portals are closed but I have reason to believe the portal in the village post office is clear. Is the only alternative physically trudging my way to the village through deep snow? I could die before... before I die the *right* death somewhere else. I believe it's called a sacrifice. I remember freezing to death, once. It was not something I care to repeat."

"Sadly, the answer is yes. Trudge you must."

Kit assumed his defiant stance. "And there's no magic loophole to be had?"

Jack's voice sounded distant as he recited more of his powers. "What-was and what will be, have no bearing on my present stand. I am the ruler of the trees, plants, and flowers, and woodland creatures —

all things great and small in the flora and fauna of the Green Lady's realms. I infuse the Hall with backbone. But I tell you this, straight from the keyhole of truth, no loophole exists to alter the Hall's portals. You might say they're frozen until further notice."

Kit ran his fingers through his silver shock of hair. "Right then, that's me off on a freezing hike. Wish me luck."

Jack's escutcheon plate vanished in a popping sound and immediately reappeared colorless – the equivalent gesture of an indifferent human shrug. "And I ground the landscape for Bash – the new Mistress of the Green, as foretold."

Kit nodded, trying to look suitably impressed. "If she survives, she will be over the moon."

Jack grunted. "I rule the moon as well, tell her. And she will have to mind her P's and Q's. She can be a tad arrogant, that little minx."

"I know you're aware that my telepathic link with Bash is also frozen, so, I will pass your message on at a later date if I may, but thanks anyway." Kit held his tongue, not wishing to fan the flames of the volatile energy buzzing between them. He turned to go but changed his mind, ever the diplomat. "Jack, I'm curious. Would you mind explaining why you and Bede Hall are always at odds with each other?" he said, instead. "You're allies, for heaven's sake."

Jack's scowl darkened. "Nothing gets by you, wunderkind. The Hall and I are like twins separated at birth. We're simply rattled from walking too long on the broken glass of war."

"Well, that's mystifyingly obscure. And your hostility towards me?"

"Bitterness lines the path to sweet victory."

Kit's blank expression contradicted his angry thoughts: *'All I ever got from Madam Sphinx were riddles. I've never had a straight answer from a goddess or cat or even a parrot. So, why should I have expected logic from a nature god as cagey as Jack. STILL, he might have given me SOME credit for my years studying alchemy. He has never thanked me for that. The significance is hardly lost on me that Jack inhabits a DOOR, no less – another word for portal. Jack's doorway is a metaphor for the way home. MY way home.'*

Chapter 12

UPON WAKING

My nose is under attack,
affronted by the smells of disinfectant and lavender.
I am nine years old. My name is Snow.

The year is 2012 or thereabouts

COLD STORAGE

Snow opened her eyes in the Winter Room assailed by the cloying odor of two smells at odds with each other. The heady stink of disinfectant and sweet lavender acted like evil smelling salts. She was fully awake in a heartbeat.

It was snowing in the Winter Room. A blizzard of thick flakes swirled in a whiteout around Snow's bed, and when the flurry settled, she stood in an unfamiliar room that appeared to be uncertain of its form as it immediately alternated from the Winter Room to a hospital room with a few homey touches.

Snow had breached the third floor of the Beehive Retirement Home. The woman asleep in the bed was her friend Beryl, the aged matriarch of Bede Hall, in a state of self-imposed dementia, who had essentially surrendered without a fight.

Lady Nan slumbered on her side. Her smiling lips were ruby red. Someone was refreshing her lipstick.

The floral perfume came from a sachet of lavender pinned to Beryl's pillow. It fought for its life, radiating in purple waves. But something wasn't quite right. The unstable room refused to cooperate with gravity. It waivered like heatwaves on hot pavement, oscillating

48

from clinical hospice to a lady's luxurious boudoir which made the room strangely cozy and austere at the same time.

But then, the entire retirement home was a series of designer holding rooms. Prettily decorated waiting rooms of death pretending to be homes away from home where occupants nursed small deaths of one kind or another: deaths of vitality, deaths of purpose, and mostly the deaths of what was. The only innocent breathing spaces were visiting days, and for the ones who knew how, time traveling in a perpetual dreamtime.

Peregrine Brooks stood by the window, plain as day with his back to the bed, arranging white carnations in a vase. He buried his face in the flowers and inhaled deeply. If Beryl woke in his absence, they would prove he had been there… that he was still waiting. This was his life's purpose.

Snow spotted the magic at once. Fairies had been casting glamours. Transparent images of Bede furniture had been superimposed over the stark hospital décor: The curtains of Beryl's four-poster bed hung over a standard metal bed constructed with unsightly gadgets and gears and wheels. Ben's replica of King Tut's Egyptian throne displaced a chintz armchair in the corner where Anubis, Bede Hall's guardian black cat, slept with one eye open.

Lady Nan's snow globe and hourglass sat side-by-side on her bedside table, large as life in suspended animation, sleeping as their owner slept, dead to the world, dreaming of better days, amongst jars of face cream, an open well-used red lipstick, and a forest of pill bottles.

A tiny brass key protruded from the back of an alarm clock. Its long hand pointed to twelve. Its small hand pointed to magic nine. The round dining table in the bay window displayed a gloom and doom centerpiece – a 'momento mori' of wilted flowers and rotting fruit.

A framed sepia engraving of the Great Sphinx, buried up to its neck in sand, hung on the wall as the first thing the patient would see, should she deem to wake. But it couldn't have mattered less to Beryl.

She was dreaming beside the real thing. Old Lady Nan preferred to sleepwalk through her past life where she had visited Madame Sphinx daily, with offerings of bread and beer and gold bracelets.

Lady Nan stirred almost awake and left her body, rising out of bed as Princess Ankhesenamun. She crossed the room and kissed Brooks' cheek, and for a moment, Prince Smenkhare's ka overshadowed Brooks' body. When Brooks present form returned, Ankhesenamun rejoined Lady Nan, melting into her withered body.

Thunder rumbled softly in the distance. Raindrops drizzled lazy patterns on the windowpane, blurring the trees into a Monet watercolor and drummed a comforting lullaby on the roof. The soothing rhythm urged Lady Nan to dive deeper into oblivion. She smiled under an intoxicating enchantment, but her smile churned Snow's stomach.

When Brooks placed the fresh carnations on the table, the wilted arrangement vanished. He capped the lipstick, wound the clock, and kissed Lady Nan's cheek. He whispered "Soon" and turned to leave.

Snow stepped aside at the last minute to prevent Brooks walking through her. "She's not Sleeping Beauty, Prince Charming," she shouted in a rage. "Your princess needs a serious wake-up call. This is not a final resting place; it's a coward's hidey hole!"

The door clicked closed.

Heavy winds arrived from the west and whipped the innocent rivulets on the window into turbulent white rapids. The original drizzle quickened and escalated to a heavy downpour.

But Lady Nan's contented smile continued to unleash the height, breadth, and depth of Snow's wrath. Snow marched determinedly to the bedside and screamed: "BERYL STRATFORD-SMYTH, YOU ALWAYS WERE INTOLERABLY SELFISH!" in Lady Nan's ear. "CAN YOU HEAR ME? ARE YOU EVEN LISTENING? THE HALL HAS BEEN SENDING OUT AN S.O.S. FOR WEEKS. SAVE OUR SOULS, DAMN YOU! SAVE THE HALL!... SAVE ME!"

Lady Nan startled awake. Her spirit-ka rose once more from her fake deathbed and walked towards Snow, its arms outstretched lovingly. Child and old lady stared through each other as the umbilical cord of light connecting them navel-to-navel, pulsated from pink to white.

Nine events occurred simultaneously: the crash of a thunderclap shook the building, a lightning bolt seared the sky purple, and the alarm clock rang madly. Anubis winked at Snow from the throne chair and promptly disappeared. White flakes swirled in the snow globe, silver grains of sand dropped in single file from the hourglass's ceiling to its floor and settled as powdered gold. The key in the alarm clock fell with a metallic ping to the floor, and Brooks entered the street below. He paused to listen intently, turned heel, and took the stairs to the third floor two at a time in slow motion.

Snow tugged the glowing chord and led Lady Nan towards the door even as her body sat up in bed issuing orders: "Everyone stop fussing," Lady Nan shouted. "Can't an old lady wake up in peace! All I need is a strong cup of tea with plenty of sugar... and perhaps a slice of toast and marmalade... and a telephone."

Beryl and Anna, a pair of nine-year-old friends, passed Brooks on the stairs, his body frozen in mid-step, halfway between heaven and hell. Beryl, suddenly twenty-one years old, kissed his cheek. Time began its perverse game of slow--slow, fast--fast, slow.

Upstairs, nurses came and went in Lady Nan's room like Keystone cops in a mad flurry of activity: trays were delivered and removed, thermometers and blood pressure gauges arrived, were employed, and departed. Charts were filled. The hands of the clock raced wildly — spinning twenty-four hours in nine seconds, and then, just as suddenly, it stopped.

PART 2

a haunting we will go

"Yesterday, upon the stair,
I met a child who wasn't there!
She wasn't there again today,
I wonder why she goes away.

When I came home last night at three,
The ghost was waiting there for me
But when I looked around the Hall,
I couldn't see her there at all!

Last night I saw upon the stair,
A little girl who wasn't there,
She wasn't there again today
I wonder why she goes away."

An adaption from the original poem 'Antigonish'
by William Hughes Mearns – 1899

Chapter 13

UPON WAKING

'Snowy hour'
Nine hours later
I am nine years old.
My name is Snow.

The year is the later half of 2012
or the first half of 2013

HALF AWAKE

Snow, primed for 'snowy hour', lay tucked in bed. Pookie called out: "She's waiting, Jack. Snow has a question all ready for you."

"Please apologise to her for me," Jack called back. I'm a bit off my game, tell her. Say that I'd like to try something different tonight and that I wonder if I might ask *her* a question, instead. I'll let you do the talking." He chuckled. "Tell her I may have caught a chill."

"Funny."

"Just trying to unfrazzle your nerves, Pook."

Pookie petted Unicorn, curled up on Snow's pillow. "Jack has an idea, baby girl. He wants to ask *you* a snowy hour question this evening. If that's all right?"

Snow's eyes were especially bright from her recent dream at the 'Beehive' with Lady Nan. "It'll be fun. Get well soon, Jack," she called out. "I'll have to be especially clever to catch Jack out, won't I?"

"That shouldn't be a problem," Pookie replied with a sniff. "Jack's lost his voice, so, he's going to send his question to my mind, and I will ask it."

"Jack should take some 'Syrup of Figs' for his throat," Snow suggested. "The Hall told me it cures everything."

In reply, Jack's feeble cough shook the door.

"Jack wants to know if you noticed anything familiar about Lady Nan's… *um* situation in your dream? Perhaps a bad memory of some kind or a problem?"

Snow considered her answer with her eyes glued shut, hoping the answer Jack wanted was inside her head. But her brain said nothing. She thought some more. "Lady Nan wasn't a ghost, so how did she walk out of her body?"

"That's a reasonable question, sphinx, but Jack wanted an answer."

"And a familiar problem," Snow said in her defense. "I have problems all the time."

"Perhaps revisit your dream again for a closer look."

Snow searched her brain once more. "We both have belly buttons," she announced suddenly. "I know because a cord of light ran from Lady Nan's to mine."

"*Hmm.* But was there anything that reminded you of one of those problems you say you have all the time?"

Snow shook her head.

"You were very angry with Beryl. Did you notice any other feelings? Were you angry with Brooks as well? Or even… yourself?"

Snow turned away from Pookie. "I'm rather tired, at the moment," she snapped. "Night night."

"*I think Snow's a little upset, Jack,*" Pookie telegraphed.

"*Well, ask her why.*"

"Jack obviously, knows what he wants me to say," Snow mumbled into her pillow. "So why doesn't he just tell me. It feels like he's trying to catch me out."

Chapter 14

UPON WAKING

The weather has changed. The sun is out.
I am still sitting in the window, observing a new day,
hooked onto the day I dreamed barely a moment ago,
experiencing a strange shift in time.
And then I remember Jack's prediction
that today my biggest dream will come true.
I am nine years old. It was the last day my name was Anna.

The year is remarkably insignificant
but appropriately enough, it's 1949

PRINCESS B & THE AMAZING PARKS

A rare summer day blossomed below Anna's open window. She sat with Unicorn, drinking in the scent of flowers, watching Parks trim the box hedges of the maze. "Hello," she called down.

"Ahoy, baby girl," Parks called back, fanning his face with his battered hat. His thought, 'perfect timing' played inside Anna's head. She grinned and cast her eyes on her wall clock with no hands. Parks was never wrong.

Parks lent on the handle of his old shovel, lost in thought, gazing at the sky muttering the words *thick and thin… and nigh invisible* like an incantation.

Anna studied her reflection in the mirror of the shovel blade, appraising herself. "Parks, am I too thin? Is that why I'm invisible?"

Parks smiled and patted her cheek. "Nay lass," he said gently, "If people can't see you, it's because they're thick-headed."

"I wave to Beryl from my window, but she doesn't see me, either. No-one does, but you and your family, and the cats, of course. Is Beryl thick-headed?"

"Beryl is just stubborn. Give her time, lass. She will see you soon." Parks checked the sundial's shadow against the angle of his spade. "Things happen when the time is right." He wiped his brow with his green handkerchief and chuckled. "Come to think of it, things happen when the time is wrong, too. Time is funny stuff. Aye, it's best not to fill your head trying to second guess it."

"All this talk of time confuses me. Seasons come and go, sometimes several times a day, so I never know when I am or when I should be and especially when my father will come home."

The sleeves of Snow's red coat started to materialize on her arms. She shivered as she felt herself thinning. "I'm chilly," she said. "I think I'm *going*."

Parks pulled off Snow's woolly mittens pilled with tiny pearls of ice. "We won't be needing these, young lady. Tis August. Now then, you stay here with me. It's too fine a day to mope in your attic." He tossed the mittens over his shoulder where they disappeared in a puff of green smoke, drew a circle in the earth around the two of them with the tip of his spade, and continued uttering his incantation *'thick and thin... thin and thick... nigh invisible is the trick'.*

Anna wiped her nose with the back of her hand and nodded dumbly.

"Childy, childy," Parks scolded gently as he rubbed Anna's frozen hands. "Your fingers will turn quite blue if you're not careful. Now, we can't be havin' that, can we, eh? We need those green thumbs of yours to help with this lavender. Now then, come sit by me, and we'll remember the land of Egypt together. We'll speak of it's scorching desert sands and you'll feel toasty in no time."

At this, the fairy Nimue appeared and spun a mauve veil around them singing *'Lavender blue dilly-dilly, lavender green. You'll be its dream dilly-dilly. I am its queen.'*

"No, you're not," a lavender plant replied curtly from its flowerbed. "Flora is our queen, thank you very much."

Snow repeated Parks' words "No -- time", and for a queer moment she thought Parks' face and hands were covered in green moss and that leaves had sprouted in the long grass of his hair. But it was only Nimue, saucy as ever, casting a glamor over the moment, and when Parks turned to beam his kindness once more, he'd returned to normal. His eyes were forest green, his old head white as snow, and the circumference of his hatband was stuffed with dozens of powerful Rowan twigs he stored there for good luck.

Parks reached up and plucked one for Anna and tucked it behind her ear. "There now, the Rowan sends you a warm memory." He paused as Unicorn darted from the mound in the center of the maze.

"And if I'm not mistaken, a friend to play with." Unicorn tumbled over himself chasing his tail in an effort to chew off several daisy-chains the fairies had placed around his neck.

Anna and Parks heard Beryl crying in the maze at the same time. Unicorn sat up, freed from the daisies, thumped his tail, and yowled piteously.

Anna saw Beryl in her mind's eye, crouched in the center of the maze next to the unicorn statue, in a patch of crushed flowers. Even from a distance, her anger was palpable. But then, Parks had confided often that a thread of premature sadness ran through Miss Beryl all the time.

Parks spoke soothingly to Beryl through the tangle of branches separating them and made his way to the center of the maze. His son, Stanley, had buried Unicorn there not long ago, and it had become a shrine to his memory where Beryl went to be alone, without nanny bothering her. But bother her she did, and whenever Beryl returned to the Hall, neither understood each other.

Anna held back from the maze, waiting. "Go inside the Hall, baby girl, Parks shouted over the wind. "There's a storm brewing. It's going to rain cats and dogs, and no mistake. Run up to the attic and make sure the windows are closed, there's a good lass."

A thunderclap shattered the afternoon. Heavy rain fell in solid sheets like liquid concrete.

Parks tossed his hat in the air and danced a jig. "Well, it took you long enough," he shouted at the clouds.

"Let's get you into the Hall, Miss Beryl," he chuckled. "I do believe the rainy season we've been waiting for, is here. It's centuries overdue, mind. But that's time, for you. It can't be rushed nor slowed. It comes as it comes, in its own time."

To the housemaids, Beryl was a curious little madame with strange ideas about fairies and such. To the latest nanny, Beryl was a challenge accompanied by the worrisome fear she might lose her position if her charge's temper spilled over into polite grownup conversation. Respecting her elders had been strongly emphasized as the discipline lacking in Miss Beryl's manners.

Beryl's wilful eruptions were well documented. She spoke out of turn at the worst times and disobeyed her father by running off to dig in the garden whenever she pleased. Routinely, Nannies arrived smiling and left in tears shortly after.

An outburst of Miss Beryl's temper was anticipated whenever Beryl's twin brother, Ben, left for school, and the household remained on eggshells until Master Ben was home for the holidays.

Keeping life on an even keel proved to be a continual challenge in the Stratford-Smyth household where children were expected to remain clean and tidy, quiet, obedient, and most of all, invisible.

Master Ben had left for school that morning, and Beryl had raged it was unfair, stamping her feet about her father being a bully, not letting her go as well. It was an old argument, but this time, Beryl had stormed out of the dining room in the middle of dinner, slammed a few doors behind her to make her point, and headed for her sanctuary.

Even when it was obvious that Beryl was sulking in the maze, none of the servants or her parents could reach the center. It was as if the maze changed its pathways to protect her. Only Parks and his family made their way inside it and out again, with ease.

It was a continuing source of disruption in the household when someone had to report to the mistress or master that Miss Beryl was hiding in the maze again. Naturally, Nanny was blamed, summarily dismissed, and left the next day without a letter of reference.

But there was another reason that servants left hurriedly. The ghost of Bede Hall who roamed the library and attic nursery had maids packing their bags whenever a sudden blast of cold air wandered past them. It was such a common occurrence that smelling salts had to be kept in good supply in the kitchen.

Chapter 15

UPON WAKING

I am lying in bed, listening to a summer rainstorm.
Unicorn is mewing piteously at the window.
I go to see what's the matter.
I am nine years old.
My name is unsure of itself,
which means for at least half the day, it's Anna.

The year is still 1949

A CHANCE OF RAIN

Night rain soothed Anna, luring her into an early bed without the promise of cocoa. It sluiced and shooshed and nurtured the gardens, and as it always did, it gave the topiaries an opportunity to gambol more freely under cover of darkness.

Jack Frost watched Pookie wriggle her arms free as Anna's vice-like hug, relaxed. "It's highly unlikely our charge will have a question tonight," she mused scratching her ears. "Gosh I've been waiting to do that for an hour."

"Anna's already questing which is an entirely different rabbit stew than dreaming," Jack replied.

Pookie's ears twitched with good humor. Her infectious giggle raised Anna's eyebrows. "I believe the term is 'a kettle of *fish*', she said, "but I take your point. Or rather, I give *you* a point for being clever."

Jack blushed slightly purple and coughed for attention. "Now, baby girl, instead of a bedtime story I…"

"Goodness," Pookie interrupted. "I hope you're not going to sing her a lullaby again."

"No little *Bunny*. Due to the time fluctuations indicated at this *time*, I've prepared, modified, and otherwise paraphrased a verse especially for Anna. In case you hadn't noticed, our little sphinx is in an entirely pre-Snow frame of mind. She's been ANNA all day! Did you not notice what she saw in the dining room mirror?"

"I did. Your little sphinx held me up so I could have a look. She saw Beryl daydreaming over her soup. We ended up discussing the various types of smiles a great deal more than I thought necessary."

Anna sat up in bed, her eyes still closed. "Fish," she murmured sleepily. "A turtle is calling me but it's not a real turtle."

"Jack has a goodnight poem for you," Pookie assured Anna, patting her cheek. "I don't think it's about a turtle, child, but one never knows with Jack."

"It's about winter, baby girl," Jack said slyly. "A Christmas Eve story with a winter twist."

Anna's mouth twitched but she settled deeper under the covers. "Too much Twinter," she mumbled. "Is it Christmas Eve?"

"Not tonight, little sphinx," Pookie said. "It's raining, remember. The snow is gone, and the garden is having a party."

"A garden party," Anna echoed. "Everyone is invited."

Pookie nodded for Jack to begin.

"Tomorrow is a big day," Jack said. "Your biggest dream will come true." He cleared his throat from ice fog and recited in a hypnotic voice. "*Twas the night before Beryl, and all through the Hall, not a creature was stirring on Hadrian's Wall. Snow's memories were dreamed by the fire to forgive... in the hopes that a ghost child would wake up and live.* Now, you best get to sleep little sphinx. Tomorrow is a big day."

After a time, Anna's breathing evened into silence and her eyelids trembled over the dreamtime.

"Beryl is a selfish little minx," Pookie said. "Sometimes she keeps Anna waiting on purpose. Sometimes, she's too angry to care."

"You're getting ahead of yourself," Jack whispered. Getting yourself all *stewed up*. Beryl and Anna haven't met, yet."

"They met in Egypt and before that, Pangea."

"It doesn't count if one of them can't remember."

Anna spoke from inside a dream. "Vita never keeps me waiting," she said.

Pookie's voice faltered, smothered by Unicorn's wet fur. "Tell me, Anna, who was Beryl? Who did she used to be?"

Silence.

"Please try to remember," Jack called out. "It's important, baby girl."

"Vita is a girl my age," Anna mumbled back. "I can't quite remember, but I think she has something to do with a turtle," she replied.

It was early morning. The 'before breakfast' sort of early. Anna lay in bed, listening to the sound of rain pounding the roof but Unicorn's heart-breaking cries drew her to the window. She held up Pookie to see.

Through the rivulets of rain streaming down the glass, they made out the shape of a black bowl turned upside down bobbing towards the maze. Anna knew at once it was the princess of the house in one of her tempers because she didn't glide, so much as stride purposely, marching through puddles in defiance of the weather.

Princess Beryl hesitated at the entrance and set the bowl upright where it collapsed into a magic wand that she poked into the leaves. She sniffed the posy of lavender clutched in her left hand and seemed to calm down slightly, but suddenly and viciously she attacked a puddle at the entrance. Beryl partly opened her umbrella and brandished it ahead of her, shield-like, stomping in a furious circle, that sent mud splashing up her legs and the hem of her raincoat.

She stared at the sky, allowing the rain to wash her face, and in a fit of temper, the muddy toes of her shiny black boots plodded into the maze.

Beryl's figure disappeared as she followed familiar twists and turns, and when she reached the center, the bowl blossomed again, obscuring the unicorn statue. She laid her lavender offering against it, turned on her heels, and marched back the way she came.

This time the bowl stayed inflated.

Anna held her breath until Beryl emerged from the maze, crying. She tapped on the window. Surprisingly, Beryl startled. She looked up and waved.

Unicorn became more agitated and meowed louder than ever. Anna cuddled him tighter, but he was restless to get away. In a trice, Unicorn disappeared from Anna's arms although she could still feel him purring against her.

Down below, Unicorn's form materialized and padded after Beryl, but she ignored him, tossed aside her umbrella in a temper, and ran towards the forest. Unicorn instantly rematerialized in Anna's arms, shivering, soaking wet, and burrowed into her neck.

Jack let out an impassioned meow in sympathy. "Today is the big day," he said. "Your biggest dream is about to come true. Beryl's too."

Parks suddenly stepped from the trees and intervened. He led Beryl towards the hall. "What's amiss," he asked calmly, loud enough for Anna to hear.

Beryl sniffed into Parks' handkerchief. "I'm angry and sad," she whined.

"I understand," Parks said. "Anger and sadness belong together like bread and butter. Come along with me, lass. Dry your eyes, now. There's someone who wants to meet you." He pointed to the Winter Room's window and waved. "She… *um* 'LIVES' up there." Unicorn's tail thrashed harder.

The furnishings in the Winter Room disappeared, one item at a time until only Canterbury and Anna's cot remained, hemmed in by boxes, broken chairs, piles of bedding, and hanging coats that smelled of mothballs. The stuffed body of Pigeon 2 hesitated but decided to stay.

Moments later, Beryl's footsteps approached outside the door, and Jack shouted "incoming," as the glass doorknob made a quarter turn.

Chapter 16

UPON WAKING

My name is Anna and Baby Girl
but mostly, Snow
Beryl and I are nine-years old.
We're together again!

The year is 1949 – my favorite year

IT'S RAINING, IT'S SNOWING…
and OLD JACK IS SNORING

Anna forgot her plan to hide behind the wallpaper. She stood submissively with Unicorn in her arms and waited like a servant about to be inspected.

Suddenly her nightgown seemed inappropriate, and it changed into her red coat, the only other outfit that was rightfully hers. But as the door opened, the coat vanished. Snow stood trembling, a barefoot ghost in a white nightgown, terrified of a live human being, as unsure as she had ever been in living memory. For that's what memories were – a return to life one moment at a time. Treasures kept in a box. A heart held captive in a cold room, remembered fragments of warmth and breath, and sometimes, in a happy dream, there was laughter.

It was clear that smiles were a stranger to the serious blond girl who entered. Beryl, tears long-since dried, was in charge, instantly assessing, as only a self-assured child of privilege, could. Her gaze swept the room from floor to ceiling with disapproval and finally settled on a girl of equal height who stared through her as if she were invisible.

"Parks said you wanted to see me," Beryl said, sounding like a grown-up lady who had no use for idle chit chat. She sniffed, visibly disgusted. "This is a storage room, surely you don't sleep here."

"Parks knows I'm happy when anyone sees me," Anna said.

"What's your name?" Beryl asked, shaking her umbrella dry.

"Baby Girl."

Beryl took in the shabbiness of the room and ran a finger over the lid of the nearest box. She drew a question mark in the dust. "No, your *real* name."

Unicorn mewed piteously, struggling to be free. "My name's not important," Anna said, avoiding Beryl's scrutiny. "And most of the time I can't remember it anyway. But I know who *you* are." She moved closer and looked into Beryl's eyes. "And I expect you recognize this cat."

"What cat?"

Unicorn squirmed out of Anna's arms and sought refuge under a chair. Anna watched him go in silence and refocused on Beryl's question. "I think my name is written inside a book in the library," she said. "If you have time, we could look."

Beryl grabbed a threadbare towel from the laundry pile and dried her hair. "It will be warmer down there. I can order tea and cakes. Or do you prefer cocoa in this weather? Have you had lunch? I can ask for sandwiches. They'll give me whatever I want. Are you a new servant? Do you really live up here? It's freezing. And it could use a woman's touch. I shall have a word with the housekeeper. Has that invisible cat of yours got your tongue?"

"I don't LIVE here, Miss Beryl," Anna said. "I'm a ghost, so, I can't *live* anywhere."

Beryl spoke calmly in a matter of fact tone that implied 'of course you are'. "Right. Then, you're the ghost who scares the housemaids. I have no patience with silly girls and no time for nonsense. I even let it be known that I'd seen you in the nursery, so they'd leave me alone. Of course, now that I've *met* you, we can be friends. Unless, that is, you have no need for company. I don't know much about ghosts, so it occurs to me you may prefer to be alone."

"Goodness, if you'd stop talking a moment, I could tell you that I'm as lonely and out of sorts as you are. My friends, such as they are, are a cat you can't see, Bede Hall, a door named Jack, Parks, and his son, Stanley… oh, I almost forgot… the entire Parks family are ghosts, by the way."

"Parks and his son are ghosts!"

"Every last one of them."

"Would your cat's name happen to be Unicorn?"

"It would."

"I'd love to see him once more. Is he afraid of me?"

"He's not happy about the thunderstorm, which is louder up here, and, as you know, he's nervous of strangers. Not that you're strange or anything, but being a ghost takes some adjusting. Try calling him. He's over there. Under that chair."

"Corny," Beryl called out. "Here, baby boy. Where are you?" Immediately, Unicorn materialized and ran to her, purring. "Sometimes I feel him beside me before I fall asleep," Beryl said snuggling Unicorn tight.

"That reminds me," Anna said. "I'm called baby *girl.*"

"Well, that's simply not good enough. If that's all you've got, I will find you a new name. In fact, it's high time I had a better name than Beryl, so, we'll both find new names and they'll be our special secret."

Anna scanned the bookshelf, with Pookie tucked under her arm, trying to remember which book had spoken her name. Cecilberry, a lavender fairy with purple hair, tapped a handsome leatherbound volume with her wand. Immediately, it moved forward, an inch at a time until it teetered on the edge and toppled into Anna's hands. Anna pointed at the name "Anne," on the spine. "Anne of Green Gables," she read. "Except, where the 'e' is, there's an 'i', and there's only one 'n'."

"You're getting warmer," Pookie shouted. "Sometimes, it has two 'a's *and* two 'n's."

"Sometimes isn't good enough," Beryl said crossly as if she'd heard Pookie. "A name has to be perfect. We must find new *forever* names." Her eyes narrowed. "And no-one will use them but us because they will be ordinary words that mean something. Not usual names at all."

Fat snowflakes filled the window. Beryl looked out in surprise. "It's snowing," she called over her shoulder as she ran downstairs. "It's snowing in August!"

Anna ran close behind shouting "Wait… it may not be."

But it *was* snowing. It was snowing *and* raining. Time had played a game of crisscross, causing the weather to overlap.

It gave Beryl an idea: she named herself 'Rain' from the weather in her time and renamed Anna, Snow, after the snowstorm in hers. "No-one will understand our code," Anna said.

"That's if any grown-ups bother to listen to us," Beryl sniped.

Thunder crashed around them. Rain pounded the roof senseless and rattled the window. The wind howled the girls together in an awkward bubble of shyness, but a flash of pink lightning showed two tongue-tied girls, sealing their friendship deep inside a winter that wasn't there.

Looking back on their meeting, Snow thought it strange that the word hello had never been uttered once. Beryl, as 'princess of the house', had merely conducted an interview, and it was only when Unicorn broke the formalities by showing himself that the two relaxed and let their guards down.

"It's still raining cats and dogs," Jack said. "But this storm is different. It feels healthy. But a lot more water has to flow under the bridge if the deeper healing is to begin."

"Cats and dogs… unicorns and jackals… potato potahto," Pookie replied, shaking her head sadly. "Our charge needs care more than ever, now. A corner has been turned."

Pigeon shrieked *'Rabbits rabbits rabbits,'* and flew around the room depositing a shower of moldy feathers and dust over everything before returning to his perch. *'Sometimes… that is to say, some --TIMES, memories have a tendency to fly in the face of life,'* he nattered under his wing.

Snow drew a heart in the dust next to Beryl's question mark before she wished the Winter Room back the way it was.

Chapter 17

UPON WAKING

I have a friend!
I am kidnapped by Anna.
I am a newborn. My name is Ani.

A memory surfaces - 3000 B.C. or thereabouts

NEITHER HAIL NOR SLEET

In the days that followed, the girls were inseparable. Snow allowed Rain to clear the winter room of boxes and decorate it with comfortable armchairs, even donating Canterbury and dozens of books, and Parks reopened the boarded-up fireplace.

Once a week, a terrified houseboy delivered bundles of firewood to the cold spot and raced off to the kitchen to get warm.

Pebbles of ice bounced off Bede Hall's roof and Hadrian's Wall. The grounded fairies sheltered in groups under the trees, determined to make the best of it, enchanted by lawns covered in frozen pearls. They played games of bowls with the hailstones that rolled under the low hanging branches.

Jack and Pookie, were corralled into overseeing a pair of high-spirited friends, in what had become an endless round of tea parties and stories read aloud, much to the delight of Pigeon who repeated every 'P' word like an irritating echo. Jack and Pookie bided their time engaged in telepathy. "You *do* know, don't you, that rain mixed with snow makes sleet," Jack announced.

"I *do* know that the weather in Bede has a rather arrogant sense of entitlement. We don't often get hail. The sound of hail is rather bothersome. I have sensitive ears."

"At least you can cover yours."

Pookie thumped her feet for exercise. "And, have you considered, since Anna and Beryl are friends, that we must now contend with a little minx *and* a little sphinx. Snow's life depends on us. We must be resolute. We can't let her down. She's paid the price a hundred times over."

"It's time she returned to her rightful place. It's time we set our world to rights," Jack said.

"It's been an extraordinarily long *zillennium*," Pookie replied. "First a three-headed green-eyed monster, and now, two single-minded 'princesses'. Sometimes I think twins had too much power in the good old days."

"They still do! But the *best* news is, Snow has dreamed herself into a breakthrough. This is the third day she's dreamed the same continuous dream. Maybe it's clear sailing from here on."

Pookie's ears drooped to cover her eyes, no longer thrilled watching two giddy, out of control princesses, making up for lost time.

Jack smiled at them like a benevolent uncle. "They make a great team, don't they? No more dream-hopping, pardon the phrase or should I say dream-*hoping*."

Pookie straightened her ears and sighed. "Sleet, you say… isn't that called slush?"

Rain arranged herself princess-like on the bed, gorging on caramels. "Tell me again how you came here and what you did all day before we met," she pleaded. "Consider it a royal order."

Snow giggled, delighted with her newfound spotlight. "I can't possibly say no to a princess."

'Oh, baby girl, of course you can,' Pookie telegraphed. *'Rain knows the whole story by now. You must concentrate on your mission. We have work to do.'*

But Snow, thrilled to have a captive audience, sat cross-legged on the floor like a storyteller around a campfire. "I lived behind the walls of Bede Hall inside a warren of hidden corridors flickering with tiny colored lights. The same lights I first knew in Egypt where they lived in clusters of lotus blossoms."

"They?"

"Bede's fairies. There are several colonies on the estate. Each one is 'deva' to a different plant or flower. A deva is the life-force within each species."

Rain squirmed and stuffed her mouth with a large mint caramel.

"The Hall invited me to explore and so I had the run of the place. Parks, his 'son' and many 'brothers' were the only humans who saw me. They treated me like their little sister and made me daisy crowns. They called me princess."

"Perhaps, when you were alive, you were a real one," Rain joked.

"Whenever my dream was Summer, I trailed after Parks and huddled in the long grass, crouching in the soil to watch him tend the plants. That's how I discovered Parks is King of the Landscape. He rules over the birds and animals, the weather and even, although they won't admit it, the woodland fairies. Fairies have minds of their own, but they bow to Parks and say kind things about him behind his back which is more than they say of…"

"My father?" Rain cut in.

Snow glanced at Rain's shoes with the gold buckles. "*Um…* for those who treat the place as a possession without respect."

Rain made a cozy nest from the bed pillows and teased Unicorn with a caramel wrapper, savoring the comfort of bad weather and a blazing fire. "Tell me more about fairy gossip."

Snow wriggled happily. "Well, fairies *are* insatiable tricksters. They've taught me how to play pranks on an especially rude house boy or stable boy. They adore horses but give the housecats a wide berth, just in case. They've been mistaken for moths too many times and been batted senseless for their troubles. Cats rule over them and all other creatures, especially humans, in that smug way cats have. Because, I have it on the highest authority, that the cats of Bede have an unrivalled pecking order. They're descendants of a royal ancient

Egyptian line of Abyssinian cats, and other than Parks, they take no nonsense from humans at all… ever!"

Rain tossed her blond curls. "Well, they should jolly well let *me* see them considering who I am," she sniffed.

The echo of the blue door being slammed shut in a pique of temper made Unicorn disappear.

"Fairies take on the colors of the flowers they tend. My favorites are the fairies who groom the fields of lavender along with the bees. Bede's lavender honey is a delicacy, and I spent hours watching the beekeepers and the cooks and the folk who tended the horses. I played tricks with the rows of cutlery when the butler and his helpers set the tables. I liked to pull a rose or two from the centerpieces and leave them in conspicuous places and blow out the candles in the silver candlesticks. Sometimes, I just tilted them crooked. It was amusing to see half a dozen footmen occupied for hours straightening candles."

"I do that all the time," Rain said. "It drives our butler crazy."

"Nimue, one of the higher up fairies, used to collect pills of ice from my mittens in the high winter to cool the cups of summer nectar."

Rain rubbed noses with Unicorn. "One day, I will own Bede Hall and …"

'No-one ever OWNS Bede Hall, tell her,' Jack shouted in Snow's head. *'People come and go and BORROW its rooms and gardens for a while. That is ALL, young lady!'*

Snow grimaced and mouthed 'be careful' to Rain. "I had other friends: the topiaries, and the swans in the lake on the days before the great ice sheet covered its surface. Unicorn and I often napped in the library chairs after I spent a few happy hours spinning the globe with my mind.

Once, a housemaid entered with her brooms and brushes and saw it spinning. She left service soon after. After that, no maid could be persuaded to clean the library alone. Not even for an extra shilling. I was sorry to have frightened them when all I wanted was to find Egypt on the map and lean my forehead on its cool surface. I discovered that was an easy way to daydream myself there. Sage, the topiary trimmed into the shape of the Great Sphinx, told me."

"We have no such topiary," Rain said. "But Ben will be pleased. He's mad for Egypt."

"It was created much later, after…"

Pookie placed a paw over Snow's mouth. *'Shhh! Rain mustn't know what you were about to tell her.'*

"*Um*… after I feel the pink sand between my bare toes on the summer days when I run barefoot over the fields of wet lavender in the rain." Snow patted the wallpaper over her bed. "There's a voice behind…"

Pookie shook her head to silence Snow, again. "Careful, child."

"*Um*… Parks explained to me that Bede Hall did its best to surround me with the kindness of warmer seasons when the gardens thrived under the tender care of the Green Man, and Parks should know. He's seen the Hall through good times and bad."

"I've never seen any ice to speak of on the lake," Rain said. "I think I've detected movement in the topiaries, though, and the colored lights in the flowers could easily be mistaken for fairies."

"After today, you will see them close up," Snow promised. "I'll let Nimue know to show herself. Be nice to her, she's far more full of herself than you are. Sorry, I didn't mean that to sound rude."

Rain shrugged. "It's all good. I know what I'm like. It's all an act. Well, mostly."

Snow handed Rain a licorice caramel. "Sometimes, when I drift through the hallways, I pass a servant in livery carrying trays of food or bowls of hot water. Whenever I find a rare patch of dust before the house maids erase it with their feather dusters or when the pastry cook leaves a fine coating of flour on one of the great kitchen tables from turning out the day's loaves, I write hello in it with my finger. I write hello in a lot of places to show I'm here. I write it in the window frost and the fog that mists the windowpanes when the coal fires are lit, and in the steam that fogs the morning room's mirror. I write hello as often as I can, and on other days, I remember to write thank you, as well."

"Thank heavens she remembers *something*," Jack snarked. "I hope that's a good sign."

"It's a start," Pookie agreed. "Now, it's up to us. We must put our heads together. It's not often that a rainy day gives a girl a new name."

Chapter 18

UPON WAKING

*It's a double-blustery day.
I am nine years old. My name is Snow
and possibly, Anu.*

The year is vaguely 19-something

TIDDLYPOM & MUMBLETY-PEG

Morning thunder rolled across the sky. It dropped and rumbled low over the snowy hills and rattled the bones of Snow's iron bedframe, stirring her dreams into a muddle of hot and cold memories until snowstorms and sandstorms became a confusing onslaught of stinging fairy darts.

Needles of fiery sand and freezing ice crystals whipped Snow's face as she slept.

Lightning crackled the dark room into warm sparks which danced the roses on the wallpaper, transforming the furniture and toys and piles of books into friendly shapes. For a moment, Snow woke to see her father sitting in one of the armchairs, staring at the fire that wasn't there, but she was only making a wish inside a dream.

It was mid-afternoon when Snow rapped on Jack's head. "Are you awake? I can't tell even when your eyes are open. I'm bored. I need company."

"Anything for you, little sphinx. What would you like to talk about? Keep in mind, I'm not in the mood for telling a long story, just now."

"I'm lonely too," Peri said from the wall. "I'll talk to you, sis."

Snow recognized Jack's sigh as relief. "What a splendid idea. You two can get better acquainted, and I can go back to… *er* work."

"Peri, I have a question," Snow said warily.

"Fire away."

"When were you… were *we* born?"

"It was morning, Ani."

"There's been quite a few mornings between my 'now' and your 'then'."

"Sorry. You were born first. Generally, the moment of one's death is more important in Egypt because it links directly to one's next life. You know… what constellation was nearest the horizon? Plus premonitions, omens, and dreams… that sort of thing."

Jack muttered "Oh, what have I done," from his door, left ajar on purpose to 'accidentally' hear as ordered by Pookie.

"That's what my… *our* father said, too."

"There was nothing dreamy about Dad," Peri said. "He was all science. Death in Egypt may have been about astrological rising and ascending stars based on the 'highest in the sky' and all that, but to Dad, it was pure astronomy."

Dear notebook, Snow wrote – *It's not my birthday, but after talking to Peri, I feel a thousand years older than an hour ago. Jack heard us and still called me baby girl. He never addresses my BABY brother as an infant. The unsettled wind blowing like a maniac, matches my furious mood. I am tired of being tired. Too tired to sleep. Too sleepy to wake up. Pookie was right. I'm a petulant child. Maybe that's why she's taken the day off.*

The wind worried the lace curtains. They flapped so desperately, Pigeon screeched loud enough to wake the dead, which is as it should be, because, after all, I AM a ghost, and my present mission hinges on the dynamics of waking and sleeping. So, here I sit, comforting the ghosts of a parrot and a cat. Earlier on, I had to rescue Unicorn, frantically burrowing under the covers the way a dog buries a bone. Parks had mentioned Unicorn never took to thunderstorms when he was alive, so, it's no surprise his ghostly form remains intent on escape.

The wind has several voices. It whispers feverish secrets one minute and roars curses the next. There are nights I find particularly unsettling when it howls like an injured beast. Today it lumbered across the hills, polishing Bede's landscape into a shiny crust of white enamel.

By sundown, Father hadn't come, so, I ate a piece of dry toast and one of Pookie's carrots.

I feel old and poetic... NOT to be confused with pathetic... although? Not far from it.

I'm noticing details in a lofty way. Most unlike the child me-of-me. High Winter snow fell in red papery flakes like autumn leaves that turned white by the afternoon. Father would have called it an IRONIC OPTICAL ILLUSION. He called high winter storms 'DELUSIONAL SNOW'. He said it was a farewell gift from a perverse season. Maybe he's where I get my creative words from. Although, when I asked Pookie, she burst into rabbity laughter until she had hiccups, and told me I was more like my Aunt Bash.

Father thought out loud to himself plenty of times. I tried not to pester him with childish questions. Uncle Kha taught me to always pay attention to my father's subconscious musings and to be patient if I was puzzled, because understanding would come later at the perfect time. perfect timing was big with him.

I've learned the hard way that beautiful things taste sour when there's no one to share them with. Bad weather was lovely when my father was home. We were shut-ins, together.

Lately, the winter has seemed endless, and I've had to creak the blue door open every hour or so to free it from the drifts. Fresh pink diamonds glittering on the doorstep have to be scraped away before the sun melts them into an icy glue that seals the door.

I remember things that I'd much rather not, like the deep frown lines on my father's forehead when he shook my shoulders, repeating

'PLEASE STAY WARM… CAN YOU HEAR ME?… ARE YOU LISTENING?' *several times. He was in a jumble of mixed emotions packing for his journey when he shouted like that. He'd delivered it as a warning rather than an order.*

He did that a lot, absentmindedly talking to me as he busied himself with matters clearly too important to raise his head from the maps and notes spread everywhere. But other than drinking tea when it's hot, there was nothing absentminded about my father.

I loved making him cups of sweet milky tea in his favorite mug, before I broke it, even though he always let it get cold. When he concentrated on a scientific problem, he was more lost in thought than me, which is saying a lot. It made me sad to watch him staring in despair at the sluggish sand in the hourglass he carried everywhere. Whenever he tried to speed up time by tapping the glass, the sand stopped altogether. His disappointment terrified me.

The hourglass is a family heirloom that was given to Lady Nan. She can't remember when.

Father used to rub it like the lamp in the story he read to me about a genie and a boy with too many wishes.

Yesterday, the night sky flared with horizontal stripes streaked with gold, pulsating green and pink that made the stars jump. The display was accompanied by a low hum that set me to dreaming of the time my father tried to explain what he called 'an anomaly'. Pookie told me later they were the northern lights – a sweeter sounding name than my father's 'aurora borealis'. My father was ever the consummate scientist, preferring to use the formal words for things, and oh, how he loved to simplify the similarities between yesterday, today, and tomorrow. TOMORROW IS MUCH LONGER, he said.

I asked the Hall to explain the passage of time. "Tomorrow is already here, child," it said. "Look out your window."

So, I looked. The garden was there, and Rain waved to me. She was wearing Parks' old hat and he stood with his hand on her shoulder grinning up at me. Unicorn was alive, chasing fairies that flashed red whenever he came too close.

The next moment I was beside them and winter was forgotten in a picnic of lemonade and cupcakes with the fairies taking more than their 'fair' share of the icing.

Last night the Hall built me a fine fire that crackled loud as thunder. The flame tips tangled with a pesky wind halfway up the chimney, blasting them into a resounding collision that sounded like a finale of crashing cymbals. Pulverized ash nearly put the fire out, so I fed the fire bits of broken chairs and a decaying table leg to calm it down. Pigeon 2 called out 'KEEP THAT FIRE DOWN TO A DULL ROAR' from his perch in the corner, reminding me of the time Father swore Pigeon was the class clown of exotic birds.

Canterbury rocked slowly in the wintry draught that whistled under the door. Pigeon 2 shrieked as many P words as he could in a state of over-excitement, and I moved his perch closer to the fire where he fanned his wings and made me laugh out loud. Father always reprimanded him for 'being in a flap' – a sure sign Pigeon was in the mood for a story.

"Pooh," he squawked. "Princess and the Pea... a continuing story... blustery days last forever."

I waved Beryl's tattered copy of 'House at Pooh Corner' in his direction to quieten him, but it inflamed him instead. He became positively unhinged, and I feared for Rain's china ornaments on the mantelpiece.

I'd marked the 'tiddlypom' page with one of Pidge's drab tail feathers and withdrew it in a flourish like a magic trick, brandishing it like a wand. For a strange moment, I wanted to dip the sharp end of it in ink and write a letter. But the notion soon passed, and I was back – a child in a white nightgown reading a children's tale of magic toys who befriended a lonely boy with the same name as my father. Father didn't like being called Christopher. Kit suited him but I found it difficult to call him by his first name. Sadly, he flinched when I called him Daddy or Father. He didn't think I noticed. But a child knows some things a grown up can't possibly understand.

[The more it snows, tiddelypom,
the more it goes, tiddelypom, on snowing.
And no-one knows, tiddelypom,
how cold my toes, tiddelypom, are growing.]

As I read those lines, Pigeon 2's dusty plumage transformed into their original fiery colors, including the grey feather bookmark, now a vibrant purple. The muddy blues turned iridescent turquoise, lacklustre red turned scarlet and magenta, forest greens took on the shades of lime and emerald.

A hazy memory of my father's voice played in my head. I caught it and held it briefly. "Pigeon," he'd, "you're a 'damned firebird." he'd laughed afterwards, so he wasn't cross.

Pigeon had belonged to Beryl's twin brother, Ben, and I gather, after much family squabbling, eventually passed to my father. Parrots live a long time, and even now my stuffed Pigeon 2 is very much alive to me. He's a direct link to what was. But in spite of his joyous rallying to story-time, my thoughts remain melancholy this bleak afternoon. The view from my window is autumn without the colors. I stared at it too long. It made me sleepy.

A withered treeline marks the ancient boundary of the Green Lady's territory. Even from my window I can pick out the boney arms of skeleton trees reaching for the sun's warmth. They look like exhausted soldiers after a long battle, but Jack says there's life in them, yet. They continue to flex their fleshless fingers in pitiful spasms. Today, a tree nymph waved to me from inside his twiggy nest, open to the elements, it looked like a cage rattling in the wind. His sorrowful wave depressed me. He looked so defeated, exposed without a curtain of leaves to hide behind. His mood infected me.

And now, the Winter Room is damp, bereft of life. The fire is almost out, and I haven't the heart to feed it again. I don't know where Pookie is, so it was Jack who finally called me out. He berated me in a way he knew would get my attention. He called me 'Keeper of the Flames', in a sarcastic way, guaranteed to hit a nerve. Sure enough, his words hit home: 'What would your father want you to do?' he snapped. And he reminded of a nightmare I once had of my father's 'death by winter'. Jack continued to rant: 'Kit knew better than anyone that falling asleep in winter was life threatening! Not for nothing, he commanded you to keep warm. Are you doing that baby girl? Are you!' All I heard was blah blah blah 'baby girl.'

I got all nostalgic after that. Vision after vision ran through my mind's eye of details I usually let pass. I suddenly became aware how magnetic clusters of snow crystals collected in the corners of the ceiling and fancied they'd been spun into steel cobwebs by the fairies.

Phew! I nearly disappeared, there. I was that older me-of-me. These are definitely NOT Snow's childish thoughts. She obsesses about tea and jam.

Gotta go. Pookie just arrived. Enough of the poetry. I hope summer will materialize tomorrow, and Rain or Vita will bring a breath of life into the attic. And considering Vita is a ghost, I'm not going to hold my own 'breath'.

Chapter 19

UPON WAKING

I am full of hope
Bede Hall is playing a game
I just might win
I am nine years old. My name is Snow.

The year is either 1949, 2023 or both
or some year in-between.
It's August, and for some obscure reason that's special

AND SO, IT GOES... ON SNOWING

Snow became overexcited as she rubbed a small hole in the window frost and peered down into a summer that shouldn't be there. A thin slick of ice defied the blistering heat of August and crept over the sundial's weathered face. The rest of Bede Hall's garden grew perfectly wild the way an abandoned landscape should.

"I have the feeling I've been here before," Snow said.

Pookie chuckled. "Déjà vu… it's all the rage in Bede right now."

"*Pfft,*" Jack scoffed. "When *isn't* déjà vu the rage in Bede?"

Snow saw the same things she always did on the heart-warming days with Rain: a marble sundial leaning slightly towards the stables, a round tower with its crenellated crown that gave her happy goosebumps, a maze that looked like a giant green puzzle, and a bright carpet of flowers that shimmered like jewels. Beyond them, a topiary sphinx that only Snow could see, basked under a blazing English sun.

For as long as she could remember, Snow expected Rain to arrive

85

in the in-between time to fulfill a promise made yesterday. August was her special window of time and Snow tried to keep her hopes up.

As the morning passed, Snow allowed herself to anticipate the thrill of meeting her friend again, but the garden remained deserted. For the ninth year in a row, the girl named Rain hadn't come.

As the shadows lengthened, a fairy wind tickled Snow's neck and the green landscape faded slowly into a sheet of white paper.

The fabric of Snow's favorite cotton dress with the lavender flowers, thickened into wool as the sleeves of her red winter coat materialized on her arms. Snow pulled its hood over her white hair and turned from the window, but the sound of birdsong made her wheel around, her eyes sparkling with renewed hope.

The scene below was a frozen wasteland clear to the horizon. There were no birds. The trickster wind was playing its whistling game with the roof slates. The Saxon round tower was gone again, it's crenellations breaking through the snow's crust like a fairy ring.

Snow waded through deep drifts towards the spot where Hadrian's Wall waited under the snowy drifts. It was easy to find. A Roman road of green clay, nine-foot wide, led east-west from the wall glowing bright under the snow. Snow shivered deeper into her hand-me-down coat that once belonged to another long-lost girl and leaned her forehead against the building stones she pictured in her mind's eye.

"Tomorrow is another day," the Hall said, trying to be kind. "I'm doing my best to find your friend. I need her too. Perhaps if we called her together, she will hear us."

Snow's mirror, the twin to the one in Rain's dining room, showed her pale ghostly reflection shining back, blue as the moon, lost inside its fur-trimmed hood. "Tomorrow never stays for very long," she whispered to the wallpaper roses, but I will concentrate one last time to please you." Within her lucid vision, Snow stood back from the wall and held out her arms as if to hug the world and wished for Rain's return, harder than ever.

Tiny white snowflakes with wings danced on Snow's red mittens and spun magic sparks into the room accompanied by fairy voices chanting an old nursery rhyme like a spell. *'Rain RAIN don't stay away. Come again another day'.* Finally exhausted, Snow curled on her cot like a cat, melted into the dreamtime, and slept for goodness knows how long.

Chapter 20

UPON WAKING

I hear Jack whistling.
I am nine years old.
I have four names: Snow/Anna/Ani/Baby Girl.
I sense a new friend is in the air
Jack says she's an old friend
who I've forgotten
it sounds like something I'd do

Jack says the year is c. 152 A.D.

LIFE IN THE WALL

Wind whistled through Jack's mouth to get Pookie's attention. *"Ahem"*, he coughed. "I believe our baby girl is past due for a nap within a nap. And it's our sworn duty to remind her, yet again, that only one room under the eaves belongs to her. Even though she's barred from its time portal, the two of you have the run of the estate. Lately, Snow's been wandering off."

Snow cuddled Pookie under her chin and closed her eyes. "You know," Pookie said. "I've heard the living speak of the cold spot in the attic with something akin to dread."

"That kind of talk always makes me shake my head," Jack said rattling the doorknob.

Snow mumbled in her sleep. "In my time, the entire house is frozen deep and blue, and, if anything, the fireplace in my room offers the only heat for I don't know how long."

Jack shuddered. The sound of his door slamming shut startled Pigeon 2 into a brief flap. *'A few million years, give or take,'* he squawked, and settled back into a dream of a white temple where, for a time, he was a god.

Pookie spoke inside Jack's mind. "It's about time we invited new *life* into the attic. What say you?"

"You're referring to Vita," Jack thought back.

"I am."

Pigeon 2 fluffed out his feathers half-heartedly, refusing to wake up. *'One door slams... another creaks opens,'* he mumbled sleepily before chattering himself back to a memory of blue skies, temple incense, and white sand.

Snow shivered into a ball under the chilly bedclothes, huddled closer into her father's sweater and hid her face in Pookie's fur. She squeezed her eyes shut and made a wish. *'Daddy, I don't want to be alone anymore. Please come back.'*

"He's trying," Pookie said patting Snow's face. "Your Aunt Bash used to say that time goes by faster when you think of good things. Listen, can you hear horses? You like horses."

Snow stirred awake. "And dogs, too. I hear dogs," she said. "My father had a dog named Jack."

"Tis a grand name," Jack Frost shouted from the keyhole, in an Irish brogue.

The sounds of galloping horses grew louder. A man's gruff voice shouted at the dogs to be quiet.

"The sounds of horses and soldiers means the fort is outside," Pookie said. "Why don't you see what Vita is up to."

"Who's Vita?" Snow said still half asleep.

"You've met Vita several times," Pookie said. "One day I expect you'll remember."

Snow opened her eyes and surveyed the room. "The fire's almost out," she blurted, hopping out of bed. "I promised Father I would keep it burning. He'll be upset."

The sounds of barking dogs grew louder as Snow raced to the

window. A girl waved up from the center of a dog pack snapping at the branch in her hand.

Snow waved back. "She's there. Vita is outside," she shouted.

Snow returned to the bed and tucked the covers around Pookie. "I have to build up the fire. You stay here and keep warm."

"Staying warm is Sage advice. So, it must be obeyed," Pookie said gravely. "I'm not overly fond of strange dogs, especially mad stick-chasing ones, so if you don't mind, I'll stay here, safe, and the room will be nice and cozy when you come back. Say hello to Vita for me."

"Maybe Vita will come back with me this time," Snow rattled on. "And we can have tea and cakes." Excited now, she pulled on her boots. "And I can show her my books. She's never seen a proper book. There's plenty to do."

Pookie smiled. "I would love to meet her, again," she said. "Now, go have fun."

For a carefree hour, Snow squelched through mud, throwing sticks for the dogs until one of them caught a scent that caused a mad canine dash to a destination unknown. "Well, now we'll have some time to ourselves," Vita said, hands on hips. "What would you like to do?"

Snow pointed to her window. "I'd like you to come to the attic with me," she said. "I have so much to show you. You'll love tea with lavender honey and fairy cakes. And I promise to read you a story from a serious book. No need to look so confused. I'll show you what serious books look like with no illustrations of teddy bears and piglets. Pookie wants to meet you as well. She's a magic rabbit."

"Yes," Jack said in Snow's head. "Pookie knows all too well about the magic powers of rabbits."

The girls entered through the main entrance. Vita climbed the staircase eagerly at first but looked nervously over the banisters at the floor far below before gamely carrying on. Snow caught a sense of Vita's fear. "No worries, we're nearly there. This is the library."

The red library looked exceptionally rosy in the sunlight. The shelves of leather spines, newly polished by the housemaids, shone softly. The air smelled of lemon wax. The first drops of gentle rain spattered the mullioned windows keeping time with the mantel clock. It was a room filled with peace. The giant floor globe stood squarely in a sunbeam turning slowly of its own accord.

Snow walked over to the bookcases and swept her arm over them. "These are serious books," she said dismissively, extracting a large fat volume protruding from a low shelf. She held it aloft like an offering and carried it to a table. It creaked open from the damp. Snow fanned the sticky pages until she found what she was looking for. "This is a book about the history of Britannia," she said, turning the open book towards Vita. "And this," she tapped a page, "is a photograph of Hadrian's Wall taken after it got old."

"Taken?"

"It means being captured in ink. Like a drawing. Perhaps captured isn't the best word. It's complicated. I'll explain later. For now, you don't need to know how it's done to see the picture. Look."

"Someone has ravaged it."

"Time has ravaged it. Many hundreds of years have gone by since you and I first met. But I want to show you something more important." Snow walked over to the globe, stopped it spinning, and selected the view of Africa. "This," she pointed to Egypt, "is where I was born." She traced her finger to the British Isles. "And here" ... *tap tap tap*... "is where you and I are standing right now. Come, place your finger on this wiggly line."

Vita approached, fascinated. "I've seen maps but never one painted on a ball," she said. She touched the horizontal line that divided a triangular land mass in two and flinched from static shock. "Where is this place?"

"Follow your finger over the line and see if you can tell me."

Vita touched the word Bede printed underneath the line. "If this is where you say we are, then surely this line is the Emperor's wall. I've followed it as far as I dared but it disappears into the distance where even I won't go."

The globe started to revolve again but Snow made it stop. "This painted ball is the whole world." She traced the line of Hadrian's Wall again. "If you could fly high enough, this is what Hadrian's Wall would look like from the stars." She turned the globe. "And this is Rome where the Emperor Hadrian, who built your Wall, came from."

An anxious shadow crossed Vita's face. She almost ran to the library windows. "I shouldn't stay away long. Once, when the fort disappeared, I was almost trapped here. I was afraid I'd never get home."

Snow looked over Vita's shoulder and pointed to a grid of military buildings laid out in orderly rows. Above it, floated a transparent blanket of green snow showing the faint pattern of lines outlining the design of the maze. Twin puzzles connected by the earth. "Look," Snow whispered. "The fort is there. Do you recognize the maze in my time? Well, it won't be on the ground for 300 years, so, you're quite safe."

Vita placed both hands on the window, leaving silver fingerprints.

Snow squeezed Vita's arm. "Bede is a mystical place where realities merge. You and I can cross its boundaries any time we choose to dream it so."

As the girls watched, the misty image of the maze blew away in the wind and the view of the fort sharpened into a solid grey mass of tiled buildings in a geometric pattern, clearly the maze's twin. Fenced square fields spread around it on all sides like a giant green and brown chessboard.

A large open area contained a scatter of mud huts where smoke curled from thatched roofs. Several smaller squares within it showed pens of sheep and pigs. Another, unfenced square, indicated a sprawling garden with rows of vegetables. Stables linked to a horse enclosure with a separate paddock, hugged the area to the fort's southern flank. Nearby, in an isolated enclosure, soldiers paraded in single file in a training yard. Two, even larger open areas lay to the east and west of the fort. Both contained a jumble of lean-to workshops bustling with commerce. A narrow track spiralled off into a copse of trees, to a circle. "I'm not sure what that circle is," Snow said.

"That's the sacred spring," Vita volunteered. "The green goddess lives there."

'*She still does, tell her,*' Jack said in Snow's head.

"You shouldn't be eavesdropping on a private conversation," Snow sent back, slightly miffed.

Vita continued, happier in her role as tour guide than visitor. "The women leave the goddess gifts of food on feast days. There's a temple, too, with its own well dedicated to Mars. The soldiers sacrifice animals there on special occasions. But I hide in the trees and cover my ears so I can't hear the fuss."

"A compassionate sensitive girl," Jack mused. "I like her."

Snow heard him and smiled. "Jack likes you. And he's not easily taken with strangers. Not that we get any when the high-winter comes."

A clean paved road ran from the Hall's entrance, following the drive to the main gates in a straight line where a battalion of armored soldiers marched north.

Vita inhaled a deep breath and exhaled slowly. *Phew…* her shoulders relaxed. "It's all right, I see the dogs chasing rabbits in the settlement's garden."

"Then, we have time for tea. My own books are upstairs. They belonged to Princess Beryl and now they're mine. We can read aloud to Pigeon who isn't a pigeon at all but a parrot. And speaking of rabbits, I have a friend who wants to meet you."

Vita and Snow reached the attic's chilly passageway where the blue paint of the Winter Room's door sparkled with shiny nuggets of ice embedded in the frost. Both girls giggled at their clouds of white breath.

Jack blinked, hello to Vita. "Pleased to meet you, *again*, lass," he said. "Welcome to the Winter Room. Don't worry, it's plenty warm inside." He narrowed his eyes at Snow. "And don't you be forgetting I'm in charge of watching over you. I may not see you, but sure as fairies, I will hear you. Pookie would bury my key if I didn't."

Pookie was not only out of bed, she'd made it and fluffed the pillows into an inviting reading cave. "We meet again, Vita," Pookie said as they came through the door. I do hope Jack didn't frighten you."

"I don't waste my time frightening wee girls," Jack called out. "I have *imp-portent* work to do."

Vita returned to the door and searched Jack's face, peering intently into his eyes. "It's all right, Jack. I'm sleeping right now, so you make perfect sense to me, and in any case, I'm known for being fearless. Even the commander of the horse turns a blind eye to my pranks, and he's not known for being overly fond of children. Sometimes I think he may not even see me."

"He doesn't. Not when you're dreaming," Jack said. "The dreamtime is a world of its own, right enough. Miss Snow has lived there ever since…"

"Thin ice ahead, Jack," Pookie interrupted with a curt telepathic warning. "Think whatever you wish, Jack, but watch what you think out loud. You must be more wary talking to visitors."

"I *am* a warrior," Jack said in a huff.

Pookie shook her head. "Listen, cloth ears. I said *wary*. It means being aware of what you say. Snow is vulnerable. Exposure is one of her locked doors. It means Snow is going through a necessary phase of helplessness, right now. Bede Hall has ears and eyes and a voice, and it loves to philosophize. Honestly, sometimes the two of you wear me out."

Jack stared long and hard at Pookie's ears. "Which one of us has cloth ears? That's what *I'd* like to know," he muttered gruffly. "Hadrian's Wall may have Vita, but in case you've forgotten, Bede Hall has a heart as big as all outdoors."

Vita looked longingly at the roaring fire, the table laden with food, and the cozy armchairs, but stared at the floor, hesitant to cross the room. "I don't want to crush the flowers," she said.

"It's a carpet," Pookie said smoothing the floral design with a paw. "They're not real, see?"

Vita hung back. "But my feet are muddy." She shuffled her feet, suddenly shod in soft knitted slippers, but would venture no further.

Pookie's nose twitched. "Is there a problem, my dear?"

"I don't understand," Vita said. "You were with another girl in the lavender field, the day we met. She was crying so *she* didn't notice me. But *you* did. It was the first time anyone from the spirit world saw me. Why?"

"I go wherever my girls take me," Pookie said, proudly. "There's no 'why' about it. It was a 'when' predestined by fate. All good and proper."

"You saw Bash, my soon-to-be Aunt," Snow interrupted, "if I understand time travel correctly."

Pookie chuckled. "You don't, Snow dear, but never mind, you're a clever child and soon you will know everything there is to know."

"That's what Jack told me, as well."

"Now, let's see about that promised tea, shall we. The kettle's boiled. Now, where's the sugar?"

Pigeon ruffled himself into a tizzy pacing back and forth on his perch. *'When does the story begin? I was promised a story.'*

"I promised *Vita* a story," Snow said.

'A story begins at the beginning,' Pigeon whinged, *'Or better yet, chapter seven.'*

Vita toasted her outstretched legs, balancing a cup and saucer precariously on her laps until Snow took the saucer away and offered her the first iced teacake of her life.

"I watch your world of shadows from the Roman wall," Vita explained with her mouth full. "I know a special place where there's a door in the stones. Some days I'm able to walk though even when I'm awake."

"It works from either side," Jack said. "But neither of you girls should overuse it. Never take dream-travel lightly. Even in Bede, traveling awake can be tricky. Time portals don't take kindly to being misused. Sparingly is the rule."

Howling dogs alerted Vita to the time. "That's the Wall's way of calling me home," she said. "I have to go. Will I see you tomorrow?"

Snow waved from the window. "I'll visit *you* this time."

Jack scoffed and called back for Snow's ears alone. "Snow will see you *yesterday* and not a moment before."

"Bedtime for you, little sphinx," Pookie called out. "It's been a long day." She telepathed Jack an urgent message. "And by long, I mean fractious. Let's leave 'snowy hour' for another night, shall we."

"Righty-o. If you say so. At the end of the day, I reckon you know best, ma'am."

Pookie turned down the bedclothes and plumped the pillows. "Amnesia is no small challenge for a child already overburdened with horrendous guilt," she sent. "It's no wonder Snow resists waking up. Our girl needs to be encouraged. Let's not give her any reason to doubt the wisdom of remembering her worst fears."

"I thought you didn't like it when I lied to her," Jack said. "I'm not soft, you know. I know what's ahead for the little mite. Her worst nightmare *is* necessary. As for being wise, only time will tell."

"Lies are always white in the Winter Room," Pookie replied slipping under the covers. "But we have to let her go." She wiggled her wet nose into Snow's cheek. "Sweet dreams, little sphinx," she whispered. "You're almost home."

Chapter 21

UPON WAKING

The words, hello again, fill my head.
I am nine years old. My name is Snow/Anna/Ani/Baby Girl.

The year in my father's dream is 2014

THE WRITING'S ON THE WALL

Pookie listened to Snow from her spot at the head of the bed while Snow tidied the hearth. Snow, mesmerized by her father's account of a strange dream, had stopped brushing ashes into a dustpan and closed her eyes, the better to recall the conversation between her father and his mentor, Peregrine Brooks. She listened intently to Kit's dream the same way Pookie scrutinized her's. Except, Pookie was worried where she was enthralled. Pookie's ears flapped erratically while she waited impatiently for Snow's bubble to break.

Snow's bubble shattered suddenly. The dustpan clattered to the floor in a cloud of dust and Snow dropped to her knees, clutching her stomach.

"Crisis," Pookie telepathed Jack. "This may be it!"

Snow rocked silently, hugging herself, clearly anguished. "Wait! she whimpered. "How can I remember someone else's dream!"

"You can't… you weren't," Pookie soothed. "Baby girl, you were there playing ghost to what actually happened. Tell her, Jack."

Snow reached out an arm. "Pookie, where are you? I can't see. I can't open my eyes."

"I'm here and so is Jack," Pookie soothed. "All you have to do is listen. The panic will pass. I promise. You are quite safe."

Snow rolled onto her side and hugged her knees. "I'm *not* safe" she panted. "I want to be sick. I'm going to disappear."

Pookie hopped to Snow's side. "Concentrate on staying," she said. "Hold my paw and pay attention to Jack's voice. Take deep breaths. We've talked about panic attacks before. Remember? It was when Six died and your Aunt Bash …"

"I want to die," Snow moaned. "But I'm already a ghost. What's happening to me?"

"What's happening is your fear of waking up," Jack said.

"I wake up all the time."

"But there are different *levels* of waking up."

Snow thrashed under the bedclothes flailing her arms as if she were drowning. "The ice is breaking," she wailed. "Please help me. The water is too cold. I'm too tired to swim."

"The ice is breaking," Pookie repeated. "That means she's fighting."

Jack's voice settled gently over Snow. "It's very simple, child. You're scared of waking up. Now, I know you wake-up every morning, but this is a different sort of awakening. You've had a wee shock. You're fighting a memory you don't want to remember. It's called a nightmare. We've been through plenty of those, haven't we?"

Pookie nodded to Jack. "Thin ice," she telepathed. "If her dream breaks, we have to let her fall through. She's remembering one of Ben's memories. The day he died."

"The thing about walls is this," Jack explained in a sterner voice. "They record everything that happens. And as a special dreamer you're able to visit events that walls have seen from before you were born."

Pookie tucked the blankets firmly around Snow.

Snow's voice faltered. "Special dreamer," she mumbled in a trance. "Before I was born. It seemed so real."

"It *was* real," Pookie said. "Peregrine Brooks was your father's mentor. Now, pretend the wall in Brooks' living room is a movie screen where your dream is playing and tell me what you see."

"Brooks is sitting across from my father. Father is thirteen. They're having tea and a normal conversation after one of their intensive meditation sessions," she said. "But their exchange is anything but normal. My father is in shock and denial over an out-of-body experience that Brooks had so recently assured him were natural occurrences to be welcomed. She smiled dreamily "As it happens, that trip was with me. In fact, I rather caused it."

"You remember that!"

"Oh, yes. Clear as ice."

"Marvellous. Don't think about ice for now. Remembering is the road to …"

"Life," Jack muttered."

"Imagine my delight," Snow said. "My father had been dreaming of *me*."

"He'd been dreaming *with* you," Pookie corrected. "There's a difference."

Snow's arms and legs trembled wildly. She clutched her blanket, desperately trying to save herself. "You've spoiled everything, Pook. Why did you have to do that. My father *was* dreaming of me. He WAS!"

"Little sphinx, I've done nothing of the kind," Pookie soothed. "It's my job to steer you right whenever you're about to run your boat aground. You tend to do that a lot. And it never serves your mission. So, please, take a deep breath and see *your* dream, not your *father's*. Look again. You were never there in real time. You watched from Brooks' ceiling or behind his wallpaper. It was a spying dream. You were only a spectator. Now report it properly so we can decode its message, together. Your dreams may be entertaining but they're *not* entertainment. Replay it in your mind and I will see and hear what you experienced. Jack will join us, won't you, Jack."

"Try and stop me," Jack replied. "I wouldn't miss this for the world."

The wallpaper roses in the Winter Room morphed into dandelions that immediately aged into a field gone to seed. Seeds swirled from their stems in a whirlwind that churned them into snowflakes. The temperature dropped. Snow shivered uncontrollably as the white blizzard solidified into a blank movie screen where animated images of a scene in Brooks' living room appeared. Bede Hall provided the whirring sound of a film projector and dimmed the lights.

A charming book-lined room glowed with the last light of an autumn afternoon. The room, clearly a bachelor's domain, was minimally furnished with a pair of enormous black leather armchairs, a few strategically placed potted palms, and accentuated with Egyptian artefacts. A replica of King Tut's golden throne stood in the corner where a single finger of warm light filtered through the Venetian blinds and glanced off the King's cartouche.

Brooks and Kit sat facing each other. Brooks, cupped a large brandy glass and swirled its amber contents, never taking his eyes off Kit.

Kit looked shrunken and pale, a boy being swallowed by a chair. He leaned back with his arms crossed as if to protect himself. "I thought I'd dreamed that Anna and I flew to Bede," Kit said. "But I was mistaken. It was *Anna's* dream, and she'd just happened to fetch me from the maze while I was on the edge of sleep. I didn't have a chance. I think she might actually be a ghost. Am I going crazy?"

Brooks uncrossed his legs. "That's very funny," he said taking a sip of brandy.

"What is?"

"Do you know what a fetch is?"

Kit shook his head.

"It's a spirit who visits the living to deliver a message at the moment of their death."

"So, Anna *is* a ghost, then. Blimey, maybe Bash is right," Kit said. "Maybe Bede Hall *is* a mystical place." He stopped. "No, forget I said that. It's not possible. I'll grant you dreams are weird, but I'd probably been eating something that upset my stomach. Anyway, there's no such thing as ghosts. Right?"

Brooks raised his eyebrows. "I'd say everything in and around Bede is up for grabs. The sooner you accept that the better for everyone. And by everyone, I mean your grandmother."

Kit looked defeated. "We'd best forget the whole thing. Meditation does funny things to me sometimes. It's no big deal."

"Go on. You've gotten this far," Brooks urged. "If nothing else, you'll feel better when it's out in the open."

Kit's mouth twitched nervously. "Okay, fine. In the dream, we, Anna and I, were flying over the countryside in a wide circle like swans trying to land. It started to snow. The flakes momentarily obscured the scene below, but it must have been a blizzard because the world went white, and we landed deep into the nuclear winter I'd been charged to prevent. It was clearly, a future ice-age."

Brooks nodded reassuringly. "Breathe, Kit. Slow down."

"Bede Hall was buried up to its… up to its *attic* in snow. It reminded me of the tip of an iceberg, and underground it was as crushed as a sunken ship. Creepy would be an understatement."

Brooks leaned forward eagerly. "You mean like the wreck of Titanic we saw in the recovery documentary?"

Kit exhaled deeply. "Yes," he said with relief. "Exactly like the broken interior of a cold, dark ghost ship. Bede Hall was chilly and damp, and where Titanic's interior dripped with strands of underwater plant life, icicles dangled from Bede's ceilings, staircases, and light fixtures."

Brooks patted Kit's knee. Concern showed on his face. "You've been holding your breath ever since the day you moved into the Hall, haven't you."

"Odd that you would say that because I *did* see something that day. It was Anna. I pretended she wasn't there. I even walked through her a couple of times, but Jack saw her." Kit visibly relaxed. He unlocked his hands and brushed the white forelock from his eyes. "I've been denying it for a long time."

"You're doing fine. Keep going as long as you can."

Kit took a deep breath and plunged back into his memories. "The blue door to the Winter Room had become Bede Hall's main entrance. There were other doors either side of it that I recognized as servants' bedrooms, and the old nursery.

The door was unlocked. The room looked different from the bare bones Bash and I first saw. Pigeon was inside, dead, covered in mildew and grey dust. He'd been stuffed and yet he moved his wings and started to sing a nonsense song of tiddly pom and snow that he'd learned from Bash. The whole thing seemed real, but I assumed it was a crazy lucid dream. I believe now, it was one of those waking dreams you told me about.

There was a tiny box room stacked with rubbish and old kitchen chairs. I smashed one against the wall and improvised a campfire from its legs.

Anna showed me a portal in the crawl space, and we followed it a long way, almost to Bede Village until I chickened out. We returned to a different hallway and Anna floated us down to Lady Nan's bedroom that had become a morbid shrine. I panicked after seeing her snow globe in a glass cabinet. When Anna led me back upstairs to the Winter Room, the campfire was gone. She pulled a tattered old notebook from a shelf and gave it to me. The thing had been through the wars, but I recognized it as mine. It was the brand new notebook I'd been writing in, only moments before in the maze. Actually, I had no idea how much time had passed. Anyway, it contained the devastating date of 2023 and entries I can't bear to remember. That's when it dawned on me that the dream might be a future reality. That time-travel was true. Naturally, I panicked. I thought perhaps I'd died, and I was haunting the place."

Brooks let out an audible sigh and massaged his scalp as the last shred of daylight faded from the room. He made the rounds and switched on every lamp. "Go on," he said. "You're not nearly done."

"Anna was chirpy enough, which made the whole thing worse. Like any little girl playing house, she insisted on having a tea party. There was plenty of snow to melt for water. I watched her in a kind of daze. I don't know how I drank the tea, but I did, and then I collapsed in an embarrassing heap and blubbered like a baby for Bash to rescue me."

Brooks pressed his glass of brandy into Kit's hand. "Take a little sip. It won't hurt you," he said.

Kit swallowed a large gulp and made a face.

"I guess she did, because I woke up freaked out in the maze with Bash standing over me, demanding why I hadn't shown up for supper. And that's pretty much it. It was the middle of the night. I know because the window in the library was open and I heard the clock chime nine. And besides, Bash showed me her watch. She was some kind of upset."

Kit brushed the hair out of his eyes again and looked as if he was about to be sick. The only sound in the room was the squeak of leather upholstery as he squirmed in his chair.

All the while, Brooks' smile had grown wider as he listened. "Dear boy," he said, positively beaming when Kit took a breath. "I envy you. I've tried to time travel many times and failed." He stood and removed the brandy glass from Kit's hand, walked across the room to the decanter, replenished it, and held it up to the light as if it was an object of wonder as he paced the room, grinning like a schoolboy.

"This is your destiny," Brooks said. "How wonderful to have discovered it so young." He sniffed the swirling brandy and drained the glass. "Your Uncle Ben's throne chair was indeed meant for you. I've been keeping it dusted and ready. I see, now it's high time it *traveled* back to the Hall where it belongs."

Brooks dropped back into his chair and leaned back looking pleased. "I will arrange that it's delivered without making a grand entrance. Let it blend in without incident. You made it clear when your grandmother gave you the tower, that it was to be out of bounds unless otherwise invited. It was your private science lab, you said. And everyone accepted that. Anyway, the family may not see it. And if any of them cared to look, they would see it for what it is – a family heirloom bequeathed to you by me, the legal executor of your uncle's estate."

Kit slammed his clenched fists on the chair's armrests. "But I…"

"But nothing!" Brooks shouted. "The chair has spoken. I sense it wants to rest in your Saxon tower. In fact, it wants to play, of that, I'm sure. It KNOWS you!"

Kit's terror-stricken expression left anger behind. "I don't want the thing. A haunted chair. For god's sake, Brooks, I thought you were my guardian."

"Christopher, not wanting one's destiny is unscientific. It's so unlike you. It wasn't easy to explain the concept of life inherent within an inanimate chair, to you. The how of it eludes me, still, so don't ask. But lately, since you began meditating with me, the feeling is more palpable. And, by the way, it's not a thing. Well, it's an object, true enough, but it's alive. And it wants to be your friend."

"And that's not supposed to be scary?"

"Destinies are supposed to be scary," Brooks scoffed. "They're challenges."

The lights came on and the screen fizzled out to pulsating wallpaper roses, none the worse for wear. "Okay, Jack said. "We're not out of the woods yet, so, let's go over it, point by point."

Snow sat up, slightly recovered, and sipped her own cup of tea, grown cold. She stared over the rim of her cup and sighed. "Oh, Pookie, I do so hate being dead."

"We'll need to hear your own account of the day you first met your father in the Winter Room," Jack said at long last.

"The third floor was always deserted," Snow began. "Only the kitchens bustled with life. Rupert was there stewing about some new grievance he'd imagined. The twins were bored. Bash had the bright idea to pursue the ghost in the attic. Kit held back but you know how persuasive Bash can be. Bash punched his arm, shouted 'you're it!' and ran off. Kit followed her, reluctantly at first, but he got swept along with the challenge. They chased each other up and down the stairs, playing 'you can't catch me' until a chilly blast from the cold spot stopped them in their tracks. That was the start of Bash's determination to get the key from Lady Nan.

After that, it was only a matter of days before the twins opened the blue door.

I'd written the word hello in the window frost and hidden behind the wallpaper. And then I saw the boy, Kit, my father, for the first time in real life. I hadn't been born so he couldn't recognize me. In fact, he *refused* to acknowledge I existed at all. So, the more he griped about the non-existence of ghosts, the more I haunted him day and night."

After that, Lady Nan and I had a proper reunion, and I became a member of the family. But it was a bittersweet meeting. Kit's parents and older brother couldn't see me, and Kit was afraid of me. He may even have hated me. There was a young boy as well, but I can't place him.

Bash was a sweetheart, though. She gave me you, Pookie, to stop me crying." She squeezed Pookie's paw. "You've been my loyal companion for sixty years.

And now, I've met Vita all over again, several times I think, without remembering.

And as for finding a message in last night's dream, I'd tried telling Kit he was my father, but he wouldn't listen, so I let him discover it for himself in his notebook. We explored several ruined rooms. Kit remained calm and quiet, but Lady Nan's bedroom with her memorabilia, spooked him.

When he read the page I'd marked, he burst into tears. Just as he told Brooks."

Jack sent Pookie a telepathic message. "Go on ask her."

"What else?" Pookie asked in a whispery voice. "I sense there's more."

Snow sat, a statue in a trance with a dreamy smile pasted on her face. "Well, and this is strange, one evening, Kit remembered a dream he'd had when he was a little older than I am now, and as he pictured it in his mind, I saw it too."

"Can you still see it?" Pookie asked. "Can you see it right now?"

"Yes. My father is dreaming of the High Winter. He's trudging through deep snow, searching for someone or some thing. He has no idea who or what other than he's on a mission to get home, although I know it's my mother. But he falls asleep from the cold and dies. He woke up screaming in his bedroom in Livingston. Only nine minutes had passed according to clock time. It was so real, he wrote about it in his science log the next day.

"It was *real* to a point," Jack mused. "Ahead of Kit's time, of course, but in a roundabout way, it brought the two of you together. I guess you could say your destinies were intertwined the day you wrote hello in the window."

"I think I could eat something now," Snow said. "I'm famished."

"Okay, little sphinx, warm milk with lavender honey and a piece of dry toast… then, bed. It's important that you concentrate. The gold lies buried under your fear. And by that, I mean the truth of the matter."

Snow was nibbling on her toast, when, out of the blue, she asked in a strong, clear, grown-up voice: "Why do I never wake up?"

Jack laughed out loud. "Oh, little flake, I mean *snow*flake, you just did, if only for a second. Tomorrow it may be two or three precious seconds. And then, with patience, the hours will arrive."

Chapter 22

UPON WAKING

A lost boy calls me from the wall above the bed.
I am nine years old. My name is Snow.

The year is also lost

THE LOST BOY

Snow approached the blue door with pursed lips and a determined chin. "Jack!" she exclaimed. "I have to report there's an unknown *boy* in my wall. This room is supposed to be mine alone, is it not?"

Jack raised a leafy eyebrow. "Please restrain your indignation. You'd do well to remember that the ancient land of Khem lies directly behind your wall, little sphinx. And what better companion for a lost Egyptian girl named little sphinx than a lost Egyptian boy."

"There's me!" Pookie replied from the windowsill sounding put out.

Snow looked in the mirror and studied her profile, taking the opportunity to practise her icy stare to use on Jack. "I'm Egyptian?"

Jack swallowed an icicle lodged in his throat. "Look, Snow, the boy's not lost; he's family. If you recall, and obviously you don't, you've abandoned him at least twice. Once as Anna, and another as Ani. It's time he had his say. It's time you *listened* to what he has to say. High-wintertime, in fact."

"Sibling rivalry," Pookie said, her ears trembling. "That old chestnut. Old as the hills and it never gets any easier."

Snow's voice lowered to a stage whisper. "Well, I believe he's *still* in there, Jack. What can we do to get him out?"

"Nothing," Pookie answered. "Rules are rules, and the time portals have more than most. Peri is a good lad. He won't hold a grudge. He's your brother and willing to stay nine years-old along with you, as time and twinship dictates. Best accept that for now. Jack and I will keep an eye on things. If they change, you'll be the third person to know."

Snow's gasp turned into a wide grin. "I have a brother?"

"A *twin* brother," Jack said.

Snow twirled in a happy dance. "My father's mission was to collect my mother. I don't remember him mentioning anything about a brother. Father must be there, in Egypt with… what did you say his name was?"

"In an Egypt that *was*," Pookie whispered. "Your brother's name is PERI. It sounds like peregrine for a reason."

Snow clambered to the headboard, placed an ear to the wall, and knocked. "Peri, is Father with you?"

There was a long pause in which Pigeon 2 squawked from his perch behind her. *'I believe I'm back there, too.'*

Snow sent him a withering look. "Shush Pigeon, I'm trying to listen across thousands of years."

'Well, excuse me for trying to help', Pigeon 2 squawked. The Winter Room went deathly quiet as Snow waited. *'Too rhymes with Pooh,'* Pigeon finally said, lamely, to break the silence.

"All my stares are icy, by the way," Jack mused. "Chilling glares are my specialty."

"Pigeon sends his regards to his parrot ka," Peri said after a heated discussion with his own Pigeon. "He wants you to know it wasn't his fault that I got left behind and that Father is on his way to Bede Hall."

"He's been on his way for 3000 years," Pookie sniffed.

Peri rapped out an S.O.S. – two sharp knocks followed by a count of four, and two more short knocks. "I want to come home if you'll let me."

"A veritable Pan child from Neverland or Wonderland," the Hall interjected. "Depending on the season, mind you."

Jack chuckled. "Time travel is tricky," he said. "No matter, it always works out in the long run."

'Not for all of us, it would seem,' Pigeon muttered.

Snow slammed her fists on the table. "All of you stop! This is *my* room, and I say it's time to open the crawl space door. If *I'm* not allowed to open it, maybe *Beryl* is. She's a princess. That has to count for something."

"Soon enough, baby girl, the Hall joined in. Doors are tricky too, as you well know, Jack. So, let's be practical. It's up to Kit to clear the time portals from wherever he is, at least we can all be clear on *that*."

"So, which comes first? The portal or the boy?"

"Ah," Jack said. "Now *that's* a puzzle worthy of tonight's 'snowy hour'. I'll need the rest of the day to prepare the answer. I don't relish disappointing baby girl, here," he said to the Hall, "but my hands are tied. *You* tied them when I *had* hands. And now, if I'm right, and I always am, the hands of time point to a reunion, do they not."

Snow picked up Pookie and searched her eyes. "Why on earth wouldn't I let Peri come home?"

The sudden sound of Pigeon 2 furiously attacking his cuttlebone broke the tension.

"One of you had better answer me," Snow said meeting Jack's blank expression.

"Jealousy," Pookie whispered, covering her eyes with her ears. "Here we go."

Snow brushed Pookie's ears to the side. "There's no need to be jealous of me," she said. "Unless… there's something you're not telling me."

"Oh dear," the Hall said. "Another can of wriggly worms opened too soon. Jack, you really need to find better things to do with your time."

Jack chose his words carefully. "It was a long time ago… *um*… an *extremely* long time ago, *before* your time, baby girl," he said. "It was, you might say, before *anyone's* time. His voice took on a tall-tale telling. "Jealousy arrived from a distant star and infected an exceedingly vast area of land. The biggest land mass earth has ever seen." His voice resumed his business-like mode. "Jealousy was a literal PAN-demic you might say, passed down from twin-to-twin, family-to-family, matriarch-to-matriarch for millions of years. More specifically, from your father to you. Twice, in your case. A double dose since your…"

Pookie thumped her foot. "Thin ice," she cautioned. "Melting snow!"

"My father was never jealous of me," Snow said. "Was he?"

"Of course not; he was jealous of his sister Bash, and even more profoundly, his half-brother, your Uncle Tut."

"Are you saying that *I* was jealous of Peri?"

"Let's just say, you chose to leap ahead of the sibling game just in case."

"I was a child, Jack. Besides, even if I *was* jealous, I'm not, now."

"And even though you may have lived thousands of years, you haven't aged. So, you're still a child, baby girl. The *same* child with the same karma, and the language of a wise woman."

"And did I mention… NOT jealous of my lost brother."

"That may be true, but karmic jealousy binds with a long leash. You were born 'Pan Gemini', half of a powerful force, and as such, you're held to a higher standard. The slightest infraction carries heavy penalties. Besides, the word sorry has no power. The word jealousy is equally benign. Actions speak louder than words… the bad ones more than most. The *act* of jealousy has far reaching consequences beyond your wildest dreams."

"My dreams aren't wild," Snow snapped.

The aggressive answer pushed Jack's alert button. "Well, they *are*, sad to say. Your dreams arrive out of sequence which makes them wildly unstable. Random equates to out of control. But *your* problem is memory loss. You only remember fragments that are miniscule figments of a vast picture – a four-dimensional puzzle, in fact. But you're nearly there. With patience and repetition, time accelerates without warning. Just ask your father. The finishing line is often closer than one thinks." Jack hemmed and hawed. "Look, I *could* show you how, little sphinx, but Pookie WILL show you how. There's a big difference!"

"Peri is working with Pookie?"

'She's called a key for a reason,' Pigeon 2 called out. *'Although I*

have to say, she can be a tad mercurial if left to dwell. 'Now, for Pooh's sake, let's unlock that wretched door.'

Pookie hopped to the window and spoke over her shoulder. "And you're terribly wrong, Jack, not to mention absentminded. Haven't you noticed that ever since 'movie night' our girl *has* been dreaming in sequence. If this continues it may jog some crossed wires."

"One lives in hope."

"A pretty futile place to live if you ask me."

"As it happens, I didn't. I never do. And Bede Hall suits me."

The Hall's thoughts bounced off the walls. "Are you calling me futile, Pook?"

Snow wandered off, mumbling in a daydream. "Anyway, it doesn't matter."

Pigeon chattered to himself under a wing. *'Quite true. And exceptionally ironic actually, since such profound utterings of wisdom are usually considered chiseled in stone.'*

Snow's mind was eons away. "Nothing matters anymore. I have a brother, and I will bring him home even if I have to go to Egypt to do it!" she whispered.

PART 3

rude awakenings

Now I lay me down to sleep,
I ask the gods my ka to keep –
To watch me safe throughout each night
and wake me with the morning light.
If I should die before I wake,
I ask the gods my ka to take.

Chapter 23

UPON WAKING

I am kidnapped by Anna.
I am a newborn. My name is Ani.
The year tried to be 2018

But it was c. 3000 B.C.

EXODUS

Unicorn stretched contentedly on a sunbeam island, ignoring the tea party. Snow poured the tea. Pookie sat on Snow's lap, smiling as Rain held her teacup suspended, hypnotized by Snow's life story.

Snow happily recited from a strong memory. "Deep in the inner sanctum of the Temple of Bast, when the cries of my newborn twin brother woke me, I found a young girl looking down at me. She smiled hello, reached into my cradle and picked me up. *'My name is Anna,'* she said, although I knew her instantly. Our thoughts, past, present, and future, were one thought."

Rain's eyes widened. "She was you?"

Snow held out a plate of cream cakes. "She was."

The Hall 'had the floor', so to speak, as it recited its own version of Snow's story to Jack and the wallpaper. Equally as enthralled as Rain, Jack listened, and kept a silent vigil over the girls' tea party out the corner of his eye.

"Anna cuddled Ani close," the Hall reminisced. "She crept through the private room where her parents, grandparents, and Uncle Kha were seated discussing a matter of great importance. Although Anna made no attempt to hide, only Kha saw her. He inclined his head, acknowledging Anna, smiled inwardly, and shifted to his persona as Master alchemist, donning his fairy glamour like a cloak. He loomed taller and brighter. Charges of static electricity snapped around him in an aura of buzzing golden bees.

Anna saw her family from every angle as she wove through the gathering, lightly touching every shoulder, progressing backwards towards the year 2018.

Hundreds of alert cats lined the temple passages, their eyes glowing florescent in the dark. A single black cat withdrew from the colony and padded after her, staying in the shadows of the tree-shaped columns that lined the halls – an alabaster forest under a canopy of stone leaves.

As Anna sleepwalked, Ani melted into Anna's body until nothing separated them. Ani became nine-years-old. Anna returned to being the child ghost of Bede Hall and re-entered fairy-tale sleep.

For hundreds of years, Anna wandered restlessly through fields of sweet-scented wildflowers that blossomed between erratic seasons. Fickle summers and winters blew hot and cold, and all the while she spent her idle hours spinning quicksilver dreams until Beryl opened the door to her room in the attic.

Both girls were nine. Both had lost their fathers. Both took new names.

For a few golden years, Snow spent her days with Rain. And when Rain became Beryl again, Snow visited their charmed past in case Rain would come back. Most days, Snow traveled wherever her dreams took her. She visited other worlds until a new friend came and she smiled once more."

"Funny," Jack said, "but only last night, Snow dreamed she was a baby in a cradle."

"So, you see," Snow said, refreshing the teapot, "babyhood advanced to childhood and I entered a period of fairy tale sleep, dreaming inside this room. Apart from Parks and his *son* Stanley, Jack Frost, the Hall, and Unicorn, my companions were the topiaries. We chased each other over the lawns, playing tag. I delighted in the summer garden hoping you would see me."

"I knew the topiaries moved. No-one believed me, not even Ben."

Snow filled a saucer with pretend cream for Unicorn. "Parks took pity on me the first day, and Stanley befriended me as an older brother."

Rain offered Unicorn a dollop of whipped cream from her finger. "I wasn't allowed to visit Parks' family, but Stanley was my secret friend who taught me how to care for the garden." Rain tickled Unicorn behind the ears. "When Unicorn died, Stanley and I buried him in the maze."

"I often visited Parks' cottage," Snow said offering her empty teacup for Pookie to sip. "It was bustling with Parks' of every age. Each one of them was as unpredictable as the star-crossed seasons."

"I still can't believe that the entire Parks family are ghosts, including Stanley."

Snow cuddled Unicorn. "Parks, the elder, told me one day he hoped to be born properly. He said the moon would send him word when it was time, and his name would be Six. I believe it's any day, now."

Chapter 24

UPON WAKING

The winter is good
I am nine years old. My name is Snow.
Rain is twelve

The year is 1952 headed for 1961

THE SNOWMAN COMETH

It was still moon-dark when Pookie woke Snow by wriggling her nose deeper into Snow's ear. "Wake up it's the *good* winter," she squeaked. "The low one… right now. Come on before it disappears." For a delicious moment, Snow savored the glow from the waking fire that painted the walls pink.

The light from the banked fire turned the room rosy. Parks must have lit it while she slept and banked it for the night.

One encouraging word from Pookie was all that was needed. Snow bounded from the bed and ran to the window. The garden was whitewashed with crystals, every flowerbed dusted with fine flour, treetops wore veils of white gauze. The topiaries huddled together in a sculpture garden of frosted animals. From above, an ice palace maze, invited Snow to play inside a larger-than-life floor puzzle. Hadrian's Wall, a distant dragon's tail, slunk over the hills, its scales glistening ice-blue into the horizon.

Snow pulled on her boots and crept downstairs. She embraced the pleasant coolness of thin snow and ran over the crunchy grass to visit Sage.

. . .

Snow placed the flat of her hands tenderly on the wall above her bed. "Please thank Parks for the fire."

"You're welcome, baby girl," the Hall said.

"I'm not a baby even though I sometimes wake up in a cradle." She paused. "Why are there two winters? And two mugs of cocoa?" She listened hopefully for footsteps outside the door. "Is one for Beryl? It can't be for my father because he belongs to the *high* winter."

The Hall's sigh caused the coals to stir and the fire burst into full flame. "There are three winters. All of them bleak. Which one pleases you?"

Snow propped Pookie in the chair opposite hers and blew on her cocoa before taking a sip. Her breath pushed a hole in the marshmallow foam floating on top. Immediately, she recalled a vision of Bede's ice-covered lake. Wind howled over its icy skin, sweeping surface frost into a low-lying mist, revealing a dark hole. From faraway, she heard Beryl crying.

It wasn't the familiar sound of a girl feeling sorry for herself. It was the gut-wrenching agony of a girl in mourning.

For a long time, Snow sat dream-locked, pouting over her cocoa. "Beryl only lives in the low winters," she finally said in a hush, trying to shake off the haunting sound. "We liked to build our own Roman fort and wall, and I forgot to be sad. I suppose I like that winter and all the summers. The bad winter makes me see my father's blue coat on the horizon when it isn't there, so, it's lonelier, but I like the blazing fires. Why doesn't Beryl visit me anymore?"

"It's not up to me."

"Then who?"

"The fires you remember are Beryl's fond memories. When she's older, she will come to hate winter."

"Yes, I've seen her moping. I don't think she can even *see* me most of the time, but I keep her company just the same. There's no telling when she'll break through. She doesn't speak. We share those moments, silent and gloomy, together. Beryl obsesses about a winter lake. I saw it just now, in my cocoa. She never told me why and I never asked. A good friend would have asked."

"Both of you pine. You have strong winter memories. Dashed hopes and dreams are wintry things. Beryl and Ben are building a snowman in the back garden. Why don't you join them."

"There's not enough snow for a snowman but I *would* like some company."

No sooner than the thought of joining them occurred, Snow found herself in the garden dressed in her red snowsuit.

Beryl waved hello. "Come on, there's plenty of work for you to do," she shouted.

Ben glanced behind him. "Who are you talking to? Is your invisible friend here?"

"Maybe."

"Hello, Beryl's imaginary friend," Ben said loudly, facing the wrong direction, "whatever your name is."

Beryl concentrated on smoothing the snowman's belly. "She's quite real," she said without making eye contact.

Ben pretended to doff an invisible cap and reverted to Park's accent, addressing Beryl. "Beggin yer pardon, Miss." He turned on his heels and formally bowed to the air. "Hello, Beryl's magical friend." He held out his hand to shake. "My name's Bentley Stratford-Smyth. I'm Beryl's twin brother. I'd be pleased to make your acquaintance if you'd care to show yourself. You can call me Ben."

"She's not magic," Beryl replied sounding miffed. "She's a ghost. The one that haunts the nursery."

Ben made a harmless snowball and threw it at his sister's coat. "It was *my* nursery too. And I can't know her name because…?"

"Because she belongs to me. *Only me.* You have real school and your chums."

"It's bad luck girls aren't allowed to go to school, and I'm glad you aren't lonely all day, but all the same, I'd like to see a ghost. Papa says there's no such thing."

"It's not up to me, and there *is*. The housemaids refuse to go near the nursery. They say there's an ominous cold spot in the passage."

"Nonsense. Those muddleheaded girls would never use a big word like ominous. Hey! Where did that carrot come from?"

"Sorry, you're right. I materialized a carrot to impress you." Beryl crossed her arms and stared smugly at Ben as an orange projectile whizzed past his face. "Where did you *think* it came from?"

"No way."

"Well, *I* didn't go to the kitchen in the last few minutes. Did *you*?"

"I didn't see a disembodied carrot floating by either. It was in your pocket."

"Suit yourself." Beryl pointed to a pile of black stones at Ben's feet. "And what about those, bossy britches? If I'm not mistaken, I'd say they were snowman buttons."

Ben shrugged and sent her one of his famous lopsided grins. "Have it your way, sister-trickster."

"And a pair of snowman eyes."

"Of course, they are. How could I have been so stupid."

"My pockets aren't that big."

Ben pulled Beryl aside, facing away from the snowman, and called over his shoulder. "Now then, little ghost, let's see you move those heavy stones."

Beryl watched the snowman with a glint in her eyes.

When they turned back, the stones hadn't moved but the carrot stuck jauntily from the center of the snowman's face.

"Oh, come on," Ben shouted to the sky. "Let me see you!"

Snow whispered in his ear. "Some day you will."

Ben stuck his finger in his ear and waggled it. "Did you hear that?"

Snow gasped at the terrible thought that followed and whirled away from Beryl lest she frighten her. In an instant, Snow was back in the Winter Room gazing into a mug of cold cocoa.

How did she know such a thing... that soon, Ben would be a ghost, too.

Chapter 25

UPON WAKING

I am dreaming of death
I am nine years old. My name is Snow.

I think the year is 1961

A 'NEARLY' DEATH EXPERIENCE

Hilton Chadwick wanted Peregrine Brooks dead. He'd wanted it ever since the 18th dynasty when Brooks was Smenkhare, Pharaoh Tutankhamun's older half-brother. And in 1961, Hilton nearly succeeded.

Peregrine was loyal. He still considered himself Lady Nan's fiancé after sixty years. He had won her hand before. As Smenkhare, he had claimed her for his 'great wife' Ankhesenamun.

But romantic courtship was no match for sibling rivalry.

The only time Snow saw Hilton in the Hall, his immaculate Armani suit was overlaid by a fairy glamour, decked out in cloth of gold, from his former lifetime as Ay, the king's vizier. In those days he was taller, more tan, and rode a magnificent chariot horse. He wore a starched white kilt, a crimson skull cap, a wide collar of gold, and leather armbands embedded with precious stones and vibrant enamels. The most disconcerting thing about him were his eyes. Hilton's eyes glittered with greed. The very definition of insanity.

Jack's eyes were closed. His keyhole mouth had widened which meant he was happy, wandering in his precious forests of summer where it was great to have a real body unencumbered by wood and metal and being attached to a door frame. He sensed Snow's presence.

"You seem pensive this morning, little sphinx," he said dreamily. "What can I do to cheer you up?"

"I was thinking about life and death," Snow replied.

"Which one in particular?"

"This morning, it's mostly death. I have these curiosities. I suppose they're memories. I don't remember. I must have died here in the Hall, but where? I've looked everywhere for a sign and while every room is familiar, none leave me feeling anxious. I don't remember my death, but I assume it was traumatic, considering I'm haunting the place. Traditionally, all ghosts are anxious, aren't they? Although my friend Vita is very joyful. Perhaps she's one of those ghosts who remained attached to the place where they were happiest."

"And that's not you?"

"Well, since I forget everything, I simply don't know."

"Jogging your memory is my mission."

"Mine too," Pookie piped up from under the bedclothes.

"I know Ben and Lady Nan died here. But, did I?"

Jack took a coughing fit, and after he recovered, he remembered he was late for a business meeting with the tree nymphs. "Please don't take this as a criticism, but there *are* other ghosts here and you've never shown any interest in them. Maybe one of *them* could answer your question."

"Taraq, the Egyptian slave boy evaporates whenever I approach him, so, I don't try anymore," Snow said. "I suppose I could ask the tree nymphs, but they scurry away all the time. Perhaps I scare them. The fairies act peevish when I ask them. I think it's beneath their dignity to dwell on lowly human details. Even in a winter like this, which I sincerely apologize for, they're busy fussing over frozen roots and dormant seeds."

A drumming of bored fingers on wood issued from the door. Jack sighed, not best pleased to leave his sanctuary. "Fairies hibernate on a whim," he said in a bored tone. "They tend to be mercurial and far more active in the summertime. But you're quite correct, the commonplace never holds their interest for long. Unless, that is, Parks gives them a direct order from Flora, the Green Lady. When that happens, they're all cooperation and light. Sweetness…? not so much. They can be testy even when they comply with Parks, especially when they have to acknowledge the portal cats."

"Did I die here? It's a straightforward question."

"Ben died here and so did Brooks… twice."

"How can one die twice?"

"The twice-borns in the village spring to mind, but that's reincarnation and nearly everyone who lives in Bede has done that. But there's another way. It's rare but it happened to Brooks."

Snow settled herself into listening mode, eager for a story that wasn't about a bear with fluff for brains at Pigeon's insistence. "Go on, then."

"You weren't around when Beryl got married. Well, you were, but you'd retreated to one of your sanctuaries. That is, a dreamed-up place where Pook and I aren't allowed. It's called the deep unconscious. In layman's terms, it's the dreamtime underneath the dreamtime."

"I've seen you in my dreams loads of times."

"We're not really there, other than in your imagination. Your dreams are snapshots of what was. You aren't making them up as you go along. They're not, strictly speaking, for entertainment purposes. It's a bit like you're in summer school only it's the high winter. It's complicated. Pookie can probably explain it better."

Pookie, now perched on top of the bedclothes, answered loud and clear. "You're doing just fine, Jack."

"The dreamtime is yours alone even if you invite others to share it."

"So, that's why you're only here when I wake up?"

"*Er…* something like that… *um…* listen baby girl, I hear one of those pesky fairies calling me from the forest I just left. I'd best go have a word. It doesn't do to cross them."

"Not until you tell me about Brooks."

"I almost forgot. Okay, I'll be quick, and then I'll have to be off, sharpish. Okay?"

"Okay."

"Beryl and Ben were twenty-one. Ironically, the ritual 'key to the door' year. Peregrine and Ben went skating on the lake, but Hilton had rigged the ice to break in the center. And then, the cunning beast left a black box near it so the boys would skate over to find out what it was. Perry was the stronger skater and got there first, and … *crack*… the ice broke like a manhole cover and in Brooks went. Ben pulled him out. It was touch and go for a bit, but Ben managed to drag Perry to safety. Trouble is, Ben inched back for something precious he'd dropped – an Egyptian scarab ring Beryl had given him. A real artefact it was, and even though Ben didn't believe in enchanted amulets, it was bursting with powerful magic. In any case, he wasn't about to lose it. Well, the ice was much weaker and it caved-in long before Ben was even close. He went into the icy water but there was no Perry to save him. Perry lay on the shore, dead!"

"How horrible. No wonder Beryl suffered. She lost the two people she loved most in the whole world."

Pookie took Snow's hand. "Tell Snow the worst part," she said.

Jack's voice became faint as he edged back into his forest vigil. "Ever since that day, Perry has been suffering from guilt and loneliness, separated from the love of his life because Beryl left him without actually leaving."

"But Ben's death wasn't Brooks' fault."

Jack's hinges squeaked as his door swung back and forth impatiently. "That's not how guilt works, Snow. Look, I really *must* go. I'm afraid guilt is something you will learn for yourself, very soon."

Pookie shook her ears and glared at Jack. "Thin ice," she grumbled angrily in his head. "What Jack means, little one, is that he's sorry he has to leave so soon, and that I will finish his story."

"No need, Miss bossy britches," Jack said indignantly. "I'm not at liberty to *go* anywhere until I've done my duty." He breathed deeply and narrated from memory. "Nimue fetched Ben's scarab ring and put it in Brooks' pocket. And the moment she did, Brooks started to breathe on his own. Well, Nimue knew it was magic, but the doctors called it a medical phenomenon, commonly known as a near-death experience. A person dies and spontaneously wakes up. Let me repeat that. SPONTANEOUSLY WAKES UP. If I sound stern it's because it's important. You might say it's a message from the beyond."

Snow gasped, panting for breath.

"Precisely. Big news is meant to shake you… another kind of wake-up call. Now then, after that tragic incident, two things happened. Beryl threw the key to my door into the lake and Nimue dived for it and set it aside for the future. But it was a future without Brooks or you because Beryl retreated into her dreams. Even after she had a daughter, your grandmother Rayne, Beryl pined for the past. Brooks was, and still is, loyal to the end."

"What end?"

"Not sure I can tell you that, baby girl. I'm under tremendous pressure to… *um*… help sort out the Hall's beeswax, as it were. Part of that concerns you, but not today. Unless Pookie has something to add. Do you Pook?"

Pookie stood and straightened her ears. "Brooks near-death *event* inspired him to investigate psychic phenomenon which led him to studying medicine. Ben's death set Brooks on the path of becoming a doctor. His specialty, psychology, evolved into past-life regressions, out-of-body-experiences (OOBEs), and the various practises of meditation. He became a psychologist, heavy on the word psychic. The second time Brooks died and stayed dead, was when the Stratford-Smyth family perished in the nuclear winter that we now inhabit after the Yellowstone Caldera exploded."

"Then, if Brooks is a ghost, why isn't *he* here, haunting." Snow sat up terrified. "POOKIE? Is my father dead! Is that why he didn't come back for me?"

"Calm yourself," Pookie said. "Your father was born a natural time-traveler which is why he left to find your mother and brother in the past… and by the way, as I'm sure you've forgotten, your grandparents and Uncle Tut are there also. Pigeon is a ghost. That's why he's still over there in the corner, dead as a doornail. Scuze the reference, Jack."

'You do know I can hear you,' Pigeon squawked. *'Sent to the corner, yes… but not a dunce.'*

"I've seen Ben over by the lake," Snow said. "He's never there when I get close, though. The swans often circle a beam of green light that issues from the whirlpool created where Ben drowned."

Chapter 26

UPON WAKING

I am with Beryl.
She's dressed in her wedding gown. All is not well.
Beryl is twenty-two. I am nine years old. My name is Snow.

The year is 1962

HAPI NEVER AFTER

Bede Hall grudgingly allowed Beryl's wedding to proceed until after the vows, but as controller of the local weather, it conjured a vicious tempest that reflected its wrath for the feeble legalities of mortal ceremony and the puniness of human traditions.

Fuming, the Hall parted the blue skies like a stage curtain, and breathed power into the gathering hurricane behind it.

The wedding decorations caught the full brunt of the Hall's temper. It whipped the formal garlands festooning the garden altar and the arch made of roses to mulch and scattered a hundred abandoned chairs tumbling over the lawn.

It was just the sort of elemental party the tree nymphs hankered for. The treeline of the Green Lady's forest took on the appearance of a jungle with shrieking, leafy ape-like creatures, leaping excitedly from limb-to-limb.

The guests, blissfully unaware of a problem, calmly gravitated inside to an elaborate feast, flowing champagne, and chamber music where the absence of the bride and groom went unnoticed due to the intervention of Nimue's fairies.

The Hall, fully incensed, conducted the surrounding storm like an orchestra with a fantasia of crashing cymbals, behaving like the mad director of a stage play, toying with dramatic theatrical lighting and bone-jarring sound effects.

The bad weather had closed in the very moment Beryl shut down. But, shutting down for Beryl meant bolting from the words 'till death do us part' like a startled gazelle. She shed one white satin slipper as she tore across the open lawn to the only sanctuary she could count on, and left the other, slowly filling with rainwater, crushed at the entrance to the maze, marking the boundary where suffering suspended, and healing began.

Looking back, Snow reflected it was the definitive moment when Beryl woke up from denying her true birthright and chose magic over a life of social misery.

Three mentors scooped Beryl out of Hilton's sight: Parks opened up, Charlotte Findhorn broke the rules of magical intervention, and at Nimue's orders, her fairies closed ranks.

Beryl's bridal veil had caught on the foliage as she ran inside the green fortress of the maze, its long gauze train floated from its center like a ghost... an eery white flag waving goodbye in conditional surrender.

Parks 2, 3, 4, and 5 stood vigil in front of the maze, arms linked, barring entry until Parks 1 arrived with Brooks.

The two men skirted the abandoned slipper and entered, carrying blankets, a brandy flask, an umbrella, and a thermos of Charlotte Findhorn's healing elixir.

Weeks before the ceremony, Charlotte had woven her botanical magic into a heady potion for Beryl with the express purpose of addressing grief and bestowing stamina. In addition to her regular infusions of well-being prepared after Ben's death, Charlotte added Mimulus to face the fear of unknown things; Star of Bethlehem for shock and heartbreak; Water Violet to release self reliance; Walnut as a protection against sudden changes; Sweet Chestnut to counter extreme mental anguish; and a touch of Holly to address the jealousy still present in Beryl's bloodstream.

Snow watched from the Winter Room window as a stream of colored fairy lights preceded the emergence of Beryl, wrapped in a blanket, leaning heavily on Brooks' arm. Unicorn darted between their legs and appeared instantaneously on Snow's lap, shivering piteously.

Parks 1 walked behind Beryl and Peregrine, sheltering them with the umbrella, carrying Pookie, He stooped down, retrieved the second white slipper, and tipped out the rainwater, stained red muttering the incantation: *'blood is thicker than water; water is thinner than ice'*.

Nimue flew at the end of the procession to cleanse the maze of sorrow and seal it against the intrusive vapors that were part of Hilton Chadwick's negative energy.

For a few hours, the marquee in the garden continued to flap in an agitated wind.

But at midnight, a tamed breeze gently nudged Beryl's bridal veil, free. It wafted like smoke towards the arms of the sacred rowan tree where it settled on a welcoming branch.

In a flash, Glumly, a young tree nymph, claimed it for his wife, Contraria, who was seen wearing the rented diamond tiara for several weeks until Nimue had to demand its return.

After the living guests had departed, Snow lingered alone, like an overlooked flower girl in a wet nightgown, trailing through soggy confetti – a more intensely *departed* soul.

It was fitting that Beryl's society wedding had been 'rained' out.

Snow's dream rewound until she sat in Beryl's bedroom where Beryl prepared for a journey into the war of an arranged marriage. Pookie lay face down, dumped in a corner. Beryl sat at her dressing table, staring unseeing into the mirror. A pearl necklace was strewn amongst scent bottles, hairpins, and spilled face powder. A bouquet of white carnations had been tossed into the chaos. Beryl was wearing one pearl earring. The other was clamped in her fist.

Snow never felt closer to her friend but never more dismissed. Her thoughts turned maudlin. *'Is this yet another ghastly punishment I'm meant to endure?'* She took her place at Beryl's side, estranged.

Beryl refused to see her and yet her pulse quickened when Snow touched her hand. A notion overpowered Snow, that having lived several lifetimes she'd likely been twenty at least once or twice herself and had probably married. An icy shudder shocked her from loneliness to fear.

Lady Nan sent Snow a thought. *'ghastly or ghostly, now that's Bede irony for you.'* she said.

"My father was right," Snow mused out loud. "My great-grandmother really did have a sly sense of humor."

Snow was reminded, while not *remembering*, the day when death determined to freeze her body into a child. And why *he,* (she used 'he' as befits the legendary figure of a *man* with a scythe), determined she should retain a grown-up's persona but erase her memories and leave the shadows of the past to trouble her dreams for eternity.

Beryl had been dressed in her wedding gown by a lady's maid who retreated to livelier ground. The Hall buzzed with guests and servants under the watchful eyes of Hilton Chadwick.

Beryl stared into her mirror. Suddenly, she hurled the pearl earring into the glass where it left a sizeable chip that turned her reflection into a gaunt woman with a blemish on her cheek.

A memory stirred inside Snow of a stinging cheek. *Whatever could it mean*, she thought. She examined the white card that came with the flowers. It contained one word written by hand - 'Forever'. There was no signature, but she knew it was from Peregrine Brooks. He had drawn an ankh beneath it – the Egyptian hieroglyph for 'life'.

A memory stirred. Snow remembered the good old days when Brooks and Beryl were courting, Brooks used to tease Beryl about them being together for all time. He'd brought her a white carnation whenever they met to remind her of their pact involving future lives as their eternal commitment to each other. He dubbed his floral offerings rein-carnations to make her smile and gift him a kiss.

Snow concentrated and managed to move the bouquet a few inches.

Sympathy evaporated. "Take it," she whispered to Beryl, feeling intense anger. "Grab life while you still can. You drive that car of yours straight through the Hall's gates and don't stop until you reach Peregrine's front door. Do it now. BERYL, DO IT RIGHT NOW!"

As if in answer, Beryl grabbed the flowers and held them in front of her face. She stared over them into the mirror, showing eyes bulging with fear. She buried her head in the blooms and inhaled, sobbing, sniffed back her tears and tore the heads from their stems.

"I know you're there, Snow," she said when she was done.

Snow, feeling the urgency to begin a dream diary, scribbled furiously in case she would forget.

'Suddenly a vision of a lone chariot, careening out of control overcame me,' she wrote. *'And I knew the true identity of Hilton Chadwick, Beryl's husband-to-be. I was stunned from choking hatred. As Hilton's anguished ka reached out for me, he disappeared behind a cloud of disturbed sand.*

The screams of terrified stampeding horses hurt my head. There was a flash of overturned gold, and a magnificent black stallion spattered with blood. A slave boy tried to calm the skittish creature. The horse pawed the ground and tossed his mane. The boy looked over his shoulder in my direction. I knew that boy but had forgotten his name.

And as Hilton's vicious ka broke through the sand and grabbed my shoulders, I remembered something from a different childhood that shattered my nerve. I am inexplicably afraid of ghosts!

I detected a flutter of light in my peripheral vision and sensed the plight of an injured butterfly, but I was mistaken. It was Hapi, a miniature Ba bird, that Pigeon sent my Aunt Bash during her 'grievous bodily harm period'. The time her handfasted mate was killed by a swarm of evil chemicals. In hindsight, it boded ill for marriages in general. It had Ay's face.'

Snow put down her pen and lay her head on the table.

Pookie shivered and sat up on the floor. "Beryl locked me in a trunk that day," she said. "I didn't mind. It was the best place *for* me."

She shook away a tear. "I was spared the worst distressing scenes of marital bliss, although I heard plenty of the squabbles. I spent my time dreaming as much as possible. So, in that regard, I can't fault your need to escape inward to higher ground, Snow. Sadly, avoidance dreaming often means running to lower ground instead. After all, the dreamtime *is* cousin to the underworld."

Snow picked up her pen. Her hand flew over the page.

'Have I known the bliss of love or the bittersweet pangs of love lost? Thankfully, the answer is unclear. But I know Brooks feels it and so does my Aunt Bash.

I've had many sightings of Ben's ka. He's always by the lake. The swans often circle a stream of green light that issues from a whirlpool where he drowned. I call his name. He turns. I wave. I run towards him over the lawn – a desperate barefoot ghost seeking the relative warmth of another lifeless phantom. The grass feels like silk. I rise an inch above it to reach him faster.

Ben is kindred. I watched him grow up. He's like an older brother to me. He smiles but turns his attention towards an old woman gazing over the water. I recognize Sarah Goodman, the love of his life. So, it would seem that some loves do survive death.

A new vision swims into view. It's a family gathering, celebrating a reunion of some kind. Ben and Sarah are there, holding hands. I look for my father, but a mist separates me from the life that is. I'm barred from seeing further.

And then a disembodied voice whispered 'You are there and not there, Snow. The choice is yours. Decide!'

Chapter 27

UPON WAKING

I am faced with a formidable guide.
I am nine years old. My name is Snow
Why do so many people insist my name is Anna?

The year is of little consequence.
In Bede time, the date is April 6, my father's birthday.

MOTHER'S DAY

The old temple garden was awake. Its fragrant air greeted Snow, but it was a low primal growl that woke her. Nothing threatening. The message she received was *'Well, finally. Where have you been?'* It came from a tawny yellow dog waiting for her in the shade of a date palm across an expanse of desert.

Snow approached it, fearing nothing, but briefly hesitated when she realized the dog was a yearling lioness cub pinning her with a fixed stare. *'You are quite safe, child,'* the cat said inside Snow's head. *'Come along now, you must meet your mother. My name is Babylion,'* she growled. *'but as a royal princess of the house of Bede, you may address me as Babs.'*

Babs leapt up. *'Don't dawdle, child. There's not much time.'*

Snow followed Babs without question, towards a temple that emerged seamlessly from the stone cliff behind it. They stole up a low ramp inset with stairs cut from pink granite blocks and passed through an endless avenue of alabaster columns – a waif in a white cotton nightgown, drifting weightless following a sleek animal rippling with power. The familiar squawk of a parrot drew Snow's gaze upwards to a carved canopy of giant acanthus leaves supported by granite tree trunks.

Once inside, Babs leaped ahead, abandoning Snow to a new sensation. The hot panting breath of a cow-sized housecat, padded silently behind her, tickling her neck. Its contented purrs set the temple air trembling like a warm wind after a desert storm.

As the cat overtook Snow it transformed into a silver tigress. "Follow my tail," she hissed as her lithe form snaked through a veritable forest of stone trees. After a while, the forest opened into a clearing smelling of mint and spices encircled by low standing stones where dozens of intoxicated cats had draped themselves over its lintels.

Flickering lights and the sound of running water accompanied by chanting issued from behind a pair of enormous cedarwood doors carved in hieroglyphic spells. Babs returned to nudge one of them open with her nose. "Anna, don't keep SaRa waiting," she snarled. "She can't levitate for long."

A beautiful lady turned her head at Snow's approach and sent her a radiant smile. Snow watched her ka slowly rise from her seated body supported by two midwives.

Ani arrived first, her violet eyes and glowing transparent skin causing a murmur of delight from the priestesses. "Your daughter is a dream traveler," one of them whispered excitedly to SaRa.

Within seconds of being whisked away to a ritual bathing with water infused with lotus petals, Ani's skin resumed a natural golden tan and her dark hair turned pure white.

Babs severed the umbilical cord with her teeth and lapped up the afterbirth.

Word spread to the male cats outside, that a dreamer had been born of the house of Pan, and set off a celebrative yowling, causing Peri to turn in SaRa's womb. Two priestess midwives called for quiet as Peri followed his sister into the 18th dynasty and was pronounced healthy. A forelock of silver in his dark hair decreed he would follow his father's footsteps. A second festive yowl broke the usual stillness of the temple.

SaRa's ghostly smile matched the one on her face below.

Snow rose several feet off the floor and rotated horizontally as if swimming into a sea of light and joined the Lady SaRa, spreadeagled in midair. They hovered protectively over the pair of newborn twins laying on a bed of golden sand.

SaRa crooned to the twins that their father was on his way. Her ka circled the babies, turned and lay floating on its back, adjusted itself and serenely drifted down to settle back into SaRa's seated body.

A figure eight, the symbol of eternity, had been drawn in the sand connecting the twins. Snow knew without a doubt, one of them was her and the other was her brother, Peri. The sight of him tugged at her heart. He was beautiful. An onlooker spoke softly. "Peri resembles his father."

It wasn't fair. *She* was daddy's girl. She had waited faithfully in the freezing attic of Bede Hall while Peri thrived in a warm embracing country. This boy knew nothing of being abandoned or that her comfort had been compromised so Kit could return to Egypt to bring him home.

A cloud of microscopic lotus fairies swirled together forming a fragrant mist that hung over the pair of cradles bestowing various spells for health and happiness. After a time, a procession of feline nursemaids, led SaRa and the newborns past an animated wall where they paused to be cleansed by the aura of flashing colors before being presented to the goddess Bast, the great mother.

Bast received them in her human form, a queen with the face of a cat, wearing a clinging shift embroidered with gold. "A dreamer *and* a traveler," she marvelled. "A New Age of Gemini is begun. Goswold's prophecy has come to pass with Christopher and his sister Bathsheba, and now, doubly confirmed with Bede's next generation and Egypt's legacy through the offspring of our newly-adopted son, KaTiKha'at, and our beloved daughter SaRa, safely delivered of the Pan Gemini, Ani and Peri."

She transformed into her rarest matriarchal form – a sleek translucent white tigress with silver stripes. "Remember and celebrate this day," she declared. "A repast of onions and beer is being prepared."

. . .

Snow watched Babs' departure from the Winter Room's window. The lioness looked up at her. *'Until next time,'* she hissed before slinking over the snow to disappear into the treeline.

'If you see Babs again,' Pigeon shrieked from the corner, *whatever you do, tell her the absolute truth.* *'She's a natural lie detector, that one.'*

Chapter 28

UPON WAKING

I am about to be born twice
through the miracle of the time portal.
I am also nine years old.
My name is Snow, Anna, and Ani

The year is a big invisible X written in the sky

FATHER'S DAY

The sun drifted lazily and settled on the capstone of the great pyramid when Kit was summoned by a visitation from Her Majesty on the Giza plateau. Bast, in tigress form, cuffed Kit playfully, and when he was barely conscious, she dismissed him by washing her whiskers as if he wasn't there. When her paws were immaculate, Bast licked Kit's face to restore his wits sufficiently enough to regain his bearings. "Now, go home reluctant father," she purred. "Your children are born. One, and mark this word carefully, is in *peril*. The other is a dream traveler. This means she will disappear from time-to-time. But, have no worries on that score. She will have many happy returns."

At dusk, Bast gave out a bloodcurdling howl at the full moon from the roof of her temple echoed by roars from the Great Sphinx and Sekhmet. Three great tails flapped hard enough to rock the foundations of the temple. Cats squirmed contentedly in the beds of catnip planted for the occasion nine-months earlier. And as the temple cats lapped up saucers of beer, Ani, disappeared for nine seconds without causing a fuss. It was a test dream.

. . .

Kit walked dazedly through the marketplace, escorted by Pigeon crowing *'the Pan Gemini are born. One Perfect Prince. One Precious Princess,'* in a royal proclamation. The temple steps, lit by dozens of glowing jars, quickened Kit's pace. Kha stood halfway to the top of the stairs like a sentinel, beaming like the proud uncle he was, with arms open wide. "All went well," he called out. "Mother and offspring are in perfect health."

Pigeon flashed off in a white blur and reached Kha first where he lit on his proffered arm.

By the time Kit reached them, Kha had seated himself and was feeding Pigeon dates and nuts. He stood, dislodging Pigeon who flew to the bowl of delicacies and helped himself. Kha pulled Kit into a bear hug and thumped him on the back. "Congratulations. I need you to sit."

'Your brother-in-law is in shock,' Pigeon cackled. *'Bast gave him a bit of a rude awakening. But I do believe it's had a Positive effect. He may have even grown up a little.'*

The semi-conscious scientist side of Kit's brain wanted to know how alabaster jars could give off such bright light. Kit's alchemist-self guessed it was a secret of magic that Kha would explain sooner if he didn't ask. A shadow of worry crossed his face. "I need to catch my breath, but I want to see SaRa and the..." he smiled, incredulously. "I have a son."

Snow cringed.

"You have *two* children."

'Happy Birthday,' Pigeon said under his wing. *'Time marches on.'*

"SaRa is well," Kha repeated patting the stone beside him. "Hello? Kit? Did you hear me? I need you to sit. You need to catch up with what's happened. The children are healthy. Your family awaits but ..."

"No no no. You can't get away with but, anything. Not this time. I won't have it. Look, if something is wrong, don't soften it. Isn't part of my training toughening up by accepting the unacceptable. Well, it worked. Here I am and I need to see my wife."

"SaRa wants me to impart something... and don't look so terrified.

It's something she and I thought may happen. Something completely normal in both our ancestral lineages, where atypical presentiments are expected and welcomed as gifts. Twins born through our bloodlines arrive with preordained extrasensory abilities."

Kit tapped his sandals impatiently. "Gifts that go on giving. Yes, I'm all too aware."

'He's got the key to the door,' Pigeon sang. *'Never been twenty-seven before.'*

You were an astrophysics geek ahead of your time – a science-minded student, academic, single-minded, and ultimately logical. Bash is a natural botanist with a pretentious open mind that embraced the metaphysical world. Your destinies were written in Pangea. *Your children's future is written here in hieroglyphics* – a dual language that imparts messages in surface pictures as well as in deep esoteric thought. This way the uneducated masses understand a level of instant communication and the house of scribes can share a world of arcane knowledge only possible to digest after years of study. Translation… your daughter is a dream traveler."

As Kit stood to leave, Pigeon swooped, divebombing his head squawking *'Destination Pangea!'* Kit gathered his cloak about him. "Tell me something I don't know. Anna once transported me to the future when I was sleeping. I guess dream travelers can do that. Everyone thought Anna was a summer ghost who haunted the Hall during hot spells which, ironically, manifested in the cold spot in the attic."

"Anna didn't create that spot cold. It was cold long before she arrived," Kha said. "Contrary to the classic rules of paranormal appearances, a cold spot isn't the result of a human ka absorbing local heat in order to manifest."

Kit waved away pigeon's continual bombing passes. "There are several ghosts in Bede Hall, not the least of whom is my grandmother, who I can assure you, can be seriously chilling in many ways, but her appearance is never preceded by a blast of cold air."

Kha assumed a formal pose with his arms crossed that he kept for serious lectures. "The laws of 'ghostly physics' are mathematical proofs refuting that excesses of expelled human ectoplasm (souls of the dead) soak up unsuspecting victims wandering in the afterlife. Cold spots are rare pockets of inner-space – time voids where no heat exists, formed by powerful past-life connections. You left Anna alone in an entire world grown cold from a volcanic winter. That's as cold as it gets before life is extinguished. She knows this all too well."

Kit blinked at Kha. "Ani has a rare gift… and?"

"And she will have a tendency to physically disappear when she travels. Which can be unnerving to a parent at odds with the metaphysical world. You may not see Ani when you meet your son. Ani has been dream traveling for the better part of the afternoon. She's quite safe but, well, she's not here and we have no way of knowing where in time she is or able to call her back."

"But Ani's a helpless baby. Where could an infant possibly go?"

"Ani is never helpless when she travels. Ani can be any age from any one of her past or future lives. She can be an animal or a chair. She can also be dreaming normally like any other baby. If you see her in her cradle, that's what's happening. Dreams where Ani travels are special. There may be years when she doesn't travel. It's a 'take it as it comes' thing, I'm afraid."

"I have to go. SaRa must be worried sick."

"My sister has been schooled in the magic of alchemy since she could walk, and she has long accepted this might happen. So, no, she's not even a little upset, other than worried how *you* will react."

"Peri looks like you," Kha said. But in nine months his hair will be the counterpart of yours, white with a forelock of black."

Kit grinned. "I have a son! And my daughter Ani takes after me."

"Close but not quite."

"I was born a time traveler."

Kha leaned forward. "Time travel and dream travel are worlds apart. Time travel is physical. Dream travel is astral. Your ka left the maze with Anna but not independent of her. Your body remained in the maze in your present time. When you time travel your molecules dissemble and reassemble. Anna had to hold your hand all the way to the future, didn't she?"

"It was like Peter Pan and Wendy, with arms spread like wings, on a fingertip-to-fingertip flight."

"It bodes well that your intuition is dead on. I'm mentioning this as a vital cog in your training wheels. Take it in. Process the weirdness and move on. We need to, as you like to say, 'advance to Go' and collect our reward for playing the game."

"Winning is sweet. I came here to win back my world."

"Winning is an empty reward that lasts a few days. The true reward is destroying the enemy at its roots so that it has no ugly head left to rear in the foreseeable future. Megeara has three such heads and all the accompanying limbs as well. Annihilation is the key – ANI-hilation. Ani is the one to watch. She is a natural alchemist. She's been waiting a long time to save you."

Ani and Peri lay swaddled on a bed of lotus blossoms, foot-to-foot, heads facing north and south in the same stone sarcophagus. Kit was appalled. "This is one custom I will never agree with. I'm beginning to see why my father called Egypt a culture of death. A sarcophagus is an eternal bed for the dead."

"It is also the bed of life," Kha said. "It's the dual energy of coming and going. A sarcophagus is a landing pad for incoming time travelers, newborn kas, and a launch pad for a ka when it departs the earth. Why else would it be placed so reverently in the King's chamber of the greatest pyramid on earth. The King's chamber is a time portal leading directly to the Winter Room in Bede Hall. Ay treats it like his personal limousine. One day he will enrage Osiris enough to be sorry. So, let's bring Osiris home as soon as it's earthly possible."

Snow leant down and tucked in an escaped strand of Peri's swaddling. "I'm sorry, Peri," she whispered. "I have to steal Ani. Father will take care of you. I have to make him proud of me. My back's against the wall on this one." She watched over her baby brother for a long time before trailing after Kit.

She cornered him on the roof. "Are you still afraid of me," she asked.

Chapter 29

UPON WAKING

I am confronted by Taraq – the ghost who has been avoiding me.
Egypt is cold and dark. Airless as a tomb.
I am nine years old. My name is Anu.

The year is c. 3,000 B.C.

HAUNTINGLY FAMILIAR

The ghost of Taraq stepped in front of Snow as she approached the back of the dining room mirror. "It's time we met properly for the second time," he said after floating to the ceiling. "And by that, I mean without lies." He held out his hand. "I think we should visit Egypt. Right now, Anu."

"But I'm enjoying a spell of summer at the moment, and I never know how long it will last. Couldn't we go later, when it's cold again, and the weather will be worth missing? And my name is SNOW.

Taraq floated down eye-to-eye. "A *spell* of summer," Taraq mused out loud, savoring each word. "Couldn't have put it better myself."

"I've seen you often," Snow said shyly. "I think we were good friends, once. For a while, I thought it was you talking to me from behind my wall. Jack told me you were shy. I often hide behind the wallpaper. I have to tell you, in case you were worried, there's no shame in hiding. It's often necessary for survival."

"What? The survival of the deceased?" Taraq countered. "And I beg to differ. There *is* shame in hiding if you're denying the truth. The Egypt where we're going is far from an idyllic landscape of blue skies and searing heat. We got along like a house on fire in Bede, before Megeara arrived. We were allies. We counted on each other."

"Why would I want to go to such a place?"

"Healthy comeuppance to balance the cold, dank, airless tomb where you abandoned me... when you should have known better, springs to mind. You're not the first ghost to deal with mistakes made in the past; yours were spectacularly heartless," he added.

"Then I don't want to remember."

"Reliving is not remembering. There is healing in reliving. You might say that's where you're headed in a decidedly indirect way. Do you suppose you're beyond help? Do you want to heal? Do you want to get out of here?"

"I've remained in Bede Hall through every dream. Escape is only a temporary illusion."

"Says you. No matter, I will dispel such an illusion."

"I expect you want an apology."

"That would be nice, but sorry does nothing to ease the terrifying emotional pain that remains after physical suffering is over."

"You refer to death, I suppose."

"I do not, baby girl. I refer to fear."

"Please don't call me that."

"Would you prefer I call you baby *sister*?"

"*Was* I your baby sister?"

"You were born a few seconds after me, so yes, I call you by a truthful name. Anu is your truthful name."

Snow tossed her long white curls. "My name is Snow, thank you very much."

A constant ticking issued from the wall. Snow listened intently. "Is that a clock?"

Taraq's expression was stone. "Deathwatch beetles, I expect." he said. "Of *course*, it's a clock, baby girl. What did you expect in a time portal?"

"This is a passageway on Bede Hall's second floor. I walk here often."

"Oh, really? Look again."

The wallpaper roses were further away. So far, they floated like pink raindrops on a dazzling turquoise horizon. The roses dived like a flock of birds and swirled into fat snowflakes that fell on the capstone of the pyramid beneath them. Each flake melted on the scorching limestone with an electric sizzle.

Snow recoiled. "I don't have to do what you say. I can go home whenever I want."

"You *are* home. But be honest for once. You've never felt Bede Hall was home. In fact, you've felt quite the opposite, which is why you constantly daydream of escape. Daydreams are, on the whole, just as telling as nightmares, by the way. And in your case, you never protect yours from being seen. Parks and I discuss them often."

"How dare you!"

"I knew your father in the end time. He was my best friend. My *only* friend. He gave me permission to deal with you."

"Deal?"

"You think Kit deserted you. He did not. He deserted himself. I was there. He was a troubled soul, which is odd considering it's we *ghosts* who are supposed to enjoy that singular privilege."

"You have a weird concept of joy."

Taraq soared to the ceiling, pushed back from it, and swooped back to the floor like an Olympic swimmer. He bowed from the waist. "Thank you. Kit always said I was weird, so I take that as a compliment."

A musty smell of fungus permeated the first antechamber of Ankhesenamun's tomb, growing stronger towards the burial chamber where the thin air retained the faint scent of incense and dried flowers. Snow's gaze cut through the gloom and rested on the skeletons of two small children, once entwined in a hug. They had collapsed into a heap of bones beside an ornate gold sarcophagus. Dust, dried to clay after a flash flood, had cemented them to the floor.

Beside them lay a smashed hourglass, its sand spilled into a tiny pyramid.

"Who?" Snow stated simply.

Taraq held a lit torch above his head. "That sad heap is what's left of you and me."

Snow looked away quickly and examined the tomb paintings. "Why are the walls filled with portraits of Lady Nan? I've seen her wearing those clothes and headdresses."

"And that tells you?"

Snow shrugged. "Nothing."

Taraq narrowed his eyes and crossed his arms which made him look like a genie. "Then, allow me to enlighten you. Lady Nan, aka Beryl aka Rain, WAS Ankhesenamun. You saw her in the Beehive care home, did you not?"

Snow's frown said she'd forgotten. "Sorry?"

"Walk around. Touch things. Memories often reside in objects. Speak out anytime a thought comes into your silly head."

"What is this?" Snow said, holding up a long bar of bent metal.

"That, baby girl, is a lever for opening the mummy's mouth after embalming, in a ceremony called the 'opening of the way'. Once opened, a ka like you and me, is released.

"We were embalmed?"

"We were too insignificant for such an honor."

"Then your ka…?"

"The human body is a physical maze," Taraq said. "My ka eventually worked its way out of my body. Yours, flew like a startled bird, without saying goodbye."

Snow's lips trembled. "I was afraid."

"So, you *do* remember!"

"Remember what?"

"Your selfish act of cruelty. You chose reincarnation over dying with me so that we could reincarnate together. Ultimately, we were meant to stay brother and sister throughout the ages to come. Or we *were*, until you were born to SaRa. She gave you the same name, Ani, so you might remember."

"I hear the pecking of a bird."

"The Ba. Yes, like the ka, it's a twin form of the spirit – a bird with the face of a departed human who hovers over the place of death.

Especially the ka's offering table built in a mini chapel in the form of a carved door, anchored to the outside of every nobles' tomb.

Queen Ankhesenamun so ordered that offerings were to be left there for you and me to honor our short years of devoted service. A rare gift for servants. That false door endured until an avalanche of stone chips buried it. From that day, I wandered, lost in the valley of the Kings until I heard Tut's golden throne calling me. Osiris himself, ordered me to protect it from its enemies.

I never realized who, until Ay stole it and took it to Bede. Brooks looked after it until I arrived. It had long since passed from Brooks' care to Ben, and eventually, your father. But it was meant for another.

Your father's half-brother, your Uncle Tut, charged me to guard it until he returned. But he never did. Or that is, he *will* return with your father but in a form no-one will recognize. If, that is, you allow it."

"Somehow, I'm responsible for my twin brother, Peri, as well. It's all very confusing. I'm rather tired. I think I need a nap. Please take me back to Bede."

"I will soon," Taraq said, "but I don't fancy my chances for a happy homecoming. Jack and Pookie will berate me for telling you too much. You were supposed to remember these things yourself. Anna knows… but she still hides inside the persona of Snow who is determined to sleep. Sleep is no sane remedy for fear."

A sharp odour assailed them. Snow crinkled her nose in disgust.

"That's natron," Taraq said. "It's the embalming salt that preserves the empty shell of a body for new life. I find it ironic that you're disgusted by the smell of life." He perched cross-legged on the largest carved trunk and patted the spot beside him "Please sit."

"You seem happy. So, what do you like most about being a ghost?" Snow asked.

Taraq chuckled. "That's easy," he replied. "I love flying. That is to say, the absence of gravity. Walking through walls is a nice trick as well."

Snow nodded. "I have flying, well, *falling* dreams but I wake up in a fright."

"Well, you don't truly wake up, but I take your point."

Snow ignored Taraq's remark. "In my defense, ghostly gravity is unstable."

"It's a question of mind over matter," Taraq explained. "When nothing matters, you're safer than you think. Transform the fear of falling into a pleasurable freefall into a landscape of your choice. There's no fear when you create a dreamworld from your imagination. But I expect you know that better than anyone."

"I'm no longer a child this day. I don't know why, but sometimes I'm quite old. At least for a while. Let us talk while I understand grown up talk. I won't remember any of this for long. Soon, I will be 'baby girl' who drifts about with a rabbit doll, talking with doorknobs and walls."

"Now, *baby sister*," Taraq said. "I have a question for *you*. What was it like being born as Ani 2?"

"Even if I could remember, which I don't, I would rather not say."

"I will send you a dream of your birth. It would be better for everyone if you remember it. Please try."

"I will do my best."

Taraq grimaced, looking over his shoulder in case some unseen demon might be eavesdropping. "Listen up. There's only time to say this once. Back in the Hall it will rock your guardians like... like a Pangean earthquake.'

Snow wriggled eagerly. "Tell me. Tell me everything."

"Ani 2 ended up in Bede Hall as Anna where she was destined to meet Beryl. Who, as I already mentioned, is the reincarnation of Ankhesenamun. After a span of two thousand years, Anna, that is, *you*, stole the newborn Ani 2, thereby deserting her/*your* brother, Peri. Jealousy is a recurring theme in your family. Anu 1 left me, Taraq 1, and Ani 2 left Peri. To be more precise, Anna kidnapped herself. Now that's a trick much harder than walking through walls."

Snow thought better of answering and swallowed a snappy comeback.

Taraq saw and grinned a satisfied grin. "A vast accumulation of guilt lies between you and freedom. It's difficult to deal with. No wonder you've installed a program of self-induced amnesia in order to maintain a state of temporary memory loss."

Snow grabbed Taraq's arm. "Wait! I recently had a dream where I took Ani from her cradle. I remember trying to dismiss it, but my father had a way of imprinting his words into my brain. I'd overheard him talking to Uncle Kha. My father clearly didn't consider me as important as Peri."

"Here's a good tip. May it be something you remember for the future *and* the past. When you eavesdrop, it's vital to stay and hear the entire conversation lest you overreact needlessly. What Kit said was: *'my little girl is extra special. Peri and I will look after her together'*."

Snow covered her ears and hummed loudly. "Lalala… I can't hear you."

The sound of the door, painted ajar in the mural, creaked open. As they blinked into the darkness, a loud thump of a power breaker engaging, flooded the interior with electric light. Several wall torches snapped on the length of the sloped passageway.

Kit, Bash, Tut, Rayne and Cornelius stood in a huddle of amazement. The only sound was five pairs of sandals crunching in the gravel, spread to keep the floor dry, that echoed like rustling leaves. A distinct line of orange grit adhered to the tomb walls where the watermark of an ancient flash flood stained the paint.

Fairies, twice the size of bumblebees, flitted playfully, casting shadowy hand puppets over Queen Ankhesenamun's painted robes. A goddess with a cat's face stood beside the queen, arm in arm. Both women, painted in profile, stared momentarily at their guests before straightening their shoulders and resumed looking right, to the future.

Kit's Saxon tower looked as it always did in the high winter, itself a cylindrical time capsule entombed under snow up to its crenellations. Inside, tattered strips of wallpaper and damp sheets of loose papers had formed into a collage of torn images: the face on Mars, diagrams of geological strata, and the Yellowstone Caldera seen from space, all frozen to the walls by fungus. The golden throne gleamed from Taraq's constant polishing as its legs danced impatiently from waiting.

Outside, Parks dug his spade into the soil of the vegetable patch with something akin to anger but worse.

"Just so you know, terrifying darkness and unbearable sorrow come in the aftermath of abandonment – a second wave of torture," Taraq said to Snow.

"He's right, baby g…. *er* I mean Snow," Parks said. He thrust his spade into the soil so hard a shower of sparks erupted from a struck stone like a miniature underground volcano. "Infernal internment, I calls it." He shook his finger at Snow. "It was cowardly done, lass, and no mistake."

"I'm not long for the underworld," Taraq blurted. "If, that is, Snow wakes up in time to do the right thing."

"I can't promise anything," Snow said.

"Of course, you can," Parks said sternly. "Simply, make up your mind. Stop being a baby."

"Why would anyone's house on fire be considered a favorable omen," Snow asked.

Chapter 30

UPON WAKING

I feel as if I am on another planet.
I am nine years old. My name means Snow.
All I remember is that it begins with the letter 'N'.

The concept of years does not yet exist.

PANIC STATION EARTH

The Temple of the Magi – Pangea

Horizontal lightning flashed angrily over central Pangea, turning the sky a malignant shade of orange. For a hideous moment, the Temple of the Magi swayed unsteadily, illuminated against it as a muddy brown shadow. Thunder grumbled under the earth unleashing plumes of black fire. Grey snow continued to blanket the streets.

Pan stood shoulder to shoulder with Goswold the elder, as lethal fumes issued from fissures in the cracked paving stones of the courtyard below. The sights before them, vicious proof that Megeara's threat had come to pass, faded to insignificance compared to the battle raging on Mars.

It was past time for final preparations, the final consensus being a ridiculously long-term solution sealed into prophecy by the brotherhood before they escaped in sky boats.

But, a last minute reconciliation needed airing. "We've been at odds far too long, my friend, Pan began. "It's time for …"

A loud grating sound of stone grinding against stone conveniently interrupted his search for the right words.

And while Goswold turned away in a coughing fit, Pan peered

through the toxic murk searching for the Bede pyramid that lay to the west of the temple complex. Knowing it was there was small comfort, obscured as it was by a last hurrah of poisonous smog.

Goswold, still choking from the rising dust, leaned heavily on the balcony railing, his gaze fixated on a deep pock mark in the stone. When he pressed his index finger into it, the stone felt soft. A grim reminder that crumbling was imminent. A group of several indentations seemed to form the outline of the constellation Gemini, but then it was Goswold's responsibility to track the design everywhere. Confirming the star pattern was part of the magic. Gemini was more than a symbol of unity, its message of sibling loyalty encouraged citizens to place family far above politics.

"The arrangements? They will hold?" Goswold shouted over the din.

Pan replied telepathically. "They have a chance."

Goswold replied in kind. "The piazza has fallen. There's word that carts can no longer negotiate the accumulation of ash in the streets." There was a pause. "The brotherhood was able to get away before the fiery rain fell."

The two stared gloomily into the uncertain future. Pan traced a deep vertical drip mark etched into the stone with a fingernail, following a dried rivulet of acid that had seared a white trail in the limestone. For a moment, two old men in embroidered robes, waited for the end but the sound of splintering stone pulled them inside as half the platform disintegrated in earnest.

Goswold cleared his throat. "So, what's the latest from Osiris? My thoughts can no longer reach him."

"That's a deliberate blocking on his part," Pan said. "I felt his anguish that such a thing was necessary. My brother keeps his thoughts to himself. Even from me."

Goswold clapped his hands together in a singular gesture of *that's over now, so let's move on*'. "Down to business then?"

"If you like."

"I do *not* like. Kit is untried. He's also a non-believer of magic, clearly not ready for a mission that entails full co-operation with the supernatural world, requiring concentrated effort."

Pan wiped sweat from his eyes. "Look, Goswold," he said wearily. "Kit is who he is. Kha is preparing him at this very moment. He's the best alchemist for the job, as you well know. It is the best we can do. The *only* thing we can do. We must make the best of it."

The balcony swayed precariously as one pillar collapsed, dropping lower to the ground by several feet as it sank into the dissolving foundations. Goswold grasped Park's arm. The balcony shuddered once and ripped itself from the wall.

"And so, pandemonium begins," Pan mused.

"I think you mean it ends," Goswold said.

Pan patted the older man's hand. "Kha was even able to convince Kit to enter the portal within the Great Sphinx of the Giza plateau. No small feat, I assure you. That boy is as single-minded as his sister."

"Kha only wore the lad down after the grizzly discovery in the Cairo Museum."

"May I restate what-is. Kindly remind the council…"

"And may *I* remind *you* that the council is no more, and that the unstable core of our planet, stirred by an immortal monster, is no match for a boy!"

"Kit was the only volunteer left standing when everyone else faded into the woodwork, including by the way, a certain 'ghost' who is want to hide behind the wallpaper at any given time. That *child* of his has accumulated enough karma for a thousand lifetimes."

Goswold bowed in deference to Pan's rank of presiding nature god. "Time decrees the Pan Gemini must be born as foretold. Not a moment too soon. Not a moment too late."

Pan dragged Goswold into the inner sanctum. "Kit had to be culled from Bede with guile. Drawn out in the open, and vulnerable I might add, in order to meet an impossible challenge completely beyond his understanding. His mentor refused the task, outright. Even the sainted Hall's matriarch stood in Kit's way. It's safe to conclude, a reluctant champion sometimes has more grit than an experienced warrior."

"He's a fifteen-year-old boy afraid of his own shadow."

"No, sir. It took a magus as powerful as Kha to lure Kit from his shadow and lead him out of the desert, pummeled as he was, by unaccustomed heat and thirst, and a generous helping of fear."

"There's no point in arguing. We have no choice," Goswold griped. "Ultimately, the death throes of Pangea lead directly to Ani's birth. Our baby girl will close her eyes on Pangea and open them in Egypt with the fully-formed question, who is Pluvia? bubbling in her newborn brain. And soon enough, her question will change to who WAS Pluvia? I want to meet the girl."

Pan nodded enthusiastically. "I concur. You *need* to meet her. Come with me to Bede. There's still time if we go now. We'll meet in the red library."

The Red Library

Parks removed his gardening hat, bowing low as a courtier before Goswold. "Welcome to the red library," he said, cramming his hat back on his head.

Parks' hair of green leaves squashed under a battered hat, and shabby gardening clothes, appeared in stark contrast to the embroidered robes he'd conjured, recently swallowed by time.

"There's no need to flatter me with false grandeur. I've been here before," Goswold grumped.

"Not in living memory," Parks retorted. "By the way, just so you're not surprised, there are stowaway fairies hiding in my waistcoat pocket. I find that ignoring them is the most direct path to victory. I shall have a wee word with them later. They are essentially mischievous creatures, but fortunately my lady wife, Flora, holds great sway over them."

Goswold sniffed at Parks gardening boots. "Goodness, is that what you always wear? Where is the girl, then? I haven't got all day. Perhaps not even an hour."

The Hall took the liberty of opening several windows. In rushed a gust of north wind that spun the library's giant globe so fast its separate colors of land and water were stirred into the color of grey soup.

Abstract grey blobs flew off its surface landing in splotches on the floor, walls, and the ceiling. One continent landed on Goswold's white robe in a stain shaped like Australia.

Europe hung precariously on the chandelier. Antarctica clung to its northern hemisphere but its brother, Arctic, slipped and was unceremoniously knocked sideways.

Nimue flew from Parks' pocket, stopping in midair, hands on hips, to survey the damage. What's all this nonsense?" she shouted in red sparks.

"And who's this," Goswold said, going for witty. "I take it, it's not our *girl*."

Nimue bristled. "Obviously, I'm a fairy," she said, insulted. "And since you're here, you can help me get these rogue continents back where they belong. Can you not see that Greenland and Britannia are in each other's back yard. For goodness sake. Alchemists!"

Goswold pieced together Scandinavia from half-a-dozen fragments. And moved it a sixteenth of an inch closer to the Black Sea. But when the globe jerked to a sudden stop, South America was briefly hurled into the middle of next week – an actual emotional destination in the mythological world.

"Careful," Parks shouted to Goswold. "That's Hadrian's Wall, you're holding. Make sure Lindisfarne is not too close to Britannia's east coast."

The sticky surface of the globe was setting like concrete. Europe was forced to drop from the chandelier with an accurate splosh at the last minute. There was just enough time to tweak Asia into its rightful position. Goswold stood back to admire their handiwork.

Parks placed a magnifying glass over Egypt. "Oh, dear, the ants are still at war," he said. "The Pangeans have not yet settled in."

Goswold grunted. "It took time to find a rightful place that befitted our status. After all, we're leaders not followers."

. . .

The globe's bodies of water shone bright blue. Its land masses anchored by varnish and beeswax glowed emerald green and burnt umber. A pale shaft of moonlight glanced off Hadrian's Wall.

Goswold directed a formal greeting into the corner where Snow was half-in and half-out of the wallpaper. "Little girl," he said. "Now then, what have you got to say for yourself."

"Me?"

"I believe you're the only little girl in the room. YES, you!"

Parks held out his hand. Don't be shy, Snow. Goswold here, is one of the kindest men on earth. He wants very much to meet you before…"

"Before what?" Snow asked defiantly.

The innards of Parks' pocket shifted restlessly. He patted it flat. "Goswold, this is our little Snowflake," he said. "She's… *er*… staying with us for a spell."

"Literally," a fairy's voice shrilled from Parks' pocket.

Snow crept timidly towards Goswold powerless to refuse, drawn like a magnet to the globe where she gingerly placed both her hands on the spherical map. "It has to do with these colored shapes, doesn't it."

"You tell me, young lady!"

"I'm sorry for whatever I did," Snow whimpered.

A jolt of static electricity riveted Snow to the spot when Goswold touched her hand. "Your mistake was hardly minor. If you're unable to recall the errors of your ways you can't effectively be sorry. Can you!"

Snow evaporated. Her disembodied tears were cut short by Unicorn darting from under a chair to attack Goswold's ankles. The magus swiped away his claws and continued. "Ghost tears are a waste of emotion," he lectured. "You've been too soft with her, Parks." He pointed to Parks' pocket. "Now, keep those Bede fairies of yours under control. And the cats, too. And tell the Lady Flora I said hello. I'm pressed for time, otherwise I would love to visit Pigeon."

As Goswold's form slowly turned to mist, the sudden hum of the globe's restored energy filled the room. It sounded like the buzzing of wasps.

"I know that sound," Snow said alarmed from inside the wall. "It's the sound Taraq described to Kit of the wasps that killed his parents. Has that nasty man gone?"

Several fairies stormed out of Parks' pocket in a hiss of pique. Cecilberry, a lavender fairy, separated from the others and landed on Snow's newly materialized shoulder. "Snow, dear, please think about what you just said. There's a memory in your head waiting to come out. You were once Taraq's sister. What do you suppose that means?"

"I don't remember."

Cecilberry tapped Snow's furrowed brow in a butterfly kiss, with the tips of her wings. "If wasps killed Taraq's parents and you were his sister, it stands to reason that they also killed yours."

"We don't mean to upset you, little sphinx. Please understand that we're concerned for your health," Jack called from the attic. "And by that, I mean harming yourself."

Snow materialized in the cold spot and stared in surprise. "Need I remind you, Jack, I'm a ghost and that a ghost can never die."

Jack snapped his mouth shut so hard it made his door quake. For once in a thousand years, the key to the door was rendered useless. Pookie responded for them both. "Indeed, you do not," she said. "Indeed, you do not."

Chapter 31

UPON WAKING

I'm pretty shaken up
after witnessing the final death pangs of Pangea's cataclysm.
I have a new, extremely ancient family.
My twin sister and I rule over Pangea as the constellation Gemini.
We are stars. Ageless. Formless.
But we have fallen from the sky as rain and snow.
My name may as well be, 'mud'.

As time flies, it's way past the 200 million years mark from 2020

FROM A LASTING IMPRESSION TO A FIRST INKLING

The Winter Room

Jack was the first to notice the pulsating blue cloud hovering over Snow's bed. Its iridescent blueness flickered and sputtered like the birthday cake sparklers Bash had once delighted in, hotly declaring them absolute proof that magic wands existed. *"Pssst,"* he called out. "Pookie, are you awake? There's something I think you should see. It's like a will-o'-the-wisp, but not."

Pookie poked her head from under the covers taking care not to wake Snow.

"Something is definitely up. I feel it in my bones," Jack wheezed.

"I'm right there with you," Pookie replied. "But I feel it in my nose."

Snow sprang from her cot still asleep and had to steady herself. She reeled and flumped back down on the bed. "I'm dizzy. I get the impression I'm leaving my body. What's happening?"

"An impression isn't dangerous," Pookie said. "Stay put. You're not going anywhere."

"I beg to differ," Jack muttered.

Snow tried dashing to the window but tripped and had to grab the sill to look out. "Did either of you hear something?" Snow shrieked at the whiteout before her. "The world is gone!"

"Calm yourself, child. It's still there. Have you forgotten that you own the high winter? You've conjured a blizzard. It's all in your mind."

"It sounds like the buzzing of wasps."

"I believe that translates to the sound of a penny dropping," Jack quipped.

"A penny from heaven if we should be so lucky," Pookie remarked.

Snow's voice trembled in fear. "Why are all of you disappearing?"

"She's under *my* spell now," Nimue announced. "Fairy truth serum lasts for only a moment, but we may be able to reach her. She's a stubborn one and no mistake. Even so, I have to say, there's not an ounce of ornery in that child."

Snow sobbed, gasping for air. "I'm going. Help me. I want to stay."

"Listen to me, baby girl," Jack shouted. "I know what this is. Stay calm. It's a vision quest. It's a rare, but natural phenomena for travelers. A kind of dream whirlpool. It's very important you don't fight it. Let the dizziness take you. It's somewhere you're supposed to go, or it wouldn't be happening."

Snow tightened her hold on Pookie.

The cloud floated across the room and melted into the wallpaper. Pookie's nose twitched furiously. "Where are you, Snow dear? What do you see?" she asked, slightly breathless from Snow's bear hug. Her eyes met Jack's with a question.

"More importantly, what do you *hear*, little sphinx?" Jack added. "Is there a voice? There should be a voice."

Snow replied in a calm voice. "I can hear you just fine, Jack."

Jack raised his eyes in exasperation. "Not me or Pook, little sphinx, *another* voice."

Snow nodded sleepily. "I'm sitting beside a river that cuts through the center of a huge city. Its banks are moving apart. A woman is waving to me from the other side of a deep abyss. There's a tropical storm. The trees are being ripped from the earth. There's uprooting, and pillaging. People are screaming. Somehow, I'm witnessing all this from the vantage point of the sky."

"Good," Jack replied. "Very good. Now please look more closely and describe as many details you can...*um...* remember. Do your best."

Snow spoke with uncommon authority. "I see a mad scramble for cargo boats with room for passengers. There aren't enough boats. Some have capsized. I see oarsmen dashing the skulls of people in the water desperate to save themselves. There's a widening rift in a seam of rock exposing a stream of white-hot soup bubbling like boiling water. Blobs are shooting from it. They look like globules of honey but when they land, they're grey pebbles. Oh, wait, the pebbles have sprouted legs. And now, wings. I don't like the way they scuttle. They've taken to the air, biting and stinging."

"Is it dark?"

"Now there's a monster beside me in the sky – a three-headed hag. Someone below is on their knees. It's a young woman calling to her: "Meagera, choose me. Choose me over my sister, your majesty." Snow paused. Her expression shifted from wonder to horror. "Oh, it's me! I'm the one begging. But I don't have a sister. Or have I forgotten her, too."

Pookie wriggled out of Snow's arms. "You've done well for one dream, child. There's no need to wear yourself out. Rest for a while."

Snow grabbed hold of Pookie's leg. "Wait... I remember something. It's a 'yesterday'. I'm in a strange room with no ceiling. A balcony supported by white columns. Two men are discussing my father. Oh, one of them reminds me of Parks! I need to listen. They're not being nice about my father. One of them is listing his faults. I refuse to listen to them anymore."

Snow closed her eyes and cocked her head. "There's a tempest in the library," she continued. "Nothing as severe as a tropical storm. Parks has brought along a few fairies for support. That's it. Oh, and the name Pluvia is running through my brain. Do you know who that is?"

"We do," Pookie said. "Well done. The fact that you remembered her name on your own is wonderful."

"So, she's a *her*. Is she a friend of mine?"

"You could say she's a friend of Beryl's."

"Can I meet her?"

"Only with Beryl's permission," Jack said.

"It's no wonder my first inkling was an overwhelming surge of sibling rivalry," Snow whined. "Always having to ask for permission is humiliating."

"Karma is as karma does," Pookie mumbled.

The fallout from Snow's unleashed tantrum was instant. Snow drifted in a dark abyss for 200,000 fairy years. But it still wasn't long enough to erase a karmic mistake. Forgiving karma was impossible.

Snow's form waivered in and out of being. "She looks pale," Nimue remarked. "Wispy as a ghost. But that's good, isn't it?"

Jack gave a slight cough. "Not necessarily," he said.

"Snow is drifting," Pookie said. "Both real and metaphorically. Either way, a vision of deep snowdrifts isn't good. Snow has been emotionally out of her depth for many years."

Jack's voice trembled from the door. "Is she gone?"

"Not yet," the Hall said. "My magic is simply out of control. Goswold was right. I've been lax. And now Snow needs all of us working tirelessly to help her rally. We must be cruel to be kind. No more coaxing. We must push. We must confront! Nimue, I charge you to call up the Green Lady's medicine."

Pigeon screeched all the way from Egypt. *'Pan, Pan the Green Man, man.'*

Nimue flinched. "I take it that's an order."

"Most definitely, it is," the Hall confirmed. "Time is running out."

"I am *so* ordered, then," Nimue said. "Step back, Pookie. My green magic is very much IN control. She dived to Snow's side and circled

Snow's head chanting *'smoke and mirror, mirrors and smoke. Snow is drifting, it's time she woke'*. Her wings tickled Snow's cheek as she whispered in her ear. "The lesson of a land mass splitting in two is...? Can you think of a human equivalent?"

"Divorce?" Jack suggested.

Nimue sent Jack a withering look. "Oh, for heaven's sake, Jack. I wasn't asking *you*." She cast a stream of fairy fog into the keyhole to silence Jack and tried again. "Snow, can you think of someone at odds with themselves?"

"Hello, Nimue," Snow mumbled dreamily. "Are you doing this? Do you think you could stop, please. Perhaps I should take a nap."

"NO!" all three shouted at once.

"Stay focused," Nimue said. "You've been privy to a great lesson. You don't want to miss a single second of it."

Snow's voice came from a distant point on the horizon. "I think maybe I do," she replied.

Nimue persisted. "Yourself, for instance? A twin perhaps?"

Snow finally surrendered. She collapsed into a ball, lay on the floor, and closed her eyes. "Yes, yes, twins. A twin of me, a twin of her, a twin of him."

Nimue cast a starry blanket over her.

Pookie smoothed Snow's hair from her face. "What's your first impression, Jack? Can you make any sense of this?"

"I think Snow knew, full well, the face on Mars was ugly before she invoked it... dared it, more like, but she couldn't know it would arrive vengeful and angry. Or that the stench of its breath would peel the skin off people's bones which was reason enough for her to promptly dismiss it and close her mind."

Pookie nodded in agreement. "This is a tremendous leap forward." She looked into Snow's mind for confirmation. "The last impression Snow had of Pangea was a diamond-hard lump of raging jealousy in her throat. Jealousy with hot spikes, throttling her. She couldn't breathe for the acidic heat of melting stone. I can feel it even now."

Snow stirred in her sleep. Her sad question came, barely a whisper. "But who is the me of me remembering such upheaval?"

Chapter 32

UPON WAKING

It's an overcast wintry day.
For some reason, Pigeon is in a frenzy over cucumber.
I am nine years old. My name is Snow.

The year is a puzzle.

PUZZLING IT OUT

Jack was out when Vita called through the keyhole to Pookie. "Can I come *in* to play? I'd ask Snow to come out but it's an overcast wintry day. Not her sort of day at all. But it's perfectly splendid for cocoa by the fire and building a jigsaw puzzle or reading a story. I imagine you *do* have a fire going."

Pookie's voice sounded distracted. "Yes, yes, of course. The fire's blazing. Come in, come in. Now then, where did I put that…?" Her voice trailed off as her head was mostly inside a huge trunk under several wool sweaters that once belonged to Beryl.

Snow opened the door and was sprayed by freezing rain for her efforts. She pulled Vita into the Winter Room by her sleeve and brushed the crystalized ice from her thin shawl. "Goodness, you'll catch your death." Oh, she gasped. "I *am* sorry, I wasn't thinking. I didn't mean to offend you. It's a figure of speech."

Vita laughed. "I think we both know I'm a ghost," she said.

"In any case," Snow added. "There's nothing wrong with being a ghost as I can testify. We're a couple of little girl ghosts in need of cocoa on a bitter day."

Vita busied herself disposing the last of the ice crystals and looked away. "Where's Pigeon?"

"He's right there in front of you. Are you okay?"

"*Mmnn.* I'm fine. It's just... oh, never mind. I'm not supposed to say."

'Blustery day... here in the flesh,' Pigeon crowed. *'Delightful... The more it snows, tiddly pom, the more it goes on snowing... that's life... full of secrets... wakey wakey.'*

"I forgot to order teacakes from the Hall," Snow said. "So, we've only got plain biscuits and sandwiches." She handed Vita a towel.

Vita dried her hair by the fire. "Pretend tea will do me nicely," she said from inside a damp towel. "I'm not overly fond of eating food outside my time." She edged closer to the hearth rubbing her hands. "I'll never get over your lovely indoor fires and soft towels. If I could, I would live here forever."

'And lots of plain cuttlebone sandwiches ... Plenty of butter... no crusts... careful what you wish for.'

"*Cucumber* sandwiches, you silly bird."

'Will I like them?'

"You have for years. Honestly, I think you're getting as forgetful as me."

"Is our puzzle where we left it in the nursery," Vita wanted to know. "And can we take Pigeon with us?"

"Of course, if he likes. Any particular reason?"

"He always asks for a story and I like them very much."

Pigeon clicked his beak and preened his feathers.

"Vita, you can ask me yourself," Snow said.

'P for Puzzles,' Pigeon nattered under his wing. *'Puzzle it out... Puzzle it out ... secrets will out. If this... then that... if that... then this... puzzle it out... you know you want to... be brave, Vita...I like... I do like... ask me anything.'*

Pigeon rode to the nursery on Vita's shoulder, eying the tray of sandwiches Snow carried.

"It looks more along than I remember," Vita said of the puzzle when Snow uncovered it. "I think Pookie may have added one or two pieces."

Pigeon clutched a sandwich in his claw, pulled the cucumber out with his beak, and dropped the offending vegetable on the floor. *'Don't like cucumber ... don't like secrets.'* he screeched. *'Go on... tell her Vita... if you're her friend... tell her before it's too late.'*

Snow looked up from the jigsaw puzzle, bewildered. She stared at the piece in her hand, surprised it was there and looked about the room in a stupor. "What are you all doing here?" she asked suddenly. "Vita, didn't you have a secret you were going to tell me?"

Pigeon, extremely animated, paced back and forth on the mantelpiece. *'Story time!'* he announced excitedly, loose feathers flying every which way. *'Tell me a story... tell Snow... tell her a story, Vita... happy endings... horrific beginnings... I'll mind the 'P's'... you mind the 'Q's'!*

"You're not actually a ghost," Vita mumbled, swallowing the rest of her sandwich in one bite. "I have to go now."

"I beg your pardon?" Snow said dreamy-eyed.

Vita rose quickly and brushed breadcrumbs from her lap. "Listen carefully," she said. "SNOW... YOU ... ARE ... NOT ... A... GHOST!"

PART 4

daybreak

Chapter 33

UPON WAKING

Vita is in a temper, interrogating me.
I am nine years old. My name is Snow.
A woman named Pluvia is wailing at a monster
The monster is laughing hysterically

The year is a Pangean mystery, swallowed by time.

HOPPING MAD

Vita mouthed the word sorry for Pookie's benefit and prodded Snow awake. "I know you're not sleeping," she said loudly. "I'm sorry you're scared. You have every right to be."

"I remember dying in this very bed," Snow said without opening her eyes.

"It was a dream," Vita said rubbing Snow's hands between her own. "You're alive, Snow. You have been, ever since you arrived in the Hall. When I first saw you walking by the Wall, I could tell right away you were sleepwalking."

Pookie squeezed out of Snow's arms and wiped her eyes. "It's lucky rabbits always have pink eyes," she said to herself. "Snow mustn't know I've been crying."

Snow's voice drifted from the bed. "You do know I can still hear you, right."

Jack chuckled. "Atta girl, little sphinx. You tell her. Out of bed with you, now. This is your lucky day. Your biggest dream will come true."

"You say that a lot," Snow remarked. "I don't think you understand what truth is, or the concept of 'big', either."

"He does," Pookie interrupted. "The truth has many layers that only a nature spirit like Jack can understand. It's a great burden to have carried them for as long as he has."

Snow opened her eyes and stared through Vita. "Who told you?"

Vita smiled. "Thank you for still being my friend. I heard it from a reliable source. Look, I feel as if I'm betraying a trust. Although it wasn't a formal promise, it *was* an understanding. And I gathered it was to protect you, but Jack put a flea in my ear that *he* couldn't tell you but that someone else, he hinted, another ghost perhaps, *might* and *should*."

"And that's you?"

"Fleas in the ears are never a good sign," Pookie mumbled quietly to herself.

"Jack said you needed help."

"I don't see how I could still be alive?"

"Hi, Snow. My name's Jack, have we met? We're presently in the Winter Room of Bede Hall. Bede is a place steeped in magic. Ring any bells?"

Snow crossed her arms and turned her face to the wall.

"Okay fine. You can still listen to Vita. Pookie and I will stay out of it."

"You've been asleep," Vita began. "You are right now. Whenever you think you've awakened in a new day, you're still dreaming of an older one. Jack explained. You're a dream traveler in a self-induced coma, like Lady Nan's. Dream travel has a different set of rules. A wheel of memories spins into random dreams, so they can be, well, dreamed, which explains why they're usually out of order. It's like a game."

"Not a very fun game."

"No."

"It wasn't a cat by any chance, was it? Your reliable source?"

"No no no, it was a fieldmouse."

Snow turned over and smiled. "Doolittle?"

"Yes."

"He's a sweetheart and as far as I know, not a liar."

Vita sighed. "I'll tell you everything I know. Jack and Pookie have been trying to wake you up. Your sleep is that deep, no wait… that's wrong. You are so powerfully *against* waking up, you sabotage yourself."

Snow spoke in muffled tones from underneath the bedding. "The two of them are always on about memories. Memories memories memories, what do you remember? What? When? Where? They never stop."

"The thing is," Vita said gently. "Is that you don't *want* to remember."

"Doolittle said that?"

"He's quite the spy, is Doolittle. Pigeon as well, although he can't keep a secret to save his feathers."

'Can too,' Pigeon replied in a huff. *'how do you think I've lived so long?… cats out of the bag … secrets require keys…. keys require sunshine… out in the open to be of any use… ergo… I keep secrets… I do NOT keep keys.'*

It would be impossible for a human to live thousands of years. I've been here since the 18th dynasty. And it seems like only yesterday, I was standing on a cliff watching the destruction of Pangea. I've no idea why I was called there."

Pookie clamped her paws over her ears and raised her eyes to the ceiling.

Snow babbled uncontrollably. "I witnessed a terrible war. There was a pyramid and a woman named Pluvia. Too many secrets. Only a ghost or a time traveler can do that and to my knowledge my father is the only time traveler in the family. That makes *me* a ghost."

"He *is* a time traveler," Jack piped up. "You are *not*. This is a day of reckoning. A door opens that cannot be shut."

"*Shouldn't* be shut," Pookie corrected. "Snow dear, your memories are necessary for moving on. For moving out of this frozen-in-time place. Suppressed memories have kept you trapped."

"If I wake up, I will be alive?"

"You ARE alive and WHEN you fully regain consciousness, your life will change, but it's more complicated than that. You have to *meet* your past. Face it head on. You must make friends with it and concede the things that must be conceded. Life waits for you beyond the act of surrendering which is only slightly ahead of listening to the truth."

"Then my truth must be terrible."

"It was and it always will be if you remain stubbornly determined not to let it go. Lady Nan did the same thing. Remember?"

"Now that I *do* remember. I was the one who woke her up."

And she was comatose in a self-induced escape from the Hall and its problems. She thought it was the easiest way out. She dreamed too. But she never disconnected from Egypt, so she slipped back easily. She didn't time travel. Her body stayed in Withering, so to speak. Her ka kept her body alive."

"She was on life support," Jack said. "Brooks made sure of that."

Snow closed her eyes and nodded. "Yes. I remember seeing Lady Nan out of her body."

"It was her ka. Right now, *your* ka is speaking to Vita and Pookie and me."

"One's ka is their life-force," Snow said dreamily.

"You see, if you want to remember, you can. You knew Pluvia as…"

Snow silenced Vita with a raised hand. "And Taraq?" Snow said, still in a trance. "I've known *him* before, too. Do you know about that, Vita?"

"Not the details."

"I know them," Pookie said. "But I can't tell you. There are rules. You have to wake up because you want to… and I mean *really* want to. Even if you don't *feel* ready. Those are two different things, and when you decide, it still won't happen all at once. Sleepwalkers must wake up naturally, else they can lose their minds. It's a slippery slope, is the dreamtime."

Snow took Vita's hand. "I'm sorry to have upset you. You've gone white as a g…"

"A sheet?"

"This means we aren't ghostly sisters," Snow pouted.

"I've had to listen to Roman soldiers all my life," Vita mused. "So, I have *some* Latin. Enough to know that Pluvia refers to rain."

Pookie stifled a scream and hopped about the room bumping into furniture startling Pigeon. *'Hopping mad... rabbits, rabbits, rabbits,'* he screeched, and burst into raucous parrot laughter.

Snow rolled the word 'rain' around in her mind's eye to see it from all angles, but it made her sleepy. "My head hurts. Pookie, why on earth are you carrying on so?"

"Shock," Jack said. "We never suspected a mouse would be our strongest ally. Remind me to kiss that little fella. Anubis tries to kiss him a lot. I don't think he can help it. Again, it's a smell that overrides common sense or duty. It's a wonder we have any mice left, but Anubis is disciplined, and the Hall and I make sure our animals are safe."

"Why wouldn't I want to wake up?" Snow asked.

"It will come to you," Jack said. "There's time. You decided to hide a very long time ago. Give it time. Memories are like sparks from a banked fire. Almost out, but one can reignite and jump like wildfire. It only takes a word or a scent, and out it tumbles and there you are, awake for a few minutes... on fire."

Pookie was not to remain outdone. "You have a form of selective amnesia which means a thought arrives and rarely stays."

"I'm not a ghost," Snow repeated. I never was. I am *alive*!"

Vita nodded excitedly. "You and I met in a dream. And when you're off dreaming elsewhere, I can still watch you. We can meet whenever we dream."

Snow turned on Pookie. "And you can stop bouncing about like a Jack-in-the-box!" How could you have been so cruel!" she ranted. "Nobody knows more than you that I need to escape this existence. How could you let me suffer. I thought you were my friend! And you, Jack. All that bragging about duty and responsibility, and innocent 'snowy hour' business. What were you thinking?"

"Beryl had a Jack-in-the-box once," Jack reflected. "A long time ago, it was. Before you came, Snow. T'was nothing like me."

"I'll be leaving the Hall, first thing tomorrow," Snow announced. "And now, I'm going to take a little cat nap. Did either of you consider that Vita could be wrong? All this has made me extremely tired."

Jack snapped back into the present. "You're partly correct, baby girl, but oh, so *very* wrong."

"You can't leave," Pookie said. Tomorrow will never come until…"

But Snow was already asleep. She automatically reached for Pookie and pulled her into a bedtime hug, smiling sweetly from a dream.

Chapter 34

UPON WAKING

I hear the sound of a dull rhythmic thud
and a feeling of being loved permeates my being.
Cats are everywhere.
I am nine years old. My name is Ani.

The year is 2018 – December 21st, the summer solstice.

IMP'VASION

Sarah Goodman's chilly kitchen was warmed by regular blasts of hot air that pumped into the room every time its cat flap opened. A stream of cats entered one-by-one. Their jewelry touched a golden memory within Snow of bright sunlight reflected off white stone. A thought broke her automatic impulse to count cats. Doing so was said to counter insomnia. *'Pookie says I have to stay awake at all costs. Counting cats is dangerous. I'm needed at the Hall. Maybe my father is home.'*

Snow's dream diary -

My father is years away, fighting. The Hall's in an uproar. Tiny black creatures swarm the stairwell buzzing with destructive energy. Their claws scuttle over the roof tiles, skittering overhead. They sound like dry leaves blowing across sandpaper. The air smells of burned trees. The sky is dry with evil clouds. Acid heatwaves shimmer on the drive like tortured ghosts.

The ears of the Hall's housecats twitch without moving as they lie in wait, perfectly still, with their newly-arrived feline allies from Egypt, quivering with the instinct to fight. I float to the ceiling to be out of the line of fire and make my way through several floors until I reach the attic.

Uncle Kha sits in Father's chair in the Winter Room, staring at a cold blue fire he's conjured in the grate. His fingers are pressed together in concentration. Aunt Bash stands by the window. I hear her thoughts, centered on the maze. She sends words of love into its heart: "I am here, waiting," she murmurs. When she presses her right hand to the glass, the brown hedges of the maze burst into verdant life. For an instant, a lavender-scented breeze blows summer into the vast lawns below. Blades of brittle straw grass pulsate with a transfusion of chlorophyl before returning to a desert seconds later.

Downstairs, an odd collection of twice-born warriors collect in clusters of two or three, cloistered together inside pockets of white light snapping with power to defend the earth. Their collective energies form a barricade against a wall of ancient jealousy and hate. Against an extraterrestrial invasion of black imps.

Beryl materializes in the Winter Room as Princess Ankhesenamun, dressed in Egyptian robes, and stands behind Aunt Bash. "We need to fight now, child," she says, placing her hand on Bash's shoulder. Bash shudders. Immediately the spell of springtime shatters but a strange beauty in the winter landscape remains.

Uncle Kha stirs from his chair, walks to my bedside where I cower under the covers, and gently calls me out of my body. "Baby Girl," he whispers in a strange language I understand. "It's time, Ani. Come. We can watch your dream from your father's tower with Taraq," he says.

The clashing of Roman swords and shields, horses thundering into battle, and the screeching of a demon, fills my ears. A girl calls from inside Hadrian's Wall. "Tell them about the turtle," she shouts. "Don't forget to come back."

When I take Uncle Kha's hand, a sharp pain awakens the memory of a hundred names and places. I feel the sting of a wasp on a boy's cheek, again. And when I open my eyes, the Winter Room is bathed in the sweetness of birdsong. The morning chorus welcomes me home. Pookie's fur is wet from my tears. Pigeon greets me with his wake-up squawk talk. I miss my baby brother.

Chapter 35

UPON WAKING

I am startled... I am under attack!
I am nine years old. My name is hard-headed girl!

The year spans two portals in Hadrian's Wall

CAUGHT CATNAPPING

The floorboards creaked in the corridor outside the Winter Room, now covered in deep snow and open to the stars. Vita walked six inches below the interior floor she knew well from her summer visits when the attic was high above the ground.

Jack's eyes flew open.

Vita quickly placed a hand over the keyhole. "Shush, it's me, Jack. I don't want to wake Snow until the time is right."

"Oh, it's you. Are you out haunting tonight, little Vita? I'm loath to admit it, but ghostly footsteps creep me out. He giggled. "Don't mind me, Vita. I'm in a giddy mood."

"I'm here for an intervention. If it works, I won't be here long. If it works, you can hoop and holler loud enough to wake the dead."

Jack exhaled a long breath. "It's long past Snow's reckoning. There's a limited number of time-sensitive windows, young lady, and Snow has used up her fair share. Has anyone ever told you that you have a decidedly quaint sense of humor?"

"I was remiss the other day when I was here," Vita moaned. "Later it occurred to me that I'd missed a golden opportunity. I'm much distressed. Snow was so close. The timing was perfect, and I wasted it."

"I was aware," Jack said to Vita. "But I couldn't say anything. The rules are quite strict about overstepping one's magical powers. My 'door was locked', as it were. I wondered if you would notice."

"I only wondered WHEN she'd notice," Pookie telegraphed. *"I KNEW she would. Vita is clever. And I'm happy to say, she has a lovely surprise coming, but that's for another time. Tonight, there's a good chance she just might cross the borders of waking and sleeping. If, that is, she doesn't back down. She's a sweet girl. Too empathetic for her own good, sometimes. And for her plan to work she will have to set those kind-hearted feelings aside. Her success will take what is widely known as gumption."*

"Ah, yes," Jack telegraphed back. *"The quaint word for what Parks calls guts. I think we may count on Miss Vita doing what she clearly sees as her duty to a friend in need."*

Vita watched Jack's face change from deep to pale blue while he and Pookie compared notes. Vita tapped his nose. "Well, is your door locked now? Hello? Jack?"

"Pardon me, I was distracted momentarily" Jack wheezed. "I am unlocked but not undone. Please enter. And the best of Bede luck to you, clever girl."

Vita tiptoed past Pigeon, sleeping with his head under a wing. He opened one eye, spied Vita, chuckled to himself and promptly closed it.

"You can join my mission if you've a mind to, Pigeon," she said. "I know you're awake."

'No, you're all right,' Pigeon said. *'But I'll watch your presentation if it won't put you off. If I owned a hat, I would take it off to celebrate your daring. It's a grand day for presents, or did you mean presence? The gift that goes on giving.'*

"Now who's being quaint."

'It's hard to smile with a beak, but you always make we want to,' Pigeon squawked. *'I thank you for that. You're a dear sweet girl.'*

Vita floated across the room and stood over Snow's bed. She bent low and felt Snow's breath on her cheek. "You're no more asleep than Pigeon is," Vita muttered, her arms crossed in anger. So, you can stop pretending. No matter, it's best you just lie there and hear what I have to say."

Vita put her mouth close to Snow's ear and took a deep breath. "YOU ARE A SELFISH HARDHEADED GIRL!" she shouted. "NO-ONE IS MORE STUBBORN THAN YOU! SOMETIMES, I WONDER IF YOU ARE EVEN WORTH SAVING! STOP WASTING EVERYONE'S TIME. LIFE WON'T WAIT FOREVER. NOW, WAKE UP!"

Snow's ka jumped out of her body and stood facing Vita. The only umbilical cord visible was connected to Snow's body and her spirit form. Snow lifted it, perplexed. "I thought we were sisters in spirit," she said to Vita, sadly. "We are disconnected."

"What did you expect. We cannot be friends if you continue to play games," Vita declared.

Snow's umbilical cord stretched as she moved to the open window. "Jack says my window of opportunity is closing. There's too much winter out there. I should close it and be done."

"I should have seen how self-centered you are," Vita complained. "I don't like you very much."

'And the point goes to Vita,' Pigeon cackled, unable to stop himself.

"This isn't like you, Snow countered, "My old friend, Vita would never be so cruel. Who's put you up to this?"

"Well, if you must know, it was me. Your NEW friend, Vita, if you still want to be friends."

"I'll think about it and get back to you."

Vita brushed past Snow and slammed the window shut. "Out of the question! Friend or foe. Those are your only options. But consider this. It was out of friendship that your angry ka woke Lady Nan when she was wallowing in self-pity. It was a selfless act that ultimately led to saving Bede Hall. If you recall, the Hall thanked you profusely. And if you do, it's a sign your memories are returning. Can you handle that? Do you really want to get out of here? Decide. The time for playing hide and seek is over. This window is not locked… yet. But you are out of time. So, what's it going to be? Perpetual winter or eternal spring?"

Snow's ka visibly crumbled as the anger in her eyes drained to surrender. Her cord vanished first, and then her ka popped like a balloon. She bolted up in bed, terrified, gripping onto the blankets as if they anchored her to the earth. "Please, Vita, don't abandon me. I need your help. I want to get out of here, more than anything. I promise… no more games."

The landscape changed from winter to spring as Vita reopened the window.

Icicles formed in Jack's eyes. "Oh, Vita, dearest girl. How will Snow ever thank you."

"I know of a way," Pookie announced. "But first, I must consult with My Lady, Flora. I spy with my little eye, something beginning with 'C'," she said. "One more game should do the trick, Snow."

Chapter 36

UPON WAKING

I slip into an old dream of soldiers and horses.
I am nine years old. My name is Snow.

It is the twentieth year of Hadrian's Wall

THE SNOWBALL EFFECT

"Hmm," Vita mused. "Something beginning with 'C'. Let's see... Oh, is that it? A trick question of 'see' and not a 'C' word at all?" She tapped the top of Snow's head with a teaspoon. "You look distracted. What's going on in there?"

"I feel as if I'm slipping away into an old dream. I'm not all here. That is to say, the happy place where we were a moment ago. Strangely, I feel bigger. I'm not sure I like it."

"The fastest way out of a dream is always through it," Jack said, "Take my advice. Resist nothing. Go with it. Besides, something tells me Pookie is in control."

Snow spoke with her eyes closed. "I'm in my father's Saxon tower. I see rows of low buildings covering the Hall's maze extending as far away as the lake. Soldiers are drilling in disciplined formations inside the fort's walls. Dozens of soldiers are building roads and digging parallel ditches that run outside the fortification walls, enclosing a ragtag village of tradesmen. Well, you lived there, Vita, so you'll know."

"Today, I seem to know more than I usually know, if that's not too much of a puzzle," Vita said. "What else do you see?"

Snow clenched her jaw determined to remember. "There's a constant ringing of smithies beating bars of white hot metal into

182

swords and horseshoes. Animals are screaming in every conceivable language. Stench issues from a vast complex of stables and pens, filled with war horses, cart horses, donkeys and pigs. I recognize soap and candle makers, bakers and butchers, and a pottery kiln on a hillside belching black smoke."

Vita nodded wistfully. "And the ditches were never finished," she added. "Not in my time, nor past my lifetime when I lingered as the shadow of an old woman afraid to move on. Even during dry spells, the ground was a mire of dung and mud."

"Stay focused," Jack urged. Pookie has sent you there for a reason. I can't ask her because she's off to see the Green Lady on urgent business."

Vita stared hard into Snow's eyes. "Your expression has changed," she said. "Where are you now?"

"Three miles away in the modern village of Bede, trailing behind an old man purchasing some odd items from a shop in the high street. Oh, I recognize them. He's carrying Beryl's snow globe and her brass hourglass. The sign over the shop reads 'Clutterbucks Emporium'. It sounds rather grand but it's more or less a junk shop."

Jack made a guffaw sound. "Don't you go disparaging junk shops, Miss high and mighty sphinx. I'll have you know there's special items in the back of that shop. Art and such. Secret antiquities and magical oddities. It's a well-respected business. Been in the Clutterbucks family for decades, it has."

"I wonder who the old man is. I don't recognize him."

Jack sounded bored. "It's Mr. Leoni."

"How do you know? It's *my* dream."

"Most of the time you leave the door to the dreamtime wide open. And being a door myself, I'm naturally curious about what lies behind doors in general, that's how. Besides it's my job to guard you. Things that lurk behind doors can be dangerous."

"Jack," Vita interrupted. "I think Snow may have ventured into a dream she's not supposed to experience without a chaperone. Maybe we should wait for Pookie."

"I'm already there," Snow said. "It's a scary movie about the end of the world. A battle is raging in a place called Pangea. Can you see it, Jack?"

"I can," Jack answered. "But it's not a dream. Let's talk about something else, shall we. You don't want to bore Vita. She's your guest."

Snow ignored Vita's hand on her arm. "Was I there?"

"You were," Jack said cagily. "One of a pair of royal twin sisters, younger by nine minutes which meant your sister was queen, and *you* were only a princess. You had to defer to her, and she had to lord it over you. That's how it was back then. Times are almost different now, but not.

Every mythological being, nature god, and hero sprouted whole from Pangean legend. All manner of grotesque monsters spawned there. Megeara could smell jealousy. It wasn't just IN her blood it WAS her blood. She was already jealous of the Pan Gemini's power. So, *someone's* who shall remain nameless, sibling rivalry tipped the scales, and in so doing, attracted an immortal glutton who gorged on jealousy."

"I see her," Snow said. "A three-headed monster in the sky. Someone's calling out to her."

Jack lowered his voice. "Megeara only came to earth to feed."

"You needn't tell *me*," Pookie announced, newly returned and breathless. "I've been privy to some nasty food fights in my years, I can tell you." She smiled sweetly in the door's direction. "Jack, dear? I see you've been telling stories while I was gone."

Vita jumped to Jack's aid. "We've been sharing Snow's dreams. She saw Mr. Leoni at Clutterbuck's Emporium."

"I was a princess," Snow declared excitedly. "In a place called Pangea."

"Were you, indeed," Pookie said staring intently at Jack who disappeared from the door, entirely. "I remember when you thought Beryl was a princess. The rest of us had to mind our backs around her. The fairies played tricks on her, but she was too haughty to see them. She never could. Beryl was a handful, but she was a different child with Parks. After Ben died, Beryl felt powerless. Invisible. She'd have given everything to have her brother back so she could be jealous again."

Snow waved a towel from the attic window with a dreamy smile.

Jack telegraphed Pookie. Stop rabbiting on, Pook. Look at Snow. She's acting strange. "What are you doing, little sphinx?" his disembodied voice called out.

"I'm pretending the Hall is an ice palace and I'm a princess trapped in a tower, but it reminds me too much of something I can't quite put my finger on," Snow said, in a far off childish voice.

"Do you not recall the princess we discussed barely a moment ago?" Vita asked with a worried look on her face.

"*Hmmn?* What? I'm asking the Hall to please bring back the manicured gardens of summer so I can play tag with the topiaries and watch the fairies swarm around Parks singing the growing songs to his plants. Beryl is too old to play tag with the topiaries. It's during the time of her great sadness."

"There were many. There's nothing wrong with *my* memory," Jack said before slamming his door shut.

"Dreams are ruled by the powers of now and then," Pookie said. But eventually, 'then' catches up to the now… and here we are!"

"A place where Snow's amnesia is on again off again." Jack commented from the ether.

Snow, momentarily recovered from being a child, read her diary out loud to hear herself think, hoping it would jog her memory:

"*Sometimes,*" she read. "*I find myself wandering a desert floating above blistering sands calling for my mother. Once, in the distance, a lone chariot I recognized as my father's, scooted across the horizon. He was searching for me. I shouted 'Father, I'm here,' but the blowing sand took my voice and stung my eyes.*

The booming voice of the Great Sphinx cut through the storm and chided me; 'Child,' it growled, 'there is one other who searches for you. A child your age. Listen. He is alone and afraid. Send him comfort. In spite of your fears, your trials are not as great. You belong together.'

I know now, that was Peri.

My attic buzzes with still-life. I hear the memories of playing children locked in the walls. The winter room was once part of Beryl's and Ben's nursery suite. I have inherited their rocking horse and plenty of picture books and windup toys made of colored tin. Pigeon watches over me from his perch. My father always covered Pigeon with a cloth, but I love to see the kindness in his glass eyes. I can't bear to cover him with a white sheet. It looks too much like a shroud of snow and parrots hate being cold. For a terrible moment, I almost remembered why I'm here, but I've learned how to push those memories behind a private door that Jack and Pookie don't know about.

"You shouldn't read that stuff aloud if it's a secret," Jack remarked sounding smug. "I have excellent telepathic hearing. And just so you know, Pookie and I *are* aware of your door, but much as we'd like to, we're forbidden to open it. It must be difficult being a child with grown-up feelings. It's a shame that feelings aren't memories. They're tendencies. Although, I have to say, you've managed to turn forgetfulness into an art form."

"Thank you. I write much older than I usually am. I was about to write how winter snow cloaked, that is to say, *clogged* the lawns in Lady Nan's time. I remember how they once stretched to the lake in a swash of green velvet. These days, Hadrian's Wall and the gates of Bede Hall have disappeared under deep snow that almost covered the Saxon round tower, my father's favorite memory place."

"Where's *your* favorite memory place?" Jack asked.

Snow shrugged. "I only know it isn't here."

"Bede Hall is a veritable house of shadows," Jack said rematerializing on the door.

Snow grimaced. "That's funny because my father called them *fore*shadows. The *before* shadows that greeted us when we arrived. He left me a note the day he left, scratched in the frost of a gilt mirror. *'See you soon, love Daddy'*. I didn't find it until the next morning."

Pookie wiped away a tear with her ears and shook her head.

"Some days it's still there," Snow whispered. "The guilt within the gilt." She brightened. "Twin guilt. Twins are important around here."

"Your father is truly sorry," Jack said. "Kit never abandoned you. It was your father's nature to abandon himself."

"Am I awake? Is it time?"

"Not quite… perhaps, soon," Pookie suggested. "At least for a moment or two. Vita said goodbye. She had to go. The dogs were calling her."

Jack looked at the darkening sky. "It's almost 'snowy hour', little prin… *sphinx*. Is there anything you'd like to ask me?"

Snow yawned and stretched sleepily on the bed, arms behind her head. "Yes please, Jack… who exactly *are* the Pan Gemini?"

Chapter 37

UPON WAKING

I am playing a game with life.
I am nine years old. My name is Snow.

The year is now and then at the same time

THE COLD BLUE SPOT

The temperature in the attic shifted. Some days it was positively balmy. A limp breeze barely stirred the curtains. Snow lay draped sideways over her father's armchair, eyes closed, her legs dangling listlessly while Vita fanned her with a comic book.

"Are you going to break the ice or shall I," Jack rebuked Pookie.

"No need for unnecessary theatrics," Pookie remarked, "I was waiting for the right moment. I spy with my little eye, something beginning with S," she said.

"I give up," Snow snapped.

"Snow still hasn't solved the 'C' clue yet," Jack said in a grump. "You're not playing fair."

"Hark who's talking," Pookie replied telepathically. "As I recall, we were somewhat distracted by a story of *yours* at the time, Jack."

"Touché."

Pookie cleared her throat. "The something beginning with 'C' could very well trick Snow into the final reckoning of her lengthy ordeal, so I'm leading into it gradually."

"Be my guest. I'll stay silent then, shall I?"

Pookie's shadow crept up the wall doubling in size. "Snow dear, while surrendering can be a fine positive thing, I taught you to never give up. Now, do either of you girls notice anything new about the Winter Room that begins with S?"

"Me," Snow answered, clearly out of sorts.

"You're definitely, in the cold zone," Pookie replied.

Snow opened one eye. "Secrets. A secret tunnel?"

"Stone cold," Pookie quipped. "Guess again."

'Never give up the ghost,' Pigeon nattered from his corner. *'Until you have to.'*

Vita paused fanning. "Does anything outside the room count?" she asked eying the window.

"The view is part of the Winter Room's energy, so, yes, it counts," Pookie replied.

Jack chuckled. "I see where *this* is going," he said. "Clever begins with C."

"Jack!" Pookie shouted. "Quiet begins with Q!"

The blue door slammed shut in a huff but dutifully reopened to restore the much-needed draft.

Vita dropped the comic book in Snow's lap and walked to the window. "I have to check the fort anyway," she said. "Come on, Snow, look with me."

Snow retrieved the comic book and began fanning herself. "I'm too tired to play."

Pookie and Jack startled at once. "Now you listen to me, baby girl," Pookie admonished, all ruffled. "The Hall is quite clear regarding Bede etiquette. There's absolutely no napping of any kind when you have an invited guest. The very idea!"

"Pook's right, little sphinx," Jack agreed. "You're the host, so mind your manners."

Pigeon roused his feathers to utter *'cucumber sandwiches'* twice and resumed snoring.

"Pigeon's sleeping," Snow accused. "Is he being rude?"

Jack averted his gaze and giggled.

"Pigeon doesn't count," Pookie replied miffed. "His mission in life is to bring clarity through sarcasm and rudeness.

Jack couldn't resist the obvious. "Apparently, that's his mission in death, as well," he sniped.

Pookie bristled and flapped her ears like a wet dog. "What do you see out there, Vita dear?"

"I spy icicles melting on the eaves," Vita answered. "Which reminds me. When I passed Cyril on the way here this morning, he mentioned that sap was rising in the trees. Apparently, it's the tree nymphs favorite time of the year. Is the word, Spring?"

"A little warmer."

"Summer!" Snow declared. "Can we make some lemonade, now."

Vita winked at Pookie. "Oh, well done, Snow," she said with a smattering of applause. "What's lemonade?"

"May I speak *now*, Pook?" Jack whined.

"Be my guest."

"Little sphinx," Jack began in his teacherly voice. "Did you know that humans and trees have something VITAL in common? I'll give you a hint. Sap is a trees' lifeblood."

"*Hmmph*," Snow mumbled. "I didn't know there was going to be an exam. I thought we were playing a childish game to pass the time. Because, if you're referring to me being alive and my blood, may I remind you…"

"Okay," Jack said. "Perhaps I spoke out of turn."

"Imagine my surprise," Pookie muttered.

Snow raised her head over the back of the armchair and stared at Pookie. "I'm bored, Pook. I simply don't care. Quite frankly, I've haunted this place long enough to know there's nothing new in or outside this room, worth knowing."

Pookie released her growing frustration by thumping her feet. "Okay, Jack, it's officially your turn. Do your worst."

"When a human is bored, Jack began. "It's said their 'blood runs cold' It's a saying that usually means indifference has grown into something doctors call depression, but things can change, and a person's lifeblood can also heat up in anticipation of happy things."

"I'm a ghost, Jack. Have we met? My blood hasn't *run* cold. I *have* no blood."

"Vita already explained that you are alive."

"Vita could be wrong. She didn't know what a book was until I showed her."

Jack's voice grew demanding. "For instance, waking up to a happy new life."

"Reincarnation?" Snow replied, evidently skeptical. Her single word dripped with the ice Vita had seen melting.

"I refer to RECUPERATION. And, by the way, little sphinx, while you've been sleeping, I've been tutoring Vita for reasons I won't go into at this time. Vita's name stands for vitality. Did you know that 'vita' is the Latin word for life! You might even say your friend Vita wrote the book on life. I'd listen to her more often if I were you."

Pookie hopped up and down, waving frantically.

Jack sniffed. "I do believe Pookie has something urgent to say."

Thank you, Jack, Pookie said. "Snow, this isn't school. We're merely having a casual conversation on a particularly humid day. Please humor me by looking for your transparent umbilical cord. Can you see it?"

"It's been gone for ages. I feel quite free."

"Excellent. There must be no incumbrances."

"Now, look out the window with Vita. But this time, picture tents swamping the lawn, heavy equipment, trailers, horses, performers, music, orders shouted into a megaphone, and the people wearing strange clothes that used to frighten you."

"Aha, Snow shouted. The something beginning with 'C' is clothes. Not so very strange. I recognize them now. They're actors wearing Egyptian clothes from the days when I lived there."

Pookie shook her ears. "Close, but no. C is for Costumes; C is for Circus; C is for Carnarvon; C is for Carter; C is for Caldera, and most important of all, C is for Consequences. And that, my dear, is how you saved Bede Hall and the planet along with it."

"I saved all that?"

"You did! The bank was about to foreclose. You and Lady Nan

watched a lot of movies during those grim days. You watched them all, including the commentaries. And one day, after watching a documentary about a movie filmed on location in a stately home, you came up with a brilliant solution to turnaround the Hall's financial crisis.

It conspired that big money was to be had renting out stately properties as film locations, considering it was cheaper than building sets. *You* planted that bug in Rupert's ear. Mind you it had to travel from you through every room in the Hall and out the other side before Rupert grasped its importance, but luckily, motion pictures, movie stars, and the entire concept of celebrity perked his interest.

Because of *your* suggestion, little Taraq came to England. If it hadn't been for *you*, your father would never have been convinced to, well, *volunteer*, for travel duty. And Taraq would never have met you in so timely a fashion or become apprenticed to Brooks."

Jack picked up the tale. "Your charming, Uncle Rupert, contacted several production houses in Hollywood. My, how Hollywood did engage that boy's interest.

By *ahem* sheer chance, I don't think, an American production company was searching for a grand English mansion. So, as luck would have it, and it didn't, they cast Bede Hall to represent the estate of Lord Carnarvon in a movie about Howard Carter's discovery of King Tutankhamun's tomb."

"And incidentally," Pookie added. "Howard Carter, also happened to be a far distant cousin of your grandfather's. Coincidence? Not a chance. It was a prime example of lucid dreaming invading subliminal memory culminating in an ingenious karmic puzzle in need of…"

Jack made the sound of a drumroll on the door.

"…THIS!" Pookie said, pulling the key to the Winter Room door from her left ear.

"So, due to your quick thinking," Jack continued. "Bede Hall made a pile of money and was restored. And not long after, to everyone's relief, the circus moved on and Rupert followed it to join the biggest three ring circus of all – Hollywood."

"Most importantly, your careworn grandmother no longer had to teach private students," Pookie chimed in.

"And don't go taxing your brain trying to place the horrid child who signed up," Jack added. "That cunning little chap, his yappy dog, aptly named, Nipper, and his needy greedy parents got what they deserved. Nimue doesn't waste niceties on disruptive humans. The father, incidentally, was one of the property developers responsible for harassing the Hall in the first place, and his colleagues were whisked away to the fairy underworld where time stops. They may just wander out in a thousand years or so. If they're lucky."

Vita applauded more loudly and Pigeon joined in screeching *'Viva Vita. Long life sweet girl.'*

Snow daydreamed with a smile on her face. "I recognized the costumes because I lived and died there with Taraq. The movie biz reunited us by chance."

"Sorry... no, that never happened. For one thing, you *didn't* die with Taraq. He died alone after you left him. Consequently, you were reunited by the universal laws of comeuppance. The cause and effect phenomenon that works in wondrous ways *after* it bites you on the bum."

"But wasn't that hundreds of years ago?"

"Snow," Vita said. "You only had the dream, yesterday."

Snow shrugged. "Well, when you're a ghost time is less relevant. Is it chilly in here?"

"It's actually sweltering in here," Vita said. "And Jack taught me that time is the only thing that IS relevant but no matter. I expect you will believe the truth that you're alive, soon. I would never lie to you."

"In my defence," Snow added. "I dreamed of Egypt many times."

"That you did, little sphinx, that you did," Jack said. "And the best part of those dreams was that your actions took a huge *bite* out of your karmic debt."

"Am I awake? Is it time?"

Pookie's ears drooped accordingly. "Not quite, child."

Chapter 38

UPON WAKING

I hear footsteps.
I am nine years old. My name is Snow.
I've made a new friend.

Jack says the year must remain a mystery

CANTERBURY'S TALES

Snow left her notebook open to investigate padding footsteps outside the blue door. The hallway was empty.

"Jack, did you see anyone just now? I heard footsteps."

"No, baby girl. As usual, I can report that all's eerily quiet in the cold blue spot."

"Am I awake? Is it time?"

"Not quite… soon."

'I've been writing. Would you like to hear what I wrote?

"Did you make it a good story?"

"I didn't have to make it up. I believe it really happened. I rode Canterbury today. The sun was lovely and warm on my back. It was like a bright yellow clock, hanging in the sky with Roman numerals around its face. Its spindly hands whiled away the seasons that could never end."

"So, it's a tall tale, then, just so we're clear."

"Not at all. Sometimes I just know things. *The time portals are clearing,'* she began. *'Soon they will be safe. What comes will rewrite history yet change nothing. That's the beauty of Bede magic. I'm growing into it. Everyone says I will wake up soon. But Jack says I will have to wait a little longer.'*

Jack's smile grew more smug. "I do say that. Things come to me as well."

'I've made a new friend. Strangely, he's been a constant companion, right under my nose.

Lady Nan visited me in a dream. She told me that Canterbury graces the Winter Room with an element of nostalgic décor.' That's how she talks. *'I call him a lovely dapple-grey pony carved from wood with a red leather saddle and a white mane. I hang my coat on him sometimes, but I've never had the urge to ride him until this morning.*

My great grandmother says he's naturally steeped in horse sense, but more than that, he's a dark horse with a deep secret. A secret he's been keeping too well for her liking.'

"Or mine," Jack said. "Lady Nan and I haven't always seen eye-to-eye."

Canterbury is a time portal, and he's been in my room the whole time, since I met Beryl.

Lady Nan says that untimely hindsight is more perverse than the regular sort.' I don't know what perverse means. *She says it's the eleventh hour, and that if I'd had a mind to, I could have ridden Canterbury clear out of my nightmare before my father was even born.'*

"Trust you grandmother to break a spell," Jack sniffed condescendingly. "I would have thought Pigeon might have told you. His rules are more lenient than mine or Pookie's. I would have bet money on it. But I *will* say this: the constant sound of wood rocking against wood broke Canterbury's spell as much as cast it."

Doolittle, the fieldmouse, sat nibbling Canterbury's yarn tail as a reward for telling the truth during a tense moment when a lie would have been easier and less painful.

He sat cross-legged atop Canterbury's rump, reminiscent of Beatrix Potter's 'Tailor of Gloucester' mouse perched on a spool of thread.

"Did you know," Snow asked him, "that Beatrix Potter lives in Bede Village? Her name is different now, but she still owns a rabbit named Peter?"

Doolittle swallowed his mouthful. "Common knowledge," he said. "Did you know that Canterbury, here, has another, *bigger* secret?"

"I didn't. Does Pigeon know?"

Pigeon's voice issued from his corner perch. *'There are no secrets in Bede that I haven't uncovered at least twice,'* he cackled.

Doolittle looked up from his snack and winked sweetly, his cheeks puffed out once more with delicious string. He swallowed, burped politely, and wiped his whiskers on the sleeve of his sky-blue coat. "Think you're too old for rocking horses, do you?" he squeaked.

"The truth will out," Snow said. "Lady Nan says that all the time, but I have no idea what it means."

The mouse continued to tease. "If anything, you're too *young* for this secret."

"Are you daring me?"

"I'm *challenging* you. Aren't you the least bit curious? I promise you, it's a secret well worth knowing. And all you have to do is climb onto Canterbury's back."

Snow did as she was told and sat waiting for a horsey voice to speak, but Canterbury remained silent. And then, almost imperceptibly at first, he moved forwards and back. And as his speed increased, the Winter Room's walls faded into countryside.

For a long time, Snow rode over a straight Roman road that cut through forests, past villages, circumventing Anglo Saxon graves pushing up mounds of treasure-riddled soil. A blur of round towers and square forts flew by as Canterbury dodged ancient border skirmishes with Scots and Vikings, on and on through rain and snow.

"Look at me, Pookie," Snow shouted into the wind. "I'm riding to a new life."

The drone of creaky floorboards brought Snow back to the Winter Room with a bump. But her stay was brief. A starting pistol sounded, and Canterbury was off, carrying Snow, wearing a blue jersey sporting the number nine, the sole rider in a race against time itself, racing a wooden horse to summer.

Part of Canterbury's secret was that its hollow belly was empty which meant there were no demons left hiding inside. Every last one of them was in the crowd cheering Snow on.

Snow, no longer trapped, broke free of the eternally frozen nursery down the hall. The unfinished puzzles and bedtime stories were put away, and her inner child thrilled to the sound of horses' hooves thudding down a soft track of mud.

"Where are you off to," Jack called out.

"My next life. Vita was telling the truth. I AM alive, and I have it on good authority, my new life waits down this road. Doolittle says it isn't so far. I intend to be ten years old when I get there. That will be my starting point."

"Have a care when you arrive, little sphinx," Jack warned. "Be yourself, but not, if you know what I mean."

"I can be the me-of-me, the perpetual child who thinks like a wise woman. Because it finally dawned on me, Jack, that a child prodigy can be brilliantly ahead of his or her time. If anything, my siblings and I fall into the category of 'well ahead of the game'.

Jack agreed. "I wholeheartedly applaud your daring journey."

"Not everyone reincarnates, do they, Jack?"

The blue door rattled loudly. "No," Jack answered. "And yet everyone who does, forgets they have. The twice-borns of Bede earned their mission to return to consciousness as a family. The Stratford Smyths have too. They're exceptions to the rule. And you, little sphinx, are a Stratford Smyth and no mistake."

Snow called over her shoulder as she rode through the gates. "It's clear to me now," she shouted, "That sometimes when we save the earth, we forget to save ourselves."

"How was the winners' circle?" Pookie asked, her ears scanning for untoward sounds. "By the way, I didn't hear footsteps, earlier."

"Oh, Pookie, I wish you'd been with me. There was a topiary hare scampering ahead of me. You should have seen him."

"That was Harigold. He used to live here. Your power must be returning to have seen him. He rarely shows himself. Consider him a good omen."

"I was surprised. He's much faster than a horse."

"He has to be. Dear old Harigold hops to the moon and back, every night."

Pookie jumped on Canterbury's back and groomed her ears. "I've left a new notebook on your bed, she said from on high. "I want you to write down your latest memories as they occur as well as any new insights you may have. This is your time – an opening of the way, an Egyptian rite of passage. Relax into it and enjoy yourself. It's a reward."

Snow's pen scribbled madly by candlelight.

My Uncle Tut doesn't rest in a gold sarcophagus, she wrote. *He's presently my distant cousin, Kem. I think of him as the latest archaeologist in a long line of distinguished scholars. The souls of my grandparents no longer reside trapped inside crumbling mummy wrappings.*

The empty stables where my father wished for a black horse as a boy, smell of fresh hay. I can see a transparent black horse kicking his hooves against a stall door, hanging by its hinges.

At the end of our ride, Canterbury approached a jump, cleared it effortlessly, and landed in the Winter Room where fresh baked bread and raspberry jam were waiting for us.

Chapter 39

UPON WAKING

I hear birds. Joyous singing birds.
I am nine years old. My name is Snow/Anna/Ani/Baby Girl.

Jack says the year will be a reckoning

AN OUT OF 'BODY-MIND-SOUL' EXPERIENCE

Unusually enough, all things considered, the hands of the Winter Room clock materialized gradually. And as they formed, the ticking stopped. "We're coming up on another reckoning," Jack announced. "How many more could there be."

'A fair few,' Pigeon shrieked. *'Many a true memory is dreamed in jest.'*

Pookie's nose stopped twitching which meant she was not in the mood for silliness. "You and your parrot droppings," she grumbled. "Your timing couldn't be more...*hmph*... untimely."

"Am I awake, Pook? Is it time?" Snow asked.

Pookie hesitated. "Yes... for a second or two. Please remain calm."

"What's next?"

"STAYING awake!" Jack replied. "Reckonings require one's full attention."

"So, what does my report card say, Pook?"

"Flying colors, little sphinx: Your mind is clear. Your body is strong. And your spirit is soaring over the moon! If you wait long enough, you'll probably see Harigold, again."

Chapter 40

UPOM WAKING

I feel as if I am on another planet
I am nine years old. My name means Snow.
All I remember is that it begins with the letter 'N'.

The concept of years does not yet exist.

THE LAST DAY

A large floor globe wobbled in the library tower every time a tremor shook the Temple of Pan's foundations. Queen Pluvia gazed over the dying remnants of her territory like an anxious woman looking for her husband's ship, knowing it was already at the bottom of the sea, and she, widowed. She was so entirely upset, she felt utter relief. And then a sweet mind-numbing nothingness washed through her, and she smiled.

Princess Nixia paced nervously behind her expecting Pluvia's wrath, which she rightly deserved, but only resignation came. And since Nixia was well aware of her sister's benign nature, endlessly aligned to the spirit of goodwill, Pluvia's silence was harder to take than if she'd lashed out with venom.

The queen was clearly holding back for the sake of magic. Hate was forbidden in Pangea. Pan himself had decreed it unlawful. Hate only remained as the sole portal where human suffering dissolved during one's golden hour of alchemic transformation.

It was too late to play the victim or martyr. When fate sealed a portal, there was no turning back. Time-travel was the only exception, if that is, one had a time machine or the equivalent. A rare few of the magi had mastered the art of astral projection, and it seemed they'd taken that option to escape after the last sky ship had gone.

The stench of sulphurous fumes watered the sister's eyes as flames soared skyward etching red scorch marks on the stone walls of the temple's highest tower.

Nearer the earth, boiling water flooded the riverbanks, and white lava oozed between the warped flagstones of the market square as sizzling sludge.

For a battle, it was quiet. But then, the armed forces had fled, and the elite population of magi, unable to follow, had voluntarily left their bodies soon after.

Pockets of herd animals gravitated naturally to newly formed island habitats.

Away from the disaster's fiery core, multi-colored tesserae pinged like bullets from mosaic floors after their clay matrix vibrated into slurry.

"The word of Megeara's attack had been out for days," Pluvia said. "I purposely announced nothing for humane reasons. I had to be sure that Osiris and Pan were whisked away to safe hideaways – sanctuaries underground within the forests, or in the stars… or both."

The sound of crumbling stone from a collapsing tower, momentarily distracted her.

"Megeara was determined to undermine Pangea's stability," she continued. "The old scold could never hope to outclass us, but she's successfully annihilated our culture, at least for a while. Jealousy will flourish under her rule which means the return of hate. "Now that she's here, I see there's truth to the rumors of old housewives that I didn't want to hear: The end, when it comes, is unforgiving. It seems there's no fury like a fury scorned."

"So, it's true," Nixia mused. "The latest grapevine *does* make the bitterest wine?"

To be perverse, Pluvia drained a glass of sweet wine. "And since we're already unstable due to *personal* differences, it's safe to assume Pangea was in for a shakeup."

"Overdue, you mean."

"A rocky battle, then."

"As queen and magi, you had the power to stop her! Maybe you still do," Nixia said.

Pluvia wheeled on Nixia. "As a *perfect* queen, I had the greater power to embrace our demise. Everything has its golden era. The last hour always comes, and more often than not, it's the untouchable golden hour. Such is the nature of alchemy. The cosmos has a contrary side."

"A perfect hour for a perfect queen," Nixia replied. "I don't suppose there's time before this hour of gold thing for me to apologize, is there?" But one look in her sister's eyes stopped her mid-sentence. "Probably not," she whispered to herself.

"Our system has been corrupted beyond repair," Pluvia mused aloud. "The only way to progress is to shut it down, completely and permanently. Megeara may be doing that for selfish reasons, but ultimately, she is doing us a favor. It's better to cut our losses and colonize afresh than be taken hostage in an emotional war. It's ironic, really. Megeara is culling the very herds that she infected."

Nixia leaned her forehead on her knees. "Still…"

"Still, you want to apologize? For what? Calling down the violent end of our world? Laying down at the mercy of a bloodthirsty monster? Surely you knew jealousy was Megeara's driving passion. Ignoring a red flag from the red planet? For relentlessly complaining? Constantly undermining my authority? By acting like a spoiled child? For dividing the people to satisfy your hungry ego? For treason? Your personal dissatisfaction? For throwing vulgar fits of anger and causing no end of confusion amongst the military? I'd have to say, no. There's not enough time to apologize for that."

"I never did all that!"

"No, Nix, you did *much* more. Thousands are dead. Millions more will be displaced, to put it mildly. But there it is. What's done cannot be undone. What's begun in peace will end in destruction. We're not children needing a time out; we're grown women out of time. Supposedly wise women, at that. The furies have struck. The Bede pyramid is god knows where. Last report it was on a land flow headed north. And there goes the entire planet. Look."

The table globe had tipped erratically and was sliding towards the opposite wall. Pluvia watched it go with a blank expression. *I wonder where the real globe will end up?* she thought. Blobs of colors swam over its painted surface like blind fish. Mountains rose where they bumped together. Hurricanes dangerously nudged the earth's axis out of alignment. Explosions rocked the tiny landscape and rancid clouds of putrid rain floated above it.

Nixia braced the runaway world with her foot and madly began to arrange the pulsating blobs of land with a fingertip, smooshing Pangea back together.

"You're my sister," Pluvia stated, dispassionately. And as such, I'm honor-bound by rank and affection to forgive you. Even from your insanely selfish politics. But, from this day, our twinship identity is compromised. According to Pan's law we're no longer twins. We're sisters torn apart, manning a sinking ship."

Nixia looked up from her desperate rescue attempt to salvage the globe's solid landmass. She choked back tears. "That's a bit harsh."

"But Goswold assured me the end of Pangea will not be the end of us. It will be far worse for you, considering mystical law has been violated. If time is involved, it will be eons before our land and culture settles. Time enough, I should think, to forgive yourself and offer a substantial sacrifice to begin the long road back to us – the Pan Gemini, the royal line of Bede, Mistress of the Great Myth, keepers of the Green Majesty, and overseers of the Khem Brotherhood. We will be queens and servants, both, in our lifetimes to come."

Nixia curtsied slyly. "Have you chosen your next life? Think wisely, Majesty. Whatever you choose, will affect me. Where you go, I won't be far behind," she said.

"Or ahead, most likely," Pluvia added.

Nixia's eyes glazed over. "I beg you choose somewhere hot."

"There you go again, assuming I could do such a thing."

"I assumed you would want to."

"Ha! I most certainly do *not*. In fact, I'm personally thrilled that the future is out of my hands. I can be spared *that*, at least for the time being. What comes will be delivered from the source of all understanding. I beg you to surrender when it arrives so we can end this karmic divide. I thought nothing could permanently separate that which was created as one, but Goswold chastised me severely for my short-sightedness. He assured me that I had it unbelievably wrong. That there would be a reckoning at the eleventh hour. A rocky war, he called it. Well, that hit a little too close to home, I can tell you.

So, from the prophecy of Bede, and I quote: Megeara must be vanquished by a Pangean champion to balance the emotional fallout of abused power, restore the cycles of hot and cold, and recalibrate earth's gravity. The earth will be plunged into dark ages of plagues and fiery upheavals of rock and ash, until the double Pan Gemini are reborn. One immortal pair restored and the other, a mortal pair of ever-borns. Mars must be reduced to a freezing pockmarked cinder and its immortals gagged below the core of their cold dead planet. It will hang in space as a reminder of the day mankind came close to extinction."

"Is that all?"

"No. The '*all*' would be the permanent end of that globe over there, full scale. A hole in the sky, should you fail your birthright. The stars silenced, and Earth reduced to a ball of blue ice circling a dead sun. *That* my sister, is how powerful your emotional tantrums are because it will be up to you to repent with every fibre of your being… for a very long time, or even eternity."

Shrieks of laughter drew Peri and Pookie to the Winter Room's window. Snow was playing tag with Harigold, chasing him over snowy ground, hopelessly outmatched. Being the same color as the lawn, Harigold was difficult to see.

"You can't catch me," Harigold teased, rudely wiggling his ears before diving into a snowbank.

"Can too," Snow shouted back, dancing in a circle, and as she waved her arms like a windmill, winter changed into summer, exposing

Harigold, whose white coat was now chestnut brown. "She's very like her Aunt Bash, isn't she," Peri said.

"Peas in a pod," Pookie replied.

"It's winter again," Snow whined at teatime. "That's all I can see from my window."

"You're dreaming it so," Jack insisted.

"I miss my summer dreams."

"Then change the dream or make the best of the one you've got. You're like another girl I used to know. She had an impatient nature, also."

"Bash?" Pookie asked.

Jack paused and smiled. "I stand corrected. Like *three* girls I used to know."

It grew late. Snowy hour was over. Moonlight played over Snow's pillow where Pookie sewed a button on Snow's red coat. "Pookie," Snow whispered. "I still have a question, but Jack only allows me one."

"You can ask me, and then, it's off to dreamland," Pookie said.

"How do I change a dream if I want to? Jack says I can, and I want to."

"You concentrate. It's like meditation only different."

It took a week, but Snow sent the winter packing. First an extended spring thaw delivered squelchy mud.

A day later, Snow lay listless on her cot, limp from blistering summer heat.

Jack was in a grump. "It's always something," he said. "Too hot; Too cold; Too perfect; not good enough."

. . .

The Hall's windows, thrown open to counteract the heat, had turned the corridors into a lively network of wind tunnels. A stray zephyr snuck past Jack and wafted through the keyhole blowing Snow's fine white hair into a halo. "Jack," she shouted. "Stop letting the drafts in. Is it too much to expect that you…"

"It was *you* who changed the seasons, Goldilocks," Jack said, not meaning to accuse. "So, if you *truly* desire calm, send the wind on its way. But before you do, remember how stifling it gets up here in summer. You might want to keep a few breezes handy against the sweltering heat that gets trapped under the roof."

"By the way, there's a new sapling in town," Pookie interrupted pulling Snow's attention away from Jack's anger. She's apparently quite obnoxious. It seems Parks planted her at a particularly ominous time, or so Nimue says. One must never overstep the moon's wisdom."

Jack rolled his eyes. "Oh, goody. Another creature with a chip on its shoulder."

Pookie blanched. "It's a *she*. A she who hates her name, the heat, and the lack of wind, so, Nimue changed her name to Crabtree because of her incessant complaining. Her initial reaction is, she's enchanted with it. And knowing Nimue as I do, there may be more truth in that statement than one sapling against the forest, can manage."

"All this confusion of things changing. It does keeps one guessing, and not in a good way," Jack bellyached.

"Calm yourself, little sphinx, and know this one important thing, with one exception, TIME DOESN'T MATTER. Turn this over in your mind, one word at a time, until the understanding comes. When it arrives in a burst of knowing, you will be free. In the meantime, you're here to play. As always, the gardens or snowdrifts await your pleasure."

Snow pouted and flumped down in a chair. "The 'mean' time is unfair."

"I expect that's why it's called mean," Pookie said.

"I don't like this dream at all," Snow whinged.

"Then change it little dreamer," Jack ordered. "Control your dreams. Or they will control you."

Chapter 41

UPON WAKING

The smell of frying bacon greets me.
I'm happy that my name will remain, Snow.
It is the last day that I feel nine years old.

The year 2024 is about to be born

A NEW DAY'S YEAR

Snow woke from the smell of fried bacon. Her father, Kit Carter Stratford-Smyth was home!

Snow opened her eyes and closed them twice to be sure she wasn't dreaming. But there was her father, standing awkwardly in the doorway, staring at Snow wide eyed, as if he'd seen a ghost. Kit held out a breakfast tray as if it were a poisonous snake about to strike. His hands shook so badly, the dishes clattering together were in danger of landing on the floor.

Snow threw back the covers, and in an instant, she had one foot on the floor and was already halfway across the room.

"Anna, stop," Kit said taking a nervous step forward. "Please, get back into bed. You may be awake, but it's early days yet, so nice and easy does it. I've brought you breakfast in bed. It's your favorite." He raised the tray a few inches but lowered it instantly as its contents careened sideways.

But Snow *didn't* stop. She lunged towards her father so fiercely he was forced to set the tray on the bed and brace himself for Snow's inevitable attack.

Snow launched herself around her father's neck, noticing it took a few seconds for him to hug her back. His navy-blue coat was gone.

There were no frozen stars to brush away from its shoulders and sleeves. Birds chattered through the sunlight of the open window.

Kit pried himself loose, kissed Snow's cheek, and stroked her face in awe that it might disappear. "I have strict orders from Nimue not to overexert you," he said, holding her at arms length for scientific examination.

In Egypt, when Snow was a toddler, she had always greeted her father, returning from one of his missions, with a childish request. She used it now to amuse him.

"Where have you been? What did you bring me?" she wheedled.

"A boiled egg and soldiers," he said. "I thought it was obvious. And bacon for me. I thought we could share."

"When…? I mean, how long have you been home?"

"We arrived home together, over a year ago. I guess you don't remember. Three of us came through the maze portal, but Peri got left behind. There were anxious days, but with Pan's help, your Aunt Bash and I combined our magic to bring him home. It wasn't long before Peri rode Kephura out of the maze as confident as you please. It was quite the dramatic entrance. Shortly after that, you asked to be left alone in the Winter Room for an hour. We found you comatose when you didn't come down for supper."

"I wonder what I was thinking."

"The fairies were all over the place, dusting this and that with their powers and powders, assuring us you needed time to process Peri being home. You were in denial, they said, but wouldn't say more, other than it was a deeply private matter that would take time and that you had to forge through it alone. They kept vigil over you until Jack appointed himself your guardian. The door was still as freezing to the touch as that day you took me there in your dream of high winter."

"I'm sorry. My mind's a blank."

"Bash consulted the Lady Flora and she sent 'the Pookie' – a rabbit sprite, one of her wisest animal devas, to be your companion in sleep. As the harbinger of springtime, the Pookie was the obvious choice, considering you were locked in the winter of your past memories. Flora said the nearness of spring would bring you comfort.”

Snow stared hungrily at the toast and marmalade and studied the light refracted from a silver teaspoon. “Father, I have a new request.”

“I’m listening, Anna,” Kit said looking worried. “If it’s in my power, I will do anything to make your transition easier. You’ve been on a long gruelling journey. Ask away. Anything to break the ice… *pun intended*.”

“Father, I would like you to call me Snow. It suits me, even though there were days I wished it hadn’t.”

Kit breathed a sigh of relief. “Done and done,” he said. “Now, what would you like first, a bread and butter soldier or a piece of bacon?”

The buzzing of a bee embroidered on a throw cushion drew Snow to a newly materialized loveseat in the window. Pookie was slumped in the opposite corner – a comatose ragdoll. Snow prodded it gently. “Pook? Are you awake?”

Pookie answered in Snow’s head. “I’m not in there anymore, baby girl. But I’m always with you, here inside your mind. It’s a very grown-up way to converse. And from now on, you will be growing older.”

“It’s true, then. I’m awake!”

“Yes, but like your father said, it’s early days. And by that, I mean tomorrow is day one of a new year. You’re living the beginning reality of a truth that wants to stay. With a little practice you will remain fully conscious, except of course, when you’re dreaming normally.”

“Jack’s gone too. The blue door looks terribly empty without him.”

“Never fear, baby girl, your friend Jack will never be separated from the Hall in any way that matters. He is the Hall’s guardian and its voice. Jack Frost is Jack o’ the Green. Surprisingly, he’s also Parks one through five, and none other than the Green Man, himself.”

“Oh, Pook. Why didn’t you tell me?”

“I follow The Green Lady Flora’s wisdom and she had her reasons. Your friend, Keyhole Jack, is in essence, the immortal nature god Pan,

Flora's consort. His weather-beaten face has returned to the bark of every tree throughout the forests of Great Britain. His lifeforce is simultaneously present within each blade of Bede grass, every blossoming flower, and the whiskers of every mouse for nine miles."

He dwells in the Green Lady's Forest and his pure essence has resettled inside the bones of Bede Hall itself. He can hear you whenever you call. He is, as Jack Frost once bragged, Bede's overseer and servant, King of the trees, jackal of all things organic, ruler of the moon, protector of woodland wildlife, and master of the landscape. A 'land-*escape*' where he withdrew during the height of Megeara's powermongering tantrums for the sake of the world. Pan sacrificed his anthropomorphic form to work tirelessly undercover as a *scape*goat for the prophecy, a selfless e*scape* artist for the greater cause of humanity.

Snow saw the word 'scape' in her mind and smiled. "I see him hiding inside one of Lady Nan's word games," she said. "How is it that I know what anthropomorphic means?"

"Pan never hides," Pookie admonished. "Pan is the eternal penultimate persona of the natural world. And you've understood grown up things lately because for the longest time, you've been dreaming as Pluvia. But it was Snow, your child-self who woke up this morning. It is Snow who will take her rightful place next to Peri. Now, go outside. Everyone's waiting for you."

A New Year's Eve garden party was in full swing under a warm drizzle of January rain. No-one minded a bit. Snow pretended to be taller by walking on her toes. Even if she'd only aged a few hours, it felt better thinking of herself as almost ten.

During the afternoon, Anubis and Feathers, their daughter Snowball and son-in-law Arthur, the former Ar'tu'Ra, made the rounds prowling for whipped cream, fish paste and shrimp, and, in Arthur's case, marmite snacks, a taste for which had grown into an obsession.

The topiaries, Memory the elephant and Sage the sphinx, held court beside the maze, dignified and regal. Memory lifted her trunk high and blasted the party louder than any tin horn noisemaker. Unicorn settled behind Sage's right ear in Snowball's old spot and was enjoying his last cat nap of the year until Twiglet, a baby tree nymph, clambered onto Sage's back, crying giddy-up horsey, bouncing like a jockey and got tangled in his leafy mane.

Deerhound Jack sniffed out Harigold and Sable, and initiated a mad chase while Mabel sat under the Rowan tree with Helen, and watched them, nibbling her new cache of digestive biscuits. Helen remarked her money was on Harigold in any race because she remembered the time he'd run so fast and so far, he hadn't returned to Bede for a week. "For days, Harry's shadow could be seen on the moon," she mused, "which, for some reason, I found distinctly comforting."

Hannah had brought Beegle and Dee Dee. Beegle the monkey had promptly vanished into the treeline the moment Hannah removed his leash. Snow heard him shrieking into the trees, flushing out the startled tree nymph elders, not the most sociable guests, unused as they were to frivolity. But at the urging of Pan; Cyril, Murk, Glumly, Drab, Misery, and Gloomsbury bravely crept closer to the festivities, keeping together for protection.

Rosie, the Queen bee, held court too. Her royal servants: Buzzle, Bumble, Queenlet, Zoom, and Honeysuckle, droned a pleasant buzz that hypnotized the revelers into recalling the sweet memories of lazy summer days. A dragonfly named Sharon flew circles around a pair of scarabs let out of their library case for exercise. The sky was alive with happy wings – fluttering, flapping, beating, and undulating, wafting the scent of early roses over the party guests.

Two stuffed birds, dusted off for the occasion, Pigeon 2 and Dee Dee, the last dodo – an exhibit rescued long ago from a bonfire in the grounds of the Ashmolean Museum, fanned their creaky wings to ease the growing sticky heat lodged in their stuffing.

Pigeon, the livewire original, had flown through the Winter Room portal for a joyous reunion with Peri, soared dozens of energetic laps in the rain, swooping low over the lake, disappearing into the forest only to shoot up through the tree canopy like a multi-colored rocket shrieking *free as a bird... free as a bird.'*

Cornelius and Rayne and Tut were there in spirit. Literally, ethereal wavery forms that blinked on and off like dying lightbulbs at every sudden noise.

At long last, Sable and Mabel frolicked through Memory's topiary legs after wearing deerhound Jack to a frazzle. Jack panted, stretched like a grey shag rug under a picnic table while Pigeon held the family spellbound with news from the eighteenth dynasty.

Vita the elder, dressed as a gypsy fortune teller stared into Lady Nan's snow globe, borrowed as a prop. "I see a sister in your future," she said to Snow in a spooky theatrical voice.

Something caught Vita's eye in the contained snowstorm. She peered more closely and winked mysteriously. "*Hmm…* that's odd," she said. "I see myself standing beside you."

"You're feeling sleepy," Peri said, when the party neared midnight. "Your eyes are getting heavy," he continued, in spite of Snow claiming she'd never felt so wide awake. "You will wake when I snap my fingers at ground zero. He counted down from ten. At zero, a shower of colored confetti broke from the sky and covered the cheering crowd. He kissed Snow's cheek. "Happy New Year, sis," he shouted. "Happy New Life!"

Snow remembered who she'd been in Pangea with perfect recall. As such, she found herself newly cloned, waving hello from the ground as well as leaning out her attic window waving goodbye. She waved Pookie's arm from the window and blew her Aunt Bash a kiss. Bash waved back from the garden holding her own rabbit doll, Pookie's twin. All was in perfect order.

The moment Snow's kiss landed on Bash's cheek the confetti transformed into a gentle snowstorm and when it cleared, a crisp January day had blown the cobwebs of the previous winter beyond the moon.

The trees were ablaze with color as a second party materialized beside the first.

Party two had a maypole. Kit rode Kephura around the crowd in a victory lap to celebrate Snow's miraculous recovery. An animated banner waved behind the partygoers displaying seasons that looped continually from summer to summer.

A family of cheering fieldmice paraded Doolittle over their heads as the 'mouse of the hour' who had broken the literal deadlock that brought Snow to her senses. Katydid scampered behind with Pearl one and Pearl two, members of the Rodents Knitting Guild who had supplied gloves, socks, and scarves for the Green Lady's Small Creatures Foundation of Bede. The January weather, being too warm for wool gloves, caused the mice to wear their scarves as more of a fashion accessory, fully approved by Miss Helen, who, as always, supported them the way a delighted schoolmarm praises her students' initiative.

The party guests reminded Snow of a scene in 'Sleeping Beauty' where the palace court reanimated after their princess awoke from a hundred-year sleeping curse. And as such, at regular intervals, several 'courtiers' singled Snow out for meaningful chats, meant to bring her up to date.

First, Bash cornered Snow with a posy of carnations. They both waved at Nimue as she darted past all dash and purpose. "Nimue acted as your head nurse for a long time after we found you," Bash said casually. "And she became a tad possessive of you. Almost as overbearing as me during my bad time. Anyway, I thought you should know so you could cut her some slack if she gets too pushy. Fairies tend to dominate situations when left to themselves. They make serious lists from which they refuse to be parted.

I also want to inform you that time travel is different these days, even though Bede time still suffers from *chronic* chronological issues. Pan reopened the time portals with stricter laws in place." she patted Snow's hand reassuringly. "None of us are given free passes to visit Egypt anytime we have a hankering for old time's sake. Pan made it clear that's what library books were for."

After Lady Nan and Beryl said their piece, Snow wondered if Nimue's fairy list *did* exist somewhere, with timeslots for short appointments, as one-by-one, each twice-born stepped forward with snippets of unsolicited advice. Snow swore later that she'd seen Nimue consulting a long list-shaped speech bubble hovering above her head, several times.

SaRa watched them come and go until it was her turn. But it was Snow who sought *her* out.

"We haven't had much of a chance to talk by ourselves," Snow said. "Are you tired, Mother? Can I get you something?"

SaRa lost no time in coming to her point. "I want you to know that your father and I, Aunt Bash, Vita, Lady Nan and Beryl-the-younger, Peri, Jack and Pookie, took turns telling you stories, hoping to dislodge a memory that would break your spell," she said. "I'm so sorry we failed."

"I heard you," Snow said. "Thank you."

"Rupert dropped by six months ago for a surprise visit, but Nimue's team kept him in a modified stupor, ironically manipulating his memories during the time they were heaven bent on freeing yours. Anyway, your celebrity cousin continued to accept that his parents were on an around the world whirlwind retirement holiday. 'California dreaming' suits him a treat."

SaRa stretched her back, massaged her pregnant belly and breathed deeply.

"When will the babies come?" Snow asked.

"I think they've been waiting for you, so my guess is any day now."

Snow's eyes shone feverishly. "We're going to be a normal family."

SaRa's eyebrows shot up as she chuckled. "Normal for Bede is perfect for us. I've had time to adjust to your name, Snow, so no worries on that score. And I now have *paid* work that I love as a translator of hieroglyphics for several archaeological societies. I am truly where I belong."

"Me too."

"The lavender business is booming after being touted as a natural aid for digestion, an antiseptic, insect repellant, and sanitizer. Bede honey is marketed as 'mystical sweetness with a medicinal kick'. Your father came up with that line. He's quite taken with becoming an author.

And, speaking of your father being an author; he's writing time-travel stories for children, prompted by Bash to use scientific language so as not to pamper them."

At nine minutes past midnight, everyone sang happy birthday to Bede Hall. Old acquaintances were remembered. Bouquets of gold-colored helium balloons imprinted with the year 2023 were released into the canopy of silver stars where the constellation Gemini transmuted into gold.

Chapter 42

UPON WAKING

I am awake!
It has been decided for me
that my name will remain Snow.
I am nine years old.

The date is January 1, 2024

ROLE CALL

To celebrate Snow's re-entry into life, the Stratford-Smyths and the twice-borns held a formal gathering in the red library on the afternoon of New Year's Day.

Fairies: Sassia, Thistledown, Nimbus, Cecilberry, Ulwen, Snapdragon, Maeve, Trixie, Jeffie, and the ghost of Fioretti, zoomed about at Nimue's pleasure, replenishing the hors d'oeuvres, tweaking the floral arrangements, straightening the slender candles wobbling in their candlesticks, and recharging the enchanted punch with a stir of their wands.

Vincento and Appleby pulled the globe to the center of the room while 'the Venerable Reid' tenderly rolled out the decaying parchment of the Bede Prophecy on the table. Kem looked like a pageboy bearing four precious artefacts on a silver tray to weight its corners: a snow globe, an hourglass, Bash's rose scarab, and its turquoise twin, belonging to Kit.

Shouts of speech! speech! brought Snow to her feet, blushing. She deferred to the ghost of Lady Nan with a bow of her head. "Partying in Bede is a bit like Nimue's punch. So exhilarating, it can literally knock a person out," she announced timidly to thunderous applause and whistles.

Nick shouted, "You can say that again!"

"SHUSH!" Nimue shouted from the top of a tall bookshelf. "Or I'll turn all of you into mushrooms. Go ahead, Snow. The floor is yours."

"I tried to say I was sorry a million years ago after I broke the world," Snow began. "But I didn't truly mean it. I refused to take responsibility for my actions, and so, according to karmic law, my truth was frozen in time. I was the one who froze it. I am grateful to my shaman companions: an enchanted rabbit doll, a keyhole named Jack, Parks, and a rightly disgruntled, Bede Hall. And so, until yesterday, I remained, age nine, adrift in Bede's 'House of Reincarnations' where the scent of lavender once started an endlessly cold war. For the past year, I have caused all of you much needless suffering, and for that, I am so very, truly sorry."

After the resulting standing ovation died down to a smattering of heartfelt applause, Snow heard her next words ring out strong and clear.

"When Lady Nan was nine-years old she was my childhood friend, Beryl, my *best* friend and my great-grandmother at the same time, which, as it turns out is nothing outrageous compared to the rest of you."

"You can say that again, n'all," Helen declared.

"It's so easy to forget the foundations that support our family temple, Bede Hall. I certainly did. And speaking of foundations, and since Nimue said the floor was mine, I invite everyone to look down at the carpet and pretend it's a levelled stone platform supporting a great stone pyramid. I ask this of you to honor Bede Hall that began as a primordial hill emerging from a timeless sea before becoming a stone pyramid in Pangea. For eons it has reshaped itself from the ground up according to the dictates of every age. We are fortunate to call it home."

Snow sent a trembly smile over the assembly. "I now turn the *floor* over to Brooks who, I believe, has something to announce."

· · ·

Peregrine Brooks took his place centerstage and made everyone laugh by tapping the air around a non-existent microphone with the words "is this thing on?"

"We are here to celebrate and welcome Snow to her next phase of life," he said. "And may I say, the family genealogy that our venerable historian has compiled in the last 24 hours, verily seals Bede Hall's reputation as the House of Reincarnations. Lady Nan and I are celebrating our next phase of life, too. We are engaged to be married."

The room broke out in cheers, stamping feet, and shouts of *"it's about time!"*

Brooks nodded to a glowing Lady Nan who rejoined him at the makeshift podium, proudly displaying the diamond engagement ring he'd given her the day before, turning her hand this way and that in the candlelight to best effect. He took one gallant step to the side of his besotted fiancé.

Lady Nan continued to flaunt her ring, gesticulating with her left hand as she spoke. "Some dynasties are constructed by brotherhoods of master stonemasons," she said. "And I have no doubt our family tree harbors more than a few. Parks often likened our genealogical map to a mosaic of crazy paving. And I'd have to agree."

More general stamping of feet ensued accompanied by shouts of "Hear hear."

"One thing is certain, we remain, as always, bound by multi-faceted memories spun behind the eternal laws of forgetfulness." She paused to rest a loving gaze on Snow. "From the self inflicted amnesia of supressed memories, to the thinly veiled spins of agitated dream fragments, and the mind numbing blankets of depression, that, sad to say, has been our lot for far too long. I tell you this: throughout it all, Bede Hall, the House of Reincarnations, has been and remains, our personal stronghold of eternal alchemy and science.

Cries of 'Bede Hall forever' shook the library books so hard a few rained down and startled the cats.

"Our dependents have unwittingly borne the brunt of a singular curse of misbegotten jealousy that sadly turned our family's sibling rivalry, genetic. But even though the Pangean legacy is at the heart of our sorrows, it is also the capstone of our pyramid. As our name surely implies; mythical by name and nature, we live in extraordinary twin realms: the mystical and the physical." She raised a self-refilling glass of 'special rowan tea' prepared by Nimue. "And so, we enter a new dynasty," she said. "To the House of Reincarnations and duality."

"And to the river Styx!" Bertie Stein called out.

Nick's voice rose above the din. "Where's that river again, Snow? I don't remember."

Snow grimaced. "Very funny," she called back. "I think it runs through our backyard."

Glasses clinked, sips and gulps were taken, as cups remained full. "Wassail! To the Green Gods!" Nick called out.

The wooziness of general contentment settled over the gathering in a rosy glow of afternoon sunlight. "Drinkhail!" the gathering responded.

Nixia, a regal woman in silk robes, materialized beside Snow whose favorite dress with the lavender flowers resumed its former appearance of a plain white nightgown, in deference.

Nixia spoke from where she stood near Lady Nan after the cheering subsided. She gave a soft chuckle as her gaze swept over the crowd. "You know, I wouldn't be at all surprised if the entire Stratford-Smyth family tree was composed of only nine multidimensional, profoundly intense entities," she said, grasping and raising Lady Nan's hand in triumph showing her sister's engagement ring to full advantage.

"Case in point. Beryl Stratford-Smyth, Bede Hall's matriarch, has been *two* queens: my sister Pluvia of Pangea, and the Egyptian queen Ankhesenamun. During her Egyptian incarnation, she employed the twins Taraq 1 and Anu (presently, our very own Snow of Bede Hall) as child slaves, after they were orphaned by a plague of wasps. But true to Pluvia's nature, she mothered them as well. Goodness, someone will have to help me with the rest," she said, tearing up.

Brooks lifted Lady Nan's hand to his lips for another kiss and stepped forward again. He squinted at the ghost of King Tutankhamun in the back, and rubbed his chin. "Let's see, now. Kit's half-brother, Taraq 2 (who became Tuts 2 and 3), was Kit's teenage nemesis *and* best friend, if I remember rightly, and I do. In the eighteenth dynasty of Egypt, Tut 2 was Kit's alchemist mentor, Kha, as well as his brother-in-law. To recap, Taraq 2 (redubbed Tut by the forementioned Kit) was an English teenager in Bede, a street orphan of seven in modern day Cairo, a nine-year old boy named Kem during the height of the Bedean war, and King Tutankhamun's eighteen-year-old understudy replacement, simultaneously, 3000 years apart." He stared into his fizzing punch and blinked. "Thanks to Nimue's punch, I will need to confirm what I just said on Bertie's chart."

Bertie Stein stepped forward, briefly consulted a horizontal scroll, rolled it into a cylinder, and shrugged. "I'm with Peregrine, I'll need more punch to decipher this," he said, tapping it on each of Peregrine's shoulders in symbolic knighthood.

Snow felt the wintriest of chills shoot up her spine as Nixia brushed her shoulder. Nixia felt it, too. "I think someone just walked on my grave... in the best possible way," she announced cheerily with a sidelong wink at Snow. At that, Snow's nightgown restored itself into a summer frock of lavender flowers.

Quite abruptly, the numbers of guests in the room expanded, spilling through the walls as far as the horizon, extending to a far distant complex of fields encompassing the boundaries of Bede territory, filled with transparent animals.

Bast, Sekhmet, Osiris, and Pan appeared as four giant shadows projected against the library's back wall reaching from floor to ceiling. A dozen twice-borns stood at their feet, hands linked in a formal semi-circle.

Each presenter, beginning with Lady Nan, rose in turn, reading out a list of contemporary names linked to their famous historical counterparts.

Lady Nan waved a sheet of papyrus in the air. "According to my cheat notes, Bede Village harbors a plethora of talented geniuses. My dear friend, Vincento Leoni, Bede Village's local pharmacist, is an artist, amateur photographer and recorder of sentient details, a birdwatcher, botanist, aviator, musician, poet, engineer, scientist (both chemist and alchemist). I bow to you, *Messr*. Leonardo da Vinci."

Leoni stepped forward with his mechanical lion, Gali-leo, in tow, and bowed to Lady Nan. *"Grazzi... tutto grazzi,"* he said, sweeping his blue velvet cap to the floor. Gali-leo performed his trick of opening a cavity in his chest and deposited a tribute of white carnations at Lady Nan's feet.

"Thank you, Messr," Lady Nan continued, dipping into a demure curtsey. "Vincento informs me he has a new business partner. So, it is my pleasure to present his colleague and fellow visionary, Nick Wardencliffe who engineered the physical ground defenses of the Hall through an ingenious network of electronic power grids from his expertise as Nicola Tesla." She gathered up an armful of Gali-leo's flowers and stood beaming like an actress receiving an academy award.

"And while we're on the subject, my granddaughter Bathsheba, our own Bash, Mistress of the Green who, in spite of her scientific misgivings, joined these two inventors and gave science a valiant effort with spectacular results." She searched for her list, lost beneath the flowers.

"Bede Village boasts no less than three art dealers, two doctors, a consummate mathematician, a singularly masterful librarian, two historians and a playwright. Their numbers include: inventors, scientists, astronomers, engineers, poets, seers, botanists, herbalists, artists, writers, oracles, clairvoyants, mystic fortune-tellers, soothsayers, archaeologists, a veterinarian, many animal activists, several landscape designers, gardeners, farmers, enchanting seers, collectors of magical talismans and other treasures, handymen, physicists, teachers, mentors, virtuosos, and one saint, all possessed of the entrepreneurial spirit. In fact, long before my time, the Clutterbuck's ancestral family business presented our family with my snow globe and hourglass." Her applause brought Theodore Clutterbuck of the misnamed 'Junk Emporium', forward.

Teddy held the Winter Room's sleeping pillow aloft where three tiny winged-creatures, Hapi, Ma'at, and Pygmalion sat, wings twitching with the urge to fly.

"My name is Theodore Clutterbuck esq. collector of art and artifacts," he said. Everyone calls me Teddy. "But I used to be Theo van Gogh, Vincent's baby brother. And long before I held that singular honor, I was the tomb carver, Ta'aten (Tee) the twin brother of the tomb painter, SenTa'aten (Sent) who became Vincent van Gogh. Vincent and I have always been born together."

The yellow chair sidled forward and nudged Teddy's leg. "As for Vincent, he still resides with my wife and I. His troubled spirit entered this yellow chair, in Arles, at the moment of his death in 1890."

Hannah joined his side and beamed up at her husband. "May I proudly present my wife," Teddy announced. "The former Hannah Johns-Joanna Bonger, Van Gogh's sister-in-law (and… my former wife) who selflessly archived Vincent's paintings into unimaginable fame."

The rest of the announcements proceeded quickly.

Nixia stood. "I present to you, my sister, Pluvia-Ankhesenamun-Beryl-Rain-Lady Nan. And her twin brother, Ben, with Sarah Goodman, his living life partner."

She curtsied. "And myself: Nixia-Anu-Ani-Anna-Snow-little sphinx, and…*ahem*… baby girl."

Bertie Stein, the former Albert Einstein, waved his rolled up scroll like a graduation certificate, and shouted out. "It's my honor to acknowledge Christopher (Kit) Stratford-Smyth-Ki'TiKa'at of Egypt, and his mentor, Dr. Peregrine Brooks-Prince Smenkhare of Egypt; his sister Bash and her husband, Six, of the Parks' clan."

The names of the remaining twice-borns were read out in turn to polite applause: Newton Appleby-Sir Isaac Newton; Bill Swan-William Shakespeare; and the essential mastermind of 'winter wonderlands turned ugly and restored to summer', Clive Lucy, the scholar and author C.S. Lewis."

Herbalist: Glynis Findlay-Charlotte Findhorn-Flora, Pan's consort, the Green Lady, concoctor of serums, remedial elixirs, spells, and enchanted amulets; her apprentice, Bathsheba (Bash) Stratford-Smyth; and her own apprentice, Kem, her adopted son, a time-slip of his former childhood self, Taraq1, and, as it turns out, a chip off the old block – the master alchemist, Kha of Egypt, who transitioned smoothly to live as the pharaoh, King Tutankhamun 2nd or was it the 3rd?"

Animal husbandry fellows: Francis Fox-St. Francis of Assisi; and woodland animal specialist and psychologist, Helen Peterson-Ms. Beatrix Potter.

Our librarian/historian, the aptly named 'Venerable Reid' after 'the Venerable Bede', father of British history, and Drew Melville-Melvil Dewey, Bede village's librarian and record keeper extraordinaire, the inventor of the Dewey Decimal System.

Flora, the Green Lady, placed a hand on the back of Hannah's yellow chair which made Vincent spin slowly on one leg.

Visiting parrot, Pigeon 1, and his ghost, Pigeon 2, perched on Kit's shoulders, chortling contentedly.

In the back, keeping a low profile, stood the collective green thumbs of the 'clan Parks', Stanley Parks reincarnations from two-to-five and the strapping ghost of a young man named Six, whose untimely death marked the turning point where the Bedean war began in earnest.

"Parks one, as you are all aware, is our resident nature god, Pan, the Green Man, after his dedicated service as Stanley Parks-Capability Brown-Jack Frost and Jack of the Green; landscape designers and botanists all!

Please welcome assorted cats, fieldmice, and fairies. Rupert is in California directing moving pictures and generally rearranging the hierarchy of Hollywood's elite much to the general horror of its celebrity pecking order."

Snow spoke up shyly. "My grandfather Cornelius's distant cousin, Howard Carter, is alive in Egypt at this time. I include him here as an honorable mention who posthumously bequeathed the middle name, Carter, to each of Rayne and Cornelius's three children.

Please raise your glasses to 'The Green Man' who rules the landscape of Europa as Pan and his twin brother Osiris who rules the underworld as Osiris, the green-faced god of the Egyptians."

"Wassail!" Bill shouted enthusiastically again.

"Drink hail!" came a more slurred inebriated response.

"Nimue brews a mean punch," Nick said to his newly designated business partner, quaffing down an entire cup and watching it refill with Charlotte Findhorn's famous 'special tea' recipe. "But watch out for her temper. She has a mean wand, does Mistress Nimue."

"You have no need to a telling me of this things," Vincento replied. "I am not so much the liking. Nimue is being the bossy cow of Galileo. He does not like, also, this thing."

Brooks overheard. "Come to think of it," he reflected. "I downed a fair swig of one of Charlotte's potions on Beryl's wedding day. It didn't clear my head, but it cured my insomnia. And I've slept like a baby ever since."

Nimue, not to be mocked, tapped her wand demurely on Snow's raised glass. "Please, everyone," she called out, sweetly. "Attention… everyone?"

When the rabble ignored her and continued chatting, Nimue's wings turned red. She whistled shrilly through her fingers. "Listen up! All of you. Snow has final words to say," she shouted.

The room quieted as Snow breathed with newfound confidence. "I would especially like to honor my mentors, Keyhole Jack in all his forms and Pookie 'mystical deva of the clan rabbit'. My father dreamed himself a wife and children and a blue-black horse. My Uncle Kha dreamed his way onto an Egyptian throne. Bede Hall dreamed itself a glorious future. I'm awake now, inside the dreams that live in the house that Jack built. Jack informs me my biggest dream will come true tomorrow, and every tomorrow after that, so, you can relax. And I can assure you that the Yellowstone caldera slumbers soundly, deeply rooted under the earth in a state of suspended unconsciousness because I have dreamed it so."

The gathering drifted outside for fresh air after the collective wooziness of 'special tea' threatened to knock everyone out.

GALI-Leo inched forward and roared, unfolded his metallic wings, alarming the birds flying over the lake, where he divebombed the topiaries, and stirred the swans into a hissing fit of angry feathers.

Chapter 43

UPON WAKING

The Winter Room is warm
I am almost ten years old. My name is Snow.

The year is now

THE LAST DREAM STANDING

Snow pulled her shawl tighter to escape a persistent draft and continued to pace the length of the attic's hallway, trailing her hand over its peeling flowered wallpaper. Her progress was marked by a slash of white frost where her hand touched the red roses. She paused to trace the outline of a single red rose with the tip of a finger and watched its color slowly fade. "Much better," she said aloud to herself.

"JACK," she called out. "White roses seem more appropriate in the cold spot, don't you think? Jack! Are you awake? Jack, can you hear me?"

Jack answered in her head. "There's no need to shout so loud, little sphinx. You'll wake the dead." He gave a chuckle. "I sleep like a cat with one ear open. Which is how I know that SaRa is in labor. The Pan-Gemini are on their way. It's time for you to wake up."

"I thought I *was* awake."

"In the greater sense, you *have* awakened. But that doesn't mean you can't dream. Right now… you are dreaming. No worries. Everyone dreams, Sphinx."

.   .   .

Snow stretched contentedly under the bedclothes and lay, gloriously still. Something was different. The room's temperature was just right. Her hands tingled.

'*Wakey wakey little sphinx,*' Pigeon chattered. '*Your biggest dream has come true.*'

Snow opened one eye and caught the colorful flutter of Pigeon's wings. Glowing feathers of turquoise and emerald, crimson and yellow filled the once grey corner. She sat up. "Pigeon, are you well? You look… I mean, does the room appear different to you?"

'*Yes, a bright spark like me notices things,*' he squawked, and promptly resumed sharpening his beak.

"Have you seen Pookie? She's not here."

Pigeon stopped pecking his cuttlebone, cocked his head to one side, and stared unblinkingly at Snow. '*A bright spark such as yourself notices things, too.*' he said imitating Jack's voice. *For instance, you have a gold scarab ring on your finger that wasn't there before. As for your mentors, they've gone… flown the coop!... but no worries… I'm here and here I'll stay.*'

The blue door stood wide open. Where Jack's stern face had once provided protection was unadorned painted wood, punctuated only by a clear glass doorknob faceted like a diamond, the size of a snowball.

"Jack? Pookie? Are you there?" Snow called out, knowing Pigeon had spoken the truth and that she was alone. The scarab ring on her finger fluttered its wings.

"As it happens, you're *not* alone," a familiar voice said.

'Keyhole Jack' stood at the foot of the bed – an ageless nature god with arms and legs, skin like moss, and a smiling human mouth. He gazed lovingly at Snow, arms folded, with a slightly amused twinkle in his eye. "I'm here," he said. "I haven't abandoned you, little sphinx. You can still speak with me anytime you wish." He held out his hand. "Now jump out of bed, there's a good sphinx, it's time. Your new siblings are about to arrive."

· · ·

Vita appeared first, as an old lady, because that was *her* last memory of life.

Taraq appeared an hour later – a young boy because that was *his* last memory of life.

'Keyhole Jack' remained as promised. His true form, old as the planet, materialized wearing a tunic of green and russet foliage. Acanthus leaves framed his cheery face. Rowan twigs weaved through his hair. His eyes shone like stars, reflecting wisdom deeper than the deepest sea, and his human mouth smiled with joy. "Don't be alarmed at my appearance, baby girl," he said. "My true nature is as you see. I am the Green Man." He bowed with a courtly flourish. "My true home lies under the bark of trees."

Peri stepped out of the wall and the Hall started to breathe.

Snow appeared last. A newly awakened child holding a white rabbit made of light.

The vigil began. A pair of twins stood facing each other, each child, as old as time, holding hands across eternity.

A short way off beyond the physical boundaries of walls and time, the Stratford-Smyth clan gathered in a protective outer circle. Beyond them, a million successive circles played out like ripples on a pond. Ancestors and descendants-to-be appeared forming their chronological history like the rings of a tree, both the living and those waiting to be reborn.

The walls of the winter room became transparent. The once enclosed space vibrated with creative energy steeped in magic – a non-local place between heaven and earth, balancing the dualities of birth and death.

Bloom was born first, at 9 a.m.

Hadrian was born nine minutes later.

This time, as there was no lioness to lap up the afterbirth, the honor fell to a local fox named Callidus, happy to comply, since Bede chickens were carefully sequestered behind an impenetrable wall of enchantment.

"Choice scraps today, chum. That's royal nosh, that is," Anubis said, watching slightly horrified but intrigued all the same, as Callidus gnawed an umbilical cord on the side of his mouth.

"Better than a mouse," Callidus replied with his mouth full.

"Yech! I'd never lower myself to eat rodents of *any* description."

"Well, la di da," Callidus said licking his chops.

"You might simply hunt further afield," Anubis suggested.

"And be deprived of royal grub? I don't *think* so. Besides, Miss Bash makes me actual sandwiches. It's true, I could do without the watercress, but the cheese is quite delightful."

Anubis sniffed at the morsels left on the plate. "By the way, there's more where that came from. SaRa had twins."

Callidus, crept away to the stables, his tummy full, anticipating a tasty late night snack.

The family ate dinner in the formal dining room to celebrate Snow's victory. Snow blushed when they applauded. She glanced furtively at the mirror over the mantelpiece. It was empty. She breathed a sigh of relief. "Will someone please pass the *real* cream," she said. "I fancy a proper cup of tea for once."

Eight replicas of King Tutankhamun's golden throne had been conjured for the occasion. Four thrones faced each other on opposite sides of the long trestle table. By contrast, a ninth chair was placed at the head of the table for the guest of honor – a plain wooden kitchen chair with a straw seat, painted buttercup yellow.

Snow took her place on the yellow chair which meant her eyes were level with the tabletop. She rested her chin on her folded arms and stared into the scarab ring for only a second.

Snow woke almost immediately to the sound of babies crying. She pulled the covers over her head and reached for Pookie before she remembered Pookie had been 'volunteered' for nursery duty.

She drifted back into the half-sleep of creative reverie, taking care to keep the morning chorus in her ears, remaining as close to daybreak as possible. It was her favorite time – waking up clear and eager, apart from the early wakeup calls of hungry babies. But she made the mistake of following the birdsong into a corner of the Green Lady's forest, that for some reason, had become a grove of exotic palm trees she'd never seen before. She closed her eyes for only a second.

Snow startled from the sound of a parrot squawking, to find herself halfway across the Winter Room, shuffling slowly across a wintry floor with Pookie clamped under one arm, balancing a wobbly teacup in both hands.

She rehearsed the word 'Father' in her mind, advancing dreamily, towards Kit who was deep in thought, intently studying a map. "Father?" she said at his elbow.

"Hmm? Pardon?"

Snow clunked the teacup onto the worktable, displacing books and papers. Carefully, she stirred a dollop of lavender honey into the steaming hot tea. "*Ahem...*" she said, animating Pookie by bouncing her up and down for attention. Pookie's ears flopped into her button eyes. "Anna wants a story, please," Snow made Pookie say in a high rabbity voice.

"Pookie, please tell Anna, now is not a good time," Kit replied without taking his eyes from the map.

"There never is," Pookie stage whispered. "I'm cold. Tell me a story about summer."

Kit straightened his papers. "I said not *now*, Anna. I need to concentrate. I don't have much time." He took a long swallow of tea. "Thank you for the tea."

"Pookie says time doesn't matter," Snow said.

Kit looked over the rim of his cup. "Pookie is mistaken. Toy rabbits don't know everything. Some *times* matter very much. Right now, it matters a great deal. The time portals can be erratic, and I have a tight schedule. Windows of opportunity are few and far between." He clattered the empty cup into its saucer and picked up his pen.

Snow watched, tapping her foot, her brows knitted in a frown. She spoke a little louder. "Pookie says the fire's going out!"

Kit raised his weary head. "You know how to add more wood," he said crossly.

"There *is* no more wood."

Kit's scraped back his chair and stood. His pinched face looked more gaunt than usual, illuminated as it was by a candle that cast eery shadows on his face from below. Snow noticed with shock, that the dark circles below her father's troubled eyes looked like bruises from a fight.

"Come on then," Kit said. "I'm leaving tomorrow, and you're going to have to keep the fire going on your own."

"How long will you be gone this time?"

"A day… maybe two. You're to bundle up warm under the covers and I'll be back before you can say Jack Frost."

"With mother and… and… *him*?"

Kit ruffled Snow's white hair. "This time I know *exactly* where the portal in the village is. There's a good chance Peri is with your mother." He drew a circle on the map and tapped its center with a teaspoon. "There."

"A magic circle," Pookie shouted excitedly.

Kit startled. "Who said that?"

"Me," Anna said, in Pookie's voice. "But that map's wrong." She stroked the crawl space door. "They're in here. All you have to do, is open this door and look."

Kit stretched his arms and cracked his knuckles. "Anna, I've told you a hundred times. That door is dangerous. You must promise me you'll never open it."

"Please. Just look."

"Calm yourself, child. I know *exactly* where to look."

"But the village is gone!"

"The village is under the snow. This map shows me where to dig."

"But you're not an archaeologist like grandfather. What if you're wrong. Can we go back to Egypt if you're wrong?"

"Absolutely."

"What if a ghost comes when I'm alone?"

Kit sighed and held Snow by the shoulders. "Now, then. What have I told you! Anna?"

Snow held Pookie in front of her face. "There's no such thing as ghosts anymore," she said in a high rabbity voice. "They're all gone."

Kit pulled Pookie away, gently. "I want to hear *you* say it."

Snow recovered Pookie. "She doesn't like being dangled by the arm like that."

"Anna!"

Snow droned in a detached voice. "Ghosts are imagined memories of things that once were, and they're all gone," she said in a small flat voice. "And my name's *not* Anna."

"All that matters now is reuniting our family."

"But I heard the parrot again."

"Pigeon died a long time ago. You know that. Walls absorb sounds. It's a wall memory, nothing more."

"No, he woke me up. I felt his tail feathers brush my face."

Kit busied himself. "Telling porky pies won't work."

"Snow is too smart for that," Jack said in Kit's head.

"My daughter's name is Anna!" Kit insisted out loud. "And I'll thank you to mind your own business, Jack."

Snow narrowed her eyes and squashed Pookie under her chin.

Kit sighed and raked his hair with his fingers. "Nonsense, child. You were listening to one of your dreams."

"What do *you* listen to, Father?"

"I listen to scientific theories. But your great-grandmother had an odd theory about words," he said, dismissing Snow with a wave of his hand. "Away with you, now. We'll make time to discuss these things later. I've no time for rehashing old memories. Daydreaming is for rabbits."

"All that matters is our family," Snow solemnly repeated to Pookie. "Time doesn't matter. TIME… DOESN'T… MATTER… That's what Jack said."

"All dreams matter eventually," Pookie said. "They can't help but follow the laws of nature. Bede Hall is not what it was, but it never lies. My dear friend, Harigold, had a theory about dreams. He was always 'haring off' following one dream or another. I'm over the moon that he's home. It's lovely to see him back."

"What's a theory?"

"It's an idea whose time has come… Harigold said a person can wake up twice from the same dream. Now… listen carefully. There's a secret message in your name. I was taught these things a long time ago."

Snow printed her name, slowly and deliberately, and read each letter aloud for her father's benefit. "S…N…O…W."

"Drop the S," Pookie said. "Read what's left."

The word 'NOW' turned summersaults over the page, changing colors. The letter 'S' wriggled like a worm, formed a question mark, and rejoined its siblings.

Jack's chuckle emanated from behind the door. "NOW MATTERS," he said. "NOW is the most important time of all. It's the *only* time that matters. It's time to stay awake, little sphinx."

"But I've been awake plenty of times."

"You've woken up inside your dreams, baby girl," Jack said. "Lucid dreaming is an illusion of real time inside a universe of formless time. You're a lucky girl."

"S'NOW MATTERS," the Pookie said.

AUTHOR'S BIO

THE MANY LIVES of VERONICA KNOX

Veronica Knox writes cozy 'metaphysical' novels under the name V Knox for discriminating bookworms who savor reading long strange books as slowly as possible. Her invented genre of choice is 'art history delivered in a ghost story'.

'CHILDHOOD 1' Veronica was born in England, spent her childhood enduring the furious winters of the Canadian prairies, attended an English art college, and became a graphic designer.

'MIDLIFE 1' she obtained a Fine Arts degree from the University of Alberta and developed an imaginative take on art history that led to an untapped source for stories. She discovered that inanimate objects were rarely bereft of life. Shoes, cats, and paintings told her juicy stories.

'MIDLIFE 2', she moved to the magical Findhorn Community of

Scotland, and turned an abandoned Scottish church near Loch Ness into an art gallery dedicated to the conservation of tigers.

'**MIDLIFE 3**' She returned to Canada and delved into the creative inner worlds of autistic savants and master artists, and in one case, the unknown child in the Titanic cemetery. She explored the discrepancies between reality and lucid dreams, fished the depths of the subconscious, the afterlife, reincarnation, the anomalies of parallel lives and dimensions, the classic psyche of 'the ghostly lover', reconciled historical facts with surreal fiction, and wrote a dozen novels.

'**CHILDHOOD 2… ongoing**' *"I remain intent on listening to the ethereal echoes from objects in museums and the voices of the Italian Renaissance – the artists as well as their anonymous subjects and companions. I grant them second chances to air their grievances, tell their stories, and together we set the dreariest history books on fire."* – V KNOX

www.veronicaknox.com

CONTACTS

V KNOX WEBSITE & CURIOUS ART HISTORY BLOG
https://veronicaknox.com/

V KNOX SIGN UP NEWSLETTER FORM
https://landing.mailerlite.com/webforms/landing/f7e8a1

V KNOX AMAZON
https://www.amazon.com/V-Knox/e/B0094K0Q7Y

V KNOX FACEBOOK
https://www.facebook.com/V-Knox-Author-307047433438123/

V KNOX LINKEDIN
https://www.linkedin.com/in/veronica-knox-233bb51b/

ACKNOWLEDGEMENTS

I am indebted to the spiritual teachings of ECKHART TOLLE that continue to inspire me after twenty years, and to NAMASTE PUBLISHING for permission to quote a passage from 'A NEW EARTH'.

And, many thanks to Charity Chimni's flawless formatting skills.

So completes the Bede Trilogy… full circle.
I discovered in a time-slip adventure
there can be no legitimate prequel.
At best, a prequel runs in and out of a sequel
Ever summarizing with the accumulated secrets
hidden in 3 books that begged to be aired, later.
Thank you for taking time to read:

'TWINTER'
'TIME FALLS LIKE SNOW,
'TOMORROW AGAIN'
and 'SNOW BEHIND THE DOOR'.

If you enjoyed them, please consider telling your friends
or posting a short review.
Word of mouth is an author's best friend and much appreciated.
Cheers… reviews matter!

Veronica Knox – August 2, 2021

Vancouver Island British Columbia **Canada**

SNOW'S MEMOIR

'Bede Hall called to me in a dream, and I obeyed,' Snow wrote. *'Perhaps Beryl called too. I was needed in Bede to jumpstart a chain of incidents deemed vital to the survival of humankind. And so, it unfolded that, as a newborn infant, I dreamed my future self into Bede Hall, took up residence as its child ghost, and met Parks and Jack Frost who were aspects of the Hall, or rather, the Hall was the living essence of Pan. As an Egyptian, I was equally beholden to Pan's twin brother, Osiris.*

And so, it came about on a summer's day in 1949 that Parks introduced Beryl to me and we became fast friends. We shared everything, including the ghost of her pet cat Unicorn that had died the previous year. We were both nine-years-old.

We had many years together despite our age differences when Beryl grew into a teenager, in love with Peregrine Brooks, her twin brother, Bentley's, best friend. The three were a team of kindred spirits but when Beryl and Ben turned 21, Ben and Perry were involved in an accident. Peregrine had a near death experience. But Ben, died.

Beryl receded into mourning with no heart for friends or romance. She denied herself happiness and refused to see me. And so, like Peregrine, I was dismissed. I was left to watch Beryl's sufferings from the shadows as her invisible childhood friend.

As the family's heiress, it was Beryl's honor-bound duty to take a husband and produce an heir. After resisting for a few lonely years, she relented to her bully of a father who found an eager suitor in Hilton Cadwick, a depraved soul who craved the estate of Bede as much as he had.

Further unhappiness from Beryl's arranged marriage advanced to the responsibilities of motherhood. I stood beside Beryl throughout every ghastly day, tracking her within the Hall and the gardens where we once played, and visited her dreams until I lost interest and she froze me out.

Hilton's shady financial dealings came to light after his death, and with the Hall buried by debt, Beryl gave up. The key to the Winter Room, locked for years, was put away for safe keeping. And in a daze of confusion, Beryl packed her snow globe and hourglass, along with her happiest memories, and slipped into retirement in a seniors' home, determined to dream her years away.

Beryl's daughter, Rayne and her husband Cornelius inherited the estate. And that was when a group of local realtors, determined to demolish Bede Hall, rallied for an attack and the Hall declared war which meant it had twin wars to fight.

The Hall revealed a new plan to me. On August 2, 2013 when my father was twelve, Lady Nan was seventy-three, and I was a perpetual nine-year-old dream traveler, we were sent a trilogy of related dreams to bind the god Pan's, dream, together.

Bede Hall was up to its attic in snow in 2023 when my father, Kit, and I, broke in through the Winter Room's door. Once inside, we lit a fire using broken chair legs as fuel. We'd carried a supply of herbs for tea, with us. And when my father left on a mission, I fended for myself. There was plenty of snow to melt for water.

After that, or was it before? Lady Nan and I had a second reunion, and I became a true member of the family, except, my grandparents couldn't see me, and my father was afraid of me.

Aunt Bash gave me the rabbit doll named Pookie that I'd already been playing with for sixty years, and I met my friend, Vita, all over again without remembering. – Snow, 2023 – Bede

Twins Christopher (Kit) and Bathsheba (Bash) Stratford-Smyth who lived on Young Street in Livingston, a suburb of greater London, were twelve when their Egyptologist father went missing from his dig in Egypt.

Meanwhile, Bede Hall, their grandmother, Lady Nan's, stately home in Northumbria, was in danger and not a little angry. It felt cruelly abandoned at its hour of need, put up for sale while its matriarch, oblivious of her old home in danger of being sold to shady developers, had intentionally distanced herself from responsibilities by retreating into a fog of distracting memories. While the Hall faced being turned it into a commercial venture, or demolition, Lady Nan dreamed on about a previous life she remembered in ancient Egypt.

But the Hall had no intentions of being sold without a fight. In desperation, it summoned its considerable powers and ordered Lady Nan to wake up and return home.

Lady Nan heard but failed to comply until the voice of her childhood playmate, a ghost child who lingered in the Hall's unsettling attic 'cold spot', joined the Hall's request. The child named Snow 'lived' behind the blue door of an abandoned room known as the 'Winter Room'.

When Lady Nan regained consciousness, reconnecting with her eccentric vital self, she discovered her son-in-law, missing from an archaeological dig, was still unaccounted for. She took control by rallying her family's flagging energies in a resourceful threefold plan to save the Hall, free her lost friend, and provide a home for her daughter's grieving family.

To save money, Mrs. S, a former teacher, recalled her eldest son, Rupert, from university, homeschooled the twins, and took in a private pupil for extra income. Unfortunately, her pupil, Edgar, was a snooping bully, the son of a greedy realtor intent on acquiring the Hall by any devious means he could.

Edgar was sent to spy, and sabotaged the Hall's sudden reversal of fortunes, because after watching television with its new residents, Bede Hall hit upon a money-making scheme that left its shameless predators out in the cold.

The twins turned thirteen and adapted to life in Bede by finding the Hall's resident ghost. But Kit uncovered the village of Bede's darkest secret when he spontaneously stumbled into one of several time portals in and around the Hall. Kit glimpsed an imminent ice-age and received an implausible shock with devastating personal consequences.

The miraculous rescue of Mr. S. by Taraq, a teenage street kid in Cairo, brought an addition to the Stratford Smyth family. The twins' adopted brother accepted the Hall's strange influences even though the twins' parents and their older brother, Rupert, remained unresponsive, oblivious of its supernatural powers.

At the end of book one, Lady Nan passed away. She took her place as the head ghost of Bede Hall, seized the gauntlet of protecting the world from disaster, and recruited her enchanted childhood toys, a snow globe and a brass hourglass, to help unlock the past.

In a plan to save the Hall, the family, and the rest of the world, the twins, their newfound mentors, Taraq (renamed Tut), and several ghosts, united to form a team called the 'Twinters' – a name comprised of the words twins and winter.

In the three years since the twins first arrived to live in Bede Hall, Kit had had enough of the Hall's games. He had several disturbing secrets to keep and an impossible decision to make.

In book two, the Hall made a financial go of renting itself out to a movie production company requiring elaborate sets in a regal stately home – a venture that transformed its dodgy bank balance from red to black and temporarily quashed the bloodthirsty land developers. But an even more bloodthirsty predator arrived, one of supernatural origins deep in Pangea's past. The movie biz toppled. The twins' parents were taken hostage, and Bede Hall was forced to take drastic measures that required Kit to time travel further than was ever thought possible.

Book two ends with Kit being pulled from a time portal in the Great Sphinx into a hostile desert, disoriented. Abandoned but for the ghost of Kha, an ally he bumped into... or rather bumped *through* in the Cairo Museum, Kit became a student of ancient alchemy in book three to accomplish his triple mission. Kit rescued his parents, prevented a volcano from erupting, and met the mother of his daughter, Anna, so she and her twin brother, Peri, could be born.

Book three found the home-front gathering for battle while Kit gathered his dormant magical wits in the ancient land of Khem (Egypt). To accomplish his quest, Kit visited Pangea and Mars after setting off from Egypt's eighteenth dynasty – his home away from home, a land dedicated to chiseling facts in stone.

BEDE HALL WAS ALIVE BUT ALL WAS NOT WELL.

Turning sixteen hadn't been easy. Turning seventeen had been a nightmare. Unbelievably, turning eighteen topped them both.

Venture into Bede
by way of this prologue –
and welcome.
But remember…
once through the portal,
you may have to stay!

THE VENERABLE BEDE HALL
Northumberland, Great Britain

There are three generations of Stratford-Smyths 'living' in Bede Hall. The fourth is the ghost of a nine-year-old girl, which makes them four generations spanning four dimensions.

Bede Hall hovers in and out of this world, visiting its past and future which means that even in the blistering heat of August it could snow at any time. It was old. The word ageless barely covered it, and the word timeless was an outright lie. Older than time was closest to the truth. But even then, strictly speaking, the Hall was older than history.

When she was alive, the elder Beryl Stratford-Smyth, the Hall's matriarch, and Lady Nan to her grandchildren, had frequently pointed out, that under the playful laws of serendipity, words often contained hidden messages. For a start, the family name contained the word myth. For another, two highly significant words, venerable (esteemed) and vulnerable (frail), perfectly framed the duality of the Hall's mindset.

While mortified by its precarious state of disrepair, Bede Hall fancifully celebrated its majestic future restored to its former position of power. More than once, its haughty delusions of grandeur had saved it from ruin. And now, being sold to local developers was simply not an option.

And while the Hall mulled over a last hurrah to save itself and the world from an embarrassingly defensive position of diminishing power, Lady Nan's transition from life to death strengthened her claim as its presiding queen.

Lady Nan's passing set her body free to shape-shift at will from old-age to childhood, and her playful nature of alternating from wise-woman to precocious nine-year-old without warning, made her seem even more eccentric. 'Beryl the younger' habitually retreated into her whimsical childhood; 'Beryl the elder' maintained a firm hold on the knowledge gained from her recent sojourn of seventy-odd-years mined from her previous lifetimes to reconcile the past and balance the trying times ahead. In so doing, Lady Nan embraced being slowly absorbed by the future, but her childhood home refused to gently crumble into the landscape without a fight.

As a child, little Beryl learned to swim with the stone mermaids who lived in the fountain. Fairies taught her the language of the flowers, woodland spirits showed her how to read the changing seasons, and old Mr. Parks the gardener, gave her botany lessons, praising her as a natural 'green thumb'.

Beryl had been proud of her thumbs, nevertheless, she remained unbearably lonely for human companionship after her twin brother was sent off to school. She played alone in the manicured flowerbeds that spread in a scented skirt around the great house and hid in the garden maze to daydream.

As a daughter, Beryl was assigned a series of governesses who routinely fled in tears after experiencing frights in the cold spot outside a room near the attic nursery. It was dubbed the Winter Room because wintry wind emanated from the keyhole of its blue door even when the rest of the house sweltered in the extreme heat of summer. And sometimes, when a crying child was heard, the wind took the shape of a blue mist and drifted through the nursery wall… or so Miss Beryl, said.

But then, grownups dismissed Beryl as a strange child whose moonbeam mind was filled with featherheaded notions. She remained bored and out of sorts until she made friends with Bede's resident child ghost – a kindred 'spirit', her own age, who 'lived' behind the locked door of the Winter Room.

The two were inseparable for twelve years until the tragic loss of Ben, Beryl's twin brother, pushed happy memories of childhood aside. Beryl grieved for a long time, refusing to be happy, and Bede's young ghost, feeling abandoned, retreated into her room, only showing herself the same day every summer in the hopes her friend would return. But Beryl focused on growing up, and it wasn't long before she married and her responsibilities as a young mother and chatelaine of a grand estate, consumed her entirely.

Beryl's busy jangle of housekeys rang through the hall's corridors louder than any ghost dragging chains. And much later, after the joys of being a grandmother waned, Beryl, now dubbed Lady Nan to circumvent her aversion to the name Nana, or worse, Gran, lapsed into a fog of pleasant daydreams to block her painful memories in a retirement home in a town called Withering.

In desperation, Bede Hall summoned her like an angry father to stave off the predator developers keen on turning it into an hotel, but it was the plaintive call for help of her childhood playmate, Snow, that stirred Lady Nan to her old self.

In generations past, Lady Nan would have been branded a witch, considering she claimed her favorite old toys, a snow globe and a brass hourglass, and her brother's beloved replica of King Tut's throne, transcended the laws of chronological time. And while her grandchildren were small, and due to her reputation as a grand storyteller, there was no reason for them to doubt her.

Teenagers Kit and Bash, short for Christopher and Bathsheba, respectively, had always experienced the natural telepathic bond of identical twins. But their idyllic school holidays spent enraptured by Lady Nan's time-travel japes failed to prepare them for the cold reality of moving to Bede Hall after their Egyptologist father went missing on a dig in the Valley of the Kings.

Fond summer memories framed in blue skies and fluffy clouds soon faded when confronted with poverty and camping out in a deteriorating ruin of damp rooms and dusty dreams. To distract themselves, the twins made a game of seeking out the rumored ghost of a lost girl who Lady Nan assured them was real.

Opening the timeless 'Winter Room's blue door with a frosty skeleton key and confronting the ghost child who still lived behind it, was daunting. In fact, in retrospect, it seemed almost ordinary after Kit time traveled to the future during an out-of-body experience.

Kit found Bede Hall buried to its rooftops in snow, locked in a volcanic winter, and while searching the ruins of the Hall, the child ghost showed him his own diary where the disaster was cited as occurring in the fall of 2020, a mere six years away. To further complicate matters, Lady Nan informed the twins they were the pair of champions prophesied to resolve Bede's old score with an ancient curse. Bash held the mystical energies as 'Mistress of the Green' that grounded Bede Hall, and Kit was the dedicated time traveler able to change the future by preventing an incident in the past.

Bash continued to thrive, following her grandmother's calling as a powerful woman aligned with natural magic. Kit, a budding scientist, rejected the notion of anything that couldn't be proven by science and was loath to embrace his new home as a wonderful adventure. Bede Hall and its village puzzled Kit until he formulated a scientific theory to explain the phenomena in a world that was beyond strange. He reasoned the exotic plant-life surrounding the Hall was causing an oddly selective mass hallucination.

The notion that Bede Hall was manipulating its new tenants in its obsession to survive, was extraordinary as much as it was *extraordinarily* dangerous.

Searching for answers with his mentor, Dr. Peregrine Brooks, led Kit to experiment with the practice of stilling his mind for a few moments each day, sitting in his great uncle's throne chair, a replica of the golden throne from King Tut's tomb. But steeped as the chair was in the tradition of mindful relaxation, to Kit it was nothing short of a dodgy time machine, and his willpower blocked any progress.

Emptying his mind always ended in horrific visions of earth's future, akin to a volcanic winter. The very words were blasting hot and chillingly frozen at the same time. And yet, Kit had witnessed it first-hand. He had *been* there.

When it proved impossible for Kit to dismiss the haunting images of earth landlocked in a freak ice-age, a newfound detachment gripped him. Kit turned a blind eye to the bizarre events he'd begun to suspect may be true and focused on saving his family.

But the worst part of Kit's refusal to cooperate with Bede Hall was that it caused a stalemate between once devoted siblings who now faced each other as opponents, scowling over a chessboard the size of Bede Hall's vast lawns. And chess, not being a friendly game at the best of times, neither of them particularly wanted to unseat the other.

In spite of Kit's denial of all things supernatural, Bede Hall's topiaries wandered over the lawns as a herd of giant green animals, faster than the human eye could detect, meeting secretly with the trees to discuss the return of their absent master, the Green Man, comparing omens and portents with the forest's colony of trickster fairies and broody tree nymphs.

Head of security, Anubis the cat, guarded the locked gates and hidden portals with his scurrying army of grapevine mice and beetles that relayed progress reports across the forest floor to the odd twice-borns in the village.

A spying colony of extraordinary cats and a network of honeybees kept a close buzz on the local developers, continually plotting the Hall's future incarnation as an hotel while the resident ghosts of Bede Hall and a contrary chair conspired to stabilize the warring factions within the Hall by gaining Kit's trust.

Meanwhile, erratic events swirled ferociously in Lady Nan's snow globe. There were days when her hourglass was encrusted with frost too hot to touch.

Kit privately toyed with the idea of using the time portal in the maze to slingshot himself back to 2010, but all things considered, the prospect terrified him. He opted for the ostrich approach of burying his head in the sand – a mockery of the real dangers his father faced in the

Egyptian desert. And so, it fell to Bede Hall's time corridors, the Great Sphinx of Egypt, the rules of twindom and the power of nine, and the Hall's chosen champions, to save the planet from becoming a ball of blue ice orbiting the sun.

With time running out, the chair misbehaved again. And as determined as Kit was to ignore his supernatural experiences in favor of scientific proof, he learned the hard way that all memories and dreams were inhabited by ghosts of one kind or another. But lives were at stake in a landscape where history was positively ancestral.

Besides, Lady Nan's wisdom continually haunted him: *If you really want something enough,* she liked to say, *a little thing like dying won't stop you.*